REFRACTION

The Illumination of the Siann Dha

Book 3

by Lisa Pelissier

www.SneakerBlossom.com

ISBN 978-1-965521-05-2

With gratitude to my beta readers:

Debe Herdtner

Tesla Mathews

And heartfelt awe for the work of my cover artist:

Helen Holmes

And a nod of appreciation to:

C.S. Lewis's *Discarded Image*

the inspiration behind Gannoir and its inhabitants

And a note for my readers:

See the ***Appendices*** at the back of the book

for pronunciations and definitions of

non-earthly words.

Check Out:

The Skies Below

Book 1 of the Illumination of the Siann Dha

Untethered

Book 2 of the Illumination of the Siann Dha

Lisa Pelissier

Lisa Pelissier

Trigger warning: *While no rape occurs in this book, it comes up as a fact in the history of several characters.*

Lisa Pelissier

Chapter 1: Tass

Darkness. Just darkness. She couldn't see. She couldn't hear. The only sensation Tass had was of the voices, the eternal, inexorable voices whispering, shouting, seductively uttering obscenities in her mind. The voices had consumed her. She was nothing and they were all. But somewhere, buried deep within all that she was, Tass was still herself. She was still Talassa Galan, best swimmer at the Calix, sister of Mailu, heroine of Garradh Gannoir. Somewhere. Somehow.

She waited, like a caterpillar in a cocoon, waiting for her rebirth. This couldn't be eternity. It couldn't. Trapped in a corner of her body, in a corner of her mind, she was a tiny grain of Tass, ready to come to life again.

Chapter 2: Xylo

"How's the patient?" Xylo asked heavily, putting a hand to his aged forehead.

Laso shook his head. "No better, no worse. They've told us that burns can take a long time to heal, especially in the bloodstream. The electricity infiltrated every vessel in her body. Healing, when it comes, will be gradual and slow." He looked at the pale form of his wife on the hospital cot.

"She's a hero, you know," Xylo said quietly. "Rahela acted as the conduit for the electricity as it poured down from the Ghalon. She was a link in the chain that healed our world."

Laso sighed. "I don't understand. I don't understand any of this. Why was Rahela so badly injured by the electricity, but Ieska and Ceres weren't?"

"We've talked about this before, you and me. And the rest of us too. I don't have answers. My best guess is that it has something to do with caste. Or age. Ieska is Esh. Ceres is young. And pregnant. I'm worried about the baby. About my grandchild."

"May Tel-Maor preserve the life of the little one," Laso said gently.

Xylo nodded. He was much more inclined to believe in the reality of Tel-Maor, the maker of their world, Gannoir, than he had been before the events that had taken him out of Luca, the land of his people since the beginning of history. There were things, many things, that he did not know. He had thought himself wise and learned. Now he knew he was little better than a fool and that his knowledge was incomplete at best. Tel-Maor, instead of being an antiquated myth, was now a possibility in his mind.

"May Tel-Maor bring healing to Rahela as well," he replied.

Laso, Rahela's husband, and Peodar, their son, had come to stay in Garradh Gannoir after his wife's injuries. Laso had kept vigil at his wife's bedside for a solid month, leaving only intermittently. Peodar, though he was also grieved, had ventured out into the community of the city of Obumbro and had made friends with some people his own age. He was able to escape the grim realities of the hospital regularly, something for which Xylo was glad.

So much had happened in the two months since the skyboulder had returned—and yet so little. It was not enough. Kleibald—and many others—had died. The elders had exonerated Gelu for his part in attempting to destroy their world. Now he, along with Xylo's son-in-law, Nadim, were ruling. Luca. He couldn't go back.

*****

Xylo wiped his feet on the woven seagrass mat before the entry to the cave and entered. "I'm home," he called. His voice echoed in the passageways. A little breeze swirled around him, and he greeted it gladly. Gaoth, the rational wind, was with him.

"Dad?" a woman's voice called.

Xylo turned down a corridor and walked toward the voice. It didn't sound like his daughter-in-law. When he entered the chamber where they usually cooked and ate, he saw with delight that it wasn't Ceres at all.

"Yasamina!" he exclaimed. "What are you doing here? Did Dano come?"

Yasamina flipped her long dark braid behind her and hugged her father. "Dano stayed in the city. We didn't want anyone to know I was coming, and since he works in government, we figured it would be better if I came alone."

"I'm glad you came," Xylo told her. "Where are the others?"

"Ceres went to pick berries for dinner, and Case took Talag to the heights to work on his gliding," Yasamina told him. Xylo's son and Ceres husband, Case, had decided to make his home in Garradh Gannoir with his father. He was helping Xylo train Talag, Xylo's grandson by his estranged and newly deceased son, Gryf. Talag was the Dynroc, the next leader of Garradh Gannoir.

Xylo grinned at the thought of his grandson soaring through the air. "I wish they taught gliding in the city. It's a useful skill."

"Ceres said Talag's been pretty excited to use his tala for something other than designating him as a member of the Esh caste," Yasamina said, looking at her tala-free arms and body.

Xylo held up his arms and his tala, full-body membranes attaching his arms to his torso, stretched out under his tunic. "It's more of an impediment than a gift most of the time," he told his daughter. Yasamina had always longed for tala. She was the only one of the Gulot caste in the family. Xylo, Case, and Talag were all of the Esh caste—fire. She was just Gulot—rock. She couldn't swim and she couldn't glide.

"You haven't told me why you came," Xylo commented. "I'm glad to see you. And if this is just a social call, I welcome it, welcome you. But given the way things have been, I suspect there is more to it than that."

Yasamina nodded. "There are rumors. Dano's not part of the inner circle, but he hears things." She looked at Xylo earnestly. "The elders are planning to arrest you," she said.

Xylo blinked in surprise. "Arrest me? For what?"

His daughter snorted. "It sounds to me like they're still deciding. Someone has it in for you, Dad. The arrest is the thing, not the crime. They don't want justice. They want you."

"But why?" Xylo asked. His old rival, Kleibald, was dead. His ex-wife—Kleibald's wife Ardanach—was also dead. The evil that Kleibald intended lived on in Gelu and in his son-in-law, Nadim, who was now the Esh-Maor of Luca. Nadim's wife, Xylo's daughter and Kleibald's stepdaughter, Aythylla, had died from the impact of the returning skyboulder. Xylo, who had been estranged from his ex-wife and children for many years, had never met his son-in-law. He held out no hope that Nadim could be an ally, however. The younger man had been part of Kleibald's entourage, and probably part of his conspiracy.

"There's talk that they're blaming you for the death of Kleibald and Ardanach. She was your ex-wife, so you had cause to hate both of them."

Xylo shook his head in frustration. "That's nonsense. I couldn't have made things turn out any differently. The skyboulder crashed into Gannoir. They died in the crash. I didn't cause the crash."

"You didn't stop it either," Yasamina pointed out. "And you were the one who orchestrated the rescue."

"The rescue," Xylo sighed, "was intended to save people. Not kill them."

"I know," Yasamina replied. "It doesn't make any sense. The other rumor is that they're going to arrest you for kidnapping."

"Kidnapping?" Xylo yelped. "Who'd I kidnap?"

"Talag," Yasamina told him. "I'm under the impression that his mother wants him back. And since Nadim is in power and he's her brother-in-law, she has the power to push for what she wants."

"Talag came with me because he wanted to," Xylo said. "And because he was obligated to. He's the Dynroc. He'll be the ruler here before long."

"I'm not sure they see it that way," Yasamina retorted.

Xylo nodded slowly. "I think you're right. It's not about justice. It's about me."

"Yes."

"I'm glad you came," Xylo said, looking at Yasamina with love in his eyes. "You're a good daughter."

"I know," Yasamina grinned. "I'm not sure they'll try anything, but I wanted you to know what they were saying."

"I think a trip to Luca is in order," Xylo said.

Chapter 3: Pax

Pax dug his fingernails into the flesh of the sea tree until the sap oozed out onto his fingers. He licked it off hungrily before it could dissolve in the seawater swirling around him.

"We can't keep living like this," his brother Laetu said. He had become adept at gill speech since he and Pax had lost themselves in the waters under the Orbokth.

"What are we going to do? Die?" Pax asked. He licked his fingers again.

"I want to go home," Laetu whined.

"Duh," Pax retorted as he scooped out another handful of sap. "If I knew how, I'd go home too."

"We can't just stay here."

"We've been here for two months," Pax pointed out. "We've tried everything. If there were a way out, we'd have found it by now."

Laetu swam in a frustrated circle around his brother. "We got in here somehow. There must be a way out. However we got in, that's the way to get back out and go home."

"Just eat," Pax ordered. He scooped a floating glob of sap and tossed it toward Laetu. It hit him in the face. Laetu wiped his face and ate the life-sustaining sap. The sap was nutritious. After they'd emptied a vine of salt oranges when they'd first found themselves in the cavern, the sap had been the only sustenance they'd had. Laetu was bored of sap. He missed his parents and his sister, Camilly. He missed his home. He missed being dry. Although he was tri-casted and could breathe underwater, he had never lived in it full time. Always he'd lived on land, slept in a bed, and been able to climb and build and do all sorts of things he couldn't do under the sea.

"Do you think they're still looking for us?" Laetu asked softly.

Pax's face softened. "You know Mom and Dad," he said. "They're still looking." Pax and Laetu were half-brothers. The people Pax called "Mom" and "Dad" were not biologically related to him at all. Laetu's mother and adoptive father, Finnan and Rhyder, had raised Pax after his mother died when he was three. Like Laetu, he was the biological son of the monster Methiant Migas.

Laetu relaxed. "You're right. They're still looking for us. Mom and Dad wouldn't give up. Not unless they found our dead bodies."

Pax grinned. "And we know they haven't found our dead bodies. We're alive."

"Unless we're really dead and don't know it," Laetu suggested.

"Laetu, we're not dead."

"What if when people die their souls go into the water and sit around eating sap?" Laetu suggested.

"What if we turn into sea monsters and grow seventeen layers of blubber? What if we sprout wings and fly around like scolopendrae? It's not going to happen. We're not dead."

"What if everyone else is dead and we're the only ones alive?" Laetu tried again.

Pax sighed and bubbles rose from his lips. "They're looking for us. They must be."

"You felt the earthquake," Laetu fretted. "What if . . ."

"Just stop!" Pax interrupted him. "We have to hold on to hope. Someone is looking for us. Someone is going to find us. The earthquake or explosion or whatever it was couldn't have killed everyone. Someone must be out there still. And we can't be that far from Garradh Gannoir."

"No one in Garradh Gannoir can swim," Laetu pointed out.

"Ceres can. And our sisters and brother. And any of the Mayim."

"Pax, I'm scared."

"It doesn't do any good to be scared."

"That doesn't help," Laetu complained.

"Just eat."

Chapter 4: Camilly

"How are they?" Camilly asked, smiling at the gnomish old man.

"The same," Dynny replied glumly.

"No worse, though," fifteen-year-old Camilly encouraged him. "You're doing a good job taking care of them." She looked at the two prone figures in the dim light of the grass hut. Tass was lying on a cot and covered with blankets. Camilly thought the darkness that covered the girl's skin looked a little lighter, but she couldn't be sure. Mailu, Dynny's other charge, was still in her stone sarcophagus. She could see the pale, scarred face of the dead girl behind the thick glass that had sealed the box against the air since the moment of Mailu's death. The belly of the dead girl was swollen so that it almost touched the glass.

Dynny gestured toward Mailu. "Baby's coming soon."

"You'll break the glass when it does?" Camilly asked.

Dynny shook his head. "Too thick to break. Bridima and Widman are going to help get it open without breaking. Breaking might hurt the baby. Might hurt Mailu."

"You think she's still alive?" Camilly asked.

"I'm taking good care of her," Dynny said. "I'm not the Dynroc anymore. I'm not anything. But I'm a good carer."

It had been his continual plaintive refrain since he had come to Cudth Deorth. Dynny had loved being the Dynroc, having the powers without which nothing could happen in Garradh Gannoir. When he had realized that he had accidentally transferred those powers to young Talag, he had been devastated. He felt he'd failed his dead master, Arros. Dynny's only comfort had been his years of training in caring for the sick and injured. Although the inhabitants of Cudth Deorth had taken pains to remind him that he was valuable and that he was doing worthwhile work, the old man was still sad.

"You are for sure a good carer, Dynny," Camilly reassured him. She leaned over and hugged the old man, her long red hair falling around his face as she did so. "I know you love Tass and Mailu."

He nodded. "And the baby."

"And the baby," Camilly agreed. "How soon do you think the baby's coming?"

Dynny scrunched up his face, concentrating. "Bridima says it'll be just a couple weeks."

"Bridima would know," Camilly replied. Bridima was the matriarch of Cudth Deorth. The mother of the oldest of the Triads, twenty-five-year-old Unaleah, Bridima, together with her best friend, Ieska, mother of another of the Triads, had twenty years earlier founded the outsiders' colony in the secret enclave on an island in the farthest reaches of Luca. Even the elders, the ruling council of Eshmaor, didn't know that Cudth Deorth existed. For the first four years, it had only been Bridima, her daughter Unaleah, and her adopted son, the Triad Gudall, and Ieska and her daughter Sadi who lived on Cudth Deorth. After that, the others gradually came.

Camilly knew they thought it was possible there were more Triads somewhere in Luca. Ieska, their liaison with the outside world, was always listening and watching, ready to take in any of the misfit tri-casted children she found.

Widman and his daughter Kari had come to Cudth Deorth sixteen years ago. A year later, Ieska had found four-year-old Ninach in an orphanage, abandoned by her parents once they realized she had the functional gills of the Mayim as well as the body-tala of the Esh. Widman had taken in the little girl and raised her along with his own daughter.

Later, the beautiful red-haired Finnan and her husband Rhyder, a Mayim couple, had come to the island with their children, Triad Laetu and their Mayim daughter, Camilly. Finnan and Rhyder had also raised the Triad boy Pax and his Gulot brother, Byid from the time they were small. That was the whole colony, unless you counted Torcalon, which Camilly didn't. Torcalon didn't live in Cudth Deorth. Like Ieska, he was a sort of liaison with the outside world. He was their ferryman, the only one who brought people in and out of the enclave.

He was also the father of Mantais Nayro—Methiant Migas, who was the father of the Triads. It was more than atonement for his son's sins. Torcalon loved all his grandchildren fiercely and gave every bit of energy in his elderly, wasted body to protect them.

Camilly wandered outside of the hut and looked up and down the shore of the small civilization. Cudth Deorth was inside of the Orbokth, the floating landmass that ringed Luca. A pool of seawater was at the center, and above, the Orbokth, the rocky part of their world, opened to the Ghalon. It was warm in Cudth Deorth, almost tropical. Plants and animals lived there that were not to be found anywhere else in Luca—maybe not in all Gannoir. It was a lush, green paradise.

"Dinner!" a voice called. It was Unaleah. Camilly made her way down to the shore to see what Unaleah had prepared. The others quickly assembled and sat at the stone benches and table.

"Where's Gudall?" Camilly asked, looking around at the assembly.

"Washing up," Bridima told her with a smile. "He was feeling well enough to work on his house this afternoon."

This was good. Gudall lacked strength due to the injuries he'd received to his lungs two months earlier. All the same . . . she glanced at the older girls. Everyone knew that building the house was Gudall's way of saying he was ready to start his own household—that he was ready to marry. But he hadn't begun courting the girl of his choice. Camilly knew that there had been tension between the four older girls when they realized that Gudall was beginning to think about marriage. Even though they were all half-siblings, there was no one else. She suspected that sweet, gentle Unaleah viewed Gudall simply as a brother—they had been raised in the same dwelling. But she wasn't entirely sure. What other options did Unaleah have? What other options did any of them have? Four of the Triads were girls; three were boys. And two of the boys were too young for the girls to consider them. And none of them were going to marry anyone unless they knew in advance they could trust them with their secrets.

Ninach was frowning at Sadi, Camilly saw. Sadi's expression was cheerful, but that was Sadi. Camilly could never tell when the girl was sad or angry. Sadi was practical. Still, the fact that Ninach considered her a rival was enough to make Camilly think that Sadi might have let something slip about her feelings for Gudall. Camilly thought sixteen-year-old Kari had been making eyes at Gudall before the mission. It didn't matter anymore. Not now that Kari was missing and probably dead. Gudall probably wouldn't have looked at her anyhow. She was too young. Camilly didn't consider herself a contender in the game for Gudall's affections. She was only fifteen to his twenty-four. He was handsome, but she'd never looked at him as anything but a brother. Ironic, since she wasn't Gudall's blood relative, and the other girls were.

Gudall walked up slowly. He looked tired but his blue eyes blazed with life. He ran a hand through his dark hair and took his seat at the table.

"How's the house coming?" Sadi asked.

Ninach glared.

"Pretty well," Gudall said. "But more slowly than I'd like. I haven't quite gotten my strength back."

"Do you want help?" Camilly offered.

The three other girls all looked at her suspiciously. Camilly wanted to roll her eyes, but she knew it wouldn't go over well, so she refrained.

"Have some soup," Camilly's mother Finnan said quickly.

They passed the soup bowl quietly. Finnan was a good cook, and fish and other meats of the sea were abundant in Cudth Deorth. They always ate well. Camilly watched her mother as her eyes roved the table. She knew what she was thinking. She was missing Laetu, Pax, and Kari, who had gone missing after the cataclysmic return of the skyboulder. Dynny was there at the table, sitting in Kari's usual place. Camilly was glad he'd come. She liked Dynny, despite his continually mournful countenance. She sighed and then said the thing that she said every night.

"Can we go back and look for them?"

She expected the usual answer—that Gudall had to heal, that they were waiting for Mailu's baby to come, that they were waiting for Tass to wake, and finally, that they were waiting for Ieska to let them know the time was right. Ieska had gone back to her job as a scientist in Lucedth.

Bridima surprised her. "We need to prepare right away."

Everyone looked up at Bridima, alarmed at her tone.

"What happened?" Camilly's father, Rhyder, asked.

Bridima exchanged a glance with Widman. "Torcalon was here today. He brought word from Ieska. She's worried. Something's afoot with the elders. There may come a time when the passage between Luca and Garradh Gannoir is either closed or heavily monitored. If we want to go there, we need to do it soon."

"Before Mailu's baby comes?" Unaleah asked.

Bridima nodded. "As soon as possible. The next time Torcalon rows over, it will be to take a team back to start searching again."

"You should have stayed there until you found them," Ninach growled. Her mousy brown hair hung loose around her shoulders, a contrast to her usual tight ponytail.

Camilly agreed with Ninach. She'd petitioned to stay in Garradh Gannoir with Xylo so she could keep looking, but Finnan and Rhyder had insisted she come back to Cudth Deorth. After all, Finnan had told her, the sea between Luca and Garradh Gannoir is connected. It was just as likely that the boys would turn up at home as turn up in Garradh Gannoir.

Camilly knew her mother's heart. She knew her mother longed to have her sons back. She wouldn't have stopped looking—not unless . . . Camilly shivered. The sea in Cudth Deorth was only connected to the main sea of Garradh Gannoir by a few narrow, undersea passages below the level where she could safely swim. Only the water could go there safely. And maybe Tass, she thought ruefully. But Tass was unconscious, and the water wasn't talking.

"I'll go," she volunteered. "I'll go now!"

"It's more a matter of who'll stay here," Widman noted gruffly. His good-natured round face was full of sorrow.

"Someone has to stay behind to take care of Mailu and Tass," Bridima said.

"That's my job," Dynny piped up.

"It certainly is," Bridima agreed compassionately. "You're good at what you do, Dynny. But we need someone here who can deal with the birth of the baby, and someone who can help get Mailu's coffin open when the time comes."

"I know I have to stay behind," Gudall noted. "I wouldn't be much use to a search yet."

Bridima nodded. "I was thinking the same, but I didn't want to keep you back if wanted to try."

Gudall shook his head regretfully. "I wish I could, but I know I can't."

Camilly cast a sideways look at Sadi and Ninach, wondering if Gudall's absence on the mission would affect their desire to join the search. The older girls said nothing.

"I'm going," Finnan said quickly. "Those are my boys out there. And I'm Mayim—I can search the sea."

"I'd like to go as well," Rhyder said. "Unless . . ." He looked at Widman.

"I want to go," Widman said flatly. "Kari is out there somewhere. I'd like to be part of the search." His face grew tight as he said his daughter's name.

Camilly looked at her father's face and read the anguish there. She knew her father wanted to be looking for his sons. She knew he didn't want to stay back while the rest of his family went away. She also knew that her father would be the best candidate to stay behind because of his skills with his hands. If anyone could open Mailu's coffin without injuring the dead girl or her baby, it was Rhyder.

"I can hold things together here," Bridima offered.

Rhyder shook his head. "I'll stay back with you. You're going to need me. And I can help Gudall with the house at the same time."

Finnan cast a loving look at her husband. Camilly wished her father had insisted on coming, but she knew she couldn't force the issue. She was proud of her father's selflessness.

"I'm coming to help," Sadi said, tossing her long black hair as though she were defying anyone who would tell her she couldn't.

"I'll come," Unaleah said quietly. "I can't bear the thought that Kari, Pax, and Laetu are out there somewhere, hurt, or sick, or . . ."

"We're going to find them," Camilly interrupted her. "They're going to be fine."

"We'll do our best," Finnan said.

"What about you, Ninach?" Bridima asked. "Will you join the search party or stay here?"

Ninach pressed her lips together. "I'll stay here."

Sadi snorted rudely.

"I wasn't part of the first mission. I see no reason I should be part of this one," Ninach answered her half-sister's unspoken objection. "Besides, someone should be here when Tass wakes up. One of her siblings. She'll feel less alone."

Ninach, Camilly reflected, had not shown much interest in her youngest sister up until then. *She's staying behind for Gudall,* she thought. *She thinks if she's the only one here, she can win him over.*

Sadi opened her mouth to argue with Ninach, but twelve-year-old Byid interrupted her. "I'm going. You'll let me, won't you? It's my brother who's missing. I know I'm just a Gulot, but we don't know that they got lost in the sea, do we? Isn't it just as likely that they wandered away on land? I can help. I promise."

"You can go," Bridima told him. "But you'll have to obey Finnan and Widman. And whoever else gives you instructions. Don't go wandering off alone. No matter what."

Joy filled the boy's face. "I won't. I won't! I promise. I just want to find Pax. And Laetu and Kari."

"The six of you—Widman, Finnan, Unaleah, Sadi, Camilly, and Byid—pack a bag after dinner. Whenever Torcalon and Ieska come, you'll need to be ready to go."

Chapter 5: Tass

Little needles of pain shot through her body, thin and barely perceptible. Tass tried to wonder about them. How badly was she hurt? Pain seemed to indicate that she was still alive, maybe even that she was getting her body back. But she couldn't open her eyes. She couldn't move. Mentally she reached out toward her limbs and found that the stinging pain grew in intensity. Would the darkness give her body back? Would she be able to inhabit her own physical form in its entirety ever again?

Laughter rang through her mind, causing her infinitely more pain that the pinpricks from her body. The darkness was still with her. Still mocking her. Paralyzing her. There was only one way to silence them, and it was almost as painful as letting them continue their evil guffaws.

In her mind, Tass chanted the spirits' refrain. *I'm worthless. I'm nothing. I'm unlovable and unloved. No one has ever loved me, and no one ever will. The darkness is all. There is no I. There is no Tass . . .*

Slowly the laughter faded, even as the ache in her soul remained.

Chapter 6: Xylo

"You both will keep up the work while I'm gone?" Xylo requested.

"Of course, Dad," Case told him. "I'll take care of Talag. He's my nephew, after all." He grinned at the boy and Talag smiled back at him.

"Don't let him out of your sight," Xylo charged his son. "I mean that. With the elders having a vendetta against me, there isn't anything they wouldn't try."

"We'll be fine, Dad," Case replied easily. "It won't be a problem."

"They've killed before," Xylo reminded him.

"I'll watch out for them," Ceres promised. "Whenever I'm not patrolling the waters, I'll keep an eye on them. And I'll watch for danger."

"No sign of the missing Triads?" Xylo asked his daughter-in-law.

Ceres shook her head. "You know I would have told you."

"We'll be okay, Papa Xy," Talag said. "I'll stay with Case. I promise."

Xylo looked at his son and grandson fondly, glad that the affection between the two had come easily. Talag had trauma, not just from the ache of losing half of his family in the crash of the skyboulder—his father, grandfather, and aunt—but in the loss of his identity. He'd lived his life thinking he was the grandson of Kleibald the Reformer, Esh-Maor and leader of Luca. He was royalty. Or he had been. While Xylo knew his grandson had been relieved to find that the blood of the would-be destroyer of the world wasn't running through his veins, it had still been a blow for him to come to terms with the loss of who he'd thought he was.

The land passage between Garradh Gannoir and Luca was now a well-traveled road. Xylo wondered how the two civilizations, which were only a day's journey apart, had remained unknown to each other for so many centuries. He took a ferry from the harbor in Obumbro, the main city of Garradh Gannoir, to the Orbokth, the rocky floating island, where the tunnel to Luca had been carved out. From there, he walked the two miles back to what he had once thought was the only pocket of life in his world. Upon emerging, he took another boat to the Lucedth clatry. The clatries were shallow floating lattices of adamantine rock upon which the metallic skyscrapers of the city rested.

Xylo was experienced at looking casual. The years he had spent in hiding from Kleibald's council of elders had prepared him well. He knew that furtive glances and stealthy steps would betray him, so he walked like someone without a care in the world.

He wondered how he was going to find out what he needed to learn. Knowing that his fiancée, Ieska, would be at work at the university, he headed for Yasamina's home. She lived near the city center on the fourteenth floor of a gleaming skyscraper. He walked up gradually, taking time to cross the bridges between the different buildings on the way. The network of bridges and ramps connected the tall buildings had been designed to flex with the movement of the sea.

He paused in the middle of a bridge about six stories above the waters and looked out over his world. The sea itself glowed a bright, unnatural turquoise, the result of the donated blood of the citizens of Luca. Light was life, and blood made light.

Xylo continued his walk toward his daughter's home. His son-in-law, Dano, greeted him at the door. Xylo's eyes widened in surprise. "Aren't you working today?" he asked.

"They let me go," Dano said darkly. He gestured for Xylo to enter the apartment.

Satchels were stacked neatly against the wall of the living room, Xylo noticed. "Going somewhere?" he asked.

"We're leaving Lucedth," Dano told him. "We want to get out before something worse happens to us. Before the elders come after us for being related to you."

"To me?" Xylo asked faintly.

"Yasamina told you about the rumors," Dano said.

"Rumors . . . rumors are not threats," Xylo defended himself.

Dano shook his head. "Rumors . . . and then I get fired. It's enough to make us cautious." He looked at his father-in-law and his expression softened. "It's not your fault. We know that. We know you had nothing to do with Kleibald's death, no matter how much you hated him. And we know you didn't kidnap Talag." He paused, searching Xylo's face for . . . Xylo didn't know what Dano was looking for. "Yasamina's expecting a baby," he said abruptly. "It's best that we go before . . . before . . ."

"Before the baby comes?" Xylo suggested, knowing his son-in-law had something much more ominous in mind.

Dano nodded. "Yeah."

"She didn't tell me," Xylo said.

"I told her not to," Dano explained. "We didn't want word to get out. You're the only one who knows. And you can't tell anyone.

If the elders knew your line was prospering, they might . . ."

"Are things that bad?" Xylo whispered.

"Maybe. Maybe not," Dano replied. "But Yasamina and I felt it would be best to play it safe. To go into hiding now, before things get bad. Once things improve, we can come back. We can start our lives again."

"Where are you going to go?" Xylo asked.

Dano hesitated awkwardly. "I'd rather not say."

Xylo nodded. "It's better if I don't know."

Dano relaxed. "Thank you for understanding."

"Can I stay here, just until Yasamina gets home?"

"Of course," Dano answered. "The elders already know we live here and that you might come here. Having you here won't increase the danger."

Xylo shook his head. "This is incredible." He strode into the living room and sat down on the sofa heavily. "That things could become so bad so quickly . . ."

"Want lunch?" Dano offered.

Xylo nodded. "And after that, I'll help you pack."

He met up with Ieska as she was leaving the university later that day. Not wanting to endanger her, Xylo simply asked her to meet him after the dark side of the Ghalon turned its face toward Lucedth that evening. She agreed without looking at him.

On top of a skyscraper, Xylo and Ieska kept their tryst.

"It's bad, Adam," she told him, using the name by which she'd known him as a young man.

"I know," he replied hoarsely. "It's my youth all over again. Kleibald won then."

Ieska shook her head. "He didn't win, Adam. You did. You became a good man. Kleibald became a bad one. He's dead. You're alive."

"He killed my son, my little Dochym," Xylo said. "And took my wife and two other children for his own."

"He didn't win. And evil is not going to win this time either." She gave him a fierce look.

He smiled at her. How he loved her. "Do you always win, my love?"

Her eyes flashed fire at him. "So far. And I don't intend to stop now."

"I don't want to lose you."

"You won't. And you're not going to lose Yasamina and Dano either. Or the baby."

"How did you know about the baby? Dano said I was the only one they told."

Ieska laughed a dry little laugh. "I saw Yasamina at the university the other day. I could tell. Mothers know."

Xylo frowned. "So anyone might know?"

"Anyone might suspect. No one would know," Ieska replied firmly.

"They're fleeing. Moving out of Lucedth," Xylo told her.

"I know. I'm helping them."

"You?" Xylo was glad but hurt that his family had seen fit to tell his fiancée but kept it a secret from him.

"I believe it has escaped the elders notice that you and I are engaged," Ieska told him. "I'm not in any danger. Besides, I have connections."

"Cudth Deorth?" Xylo asked.

Ieska shook her head. "I wouldn't endanger the Triads by

sending ordinary citizens there. The whole thing could blow up in our faces."

"I won't ask," Xylo replied. "It's better that I don't know."

"It won't be forever," Ieska comforted him. She took his hand. "Once this passes, we'll be together, all of us. You and I, and the Triads, and Dano and Yasamina, Case and Ceres, Talag, and your new grandchildren."

"It's a happy dream," Xylo answered.

"But for now, we have to figure out what to do."

"I should go back to Garradh Gannoir. The people there will support me, unlike the people here who are ruled by the elders."

Ieska nodded. "I was thinking the same thing."

"I'll go in the morning," Xylo promised.

"I'll be following you in a few days' time," Ieska told him. "There's something wrong here, something I can't quite figure out. We need to find out what happened to Pax, Kari, and Laetu. With them missing there are too many questions. I'm bringing the Triads to Garradh Gannoir."

"All of them?"

"There are only four left—five if you count Tass, but I don't. The last I heard she was still unconscious."

Xylo nodded. "Thank you. You know I believe they're still alive."

Ieska's lively black eyes met his. "I think so too. I'd know if they weren't. They're like my own children, all of them. If anything had happened, somehow, I would know."

"We'll find them," Xylo said.

"You're overly optimistic," Ieska countered.

"Hang on to hope. It's all we have."

"And each other, Adam. There's that too."

Chapter 7: Pax

"Wake up," Laetu hissed, shaking Pax by the shoulder.

Pax rolled over and tumbled out of the crevice in which he'd tucked himself to sleep. His body slowly uncoiled. "What's wrong?" he asked sleepily.

"I saw something!" Laetu fretted.

Pax clenched his eyes shut. This wasn't the first time Pax had roused him with tales of danger in the night. "Go back to sleep," he ordered. "You're just having a nightmare."

Laetu flicked his feet, throwing a current of water toward Pax. "It wasn't a nightmare. I was awake. There was a face."

"Was it mine?" Pax snorted.

"No!"

"We're the only ones here, Laetu. You couldn't have seen a face. You were dreaming. Remember when you saw the vauzigk attacking us?"

Laetu's expression darkened. "That was a dream. I admit that. But this was different. I really saw a face."

"Where?" Pax asked, frustrated. He wanted to go back to sleep. The best way to achieve that was the humor Laetu.

"Over there," Laetu gestured toward a solid section of the Orbokth.

Pax swam across the pocket of the sea in which they were confined and placed his palms on the rock. "Here?"

"A little lower," Laetu said.

Pax adjusted his position.

"And more to the left," Laetu directed without coming any closer.

Pax moved again. "Here?"

Laetu nodded. He looked scared. More scared than he'd been after the nightmare about the vauzigk, Pax noted. Pax felt the rocky wall. It was solid but not smooth. There were any number of crevices in it, perfect for small sea creatures' homes. But none were large enough to hide a person.

"I think you were dreaming," Pax said.

"I wasn't!" Laetu insisted.

Pax could tell his brother was on the verge of tears. "It's solid rock, Laetu. Solid. There are little holes in the rock, but nothing big enough for a person to hide in. Just little things. Fish. Sea snails. That sort of thing."

"Someone was there."

Pax shook his head. "It's not possible."

"What if it was Dwoyra?"

"Dwoyra's body is made out of water," Pax pointed out. "No one ever said they saw her with a face."

"She can make the water take on any shape," Laetu argued hopefully. "Maybe she manifested herself as a face."

Pax didn't think much of Laetu's idea. Dwoyra wasn't visible. The only way to encounter Dwoyra was through touch or sound. And she'd never spoken to him or to Laetu. But he didn't argue. If Laetu wanted to think it was Dwoyra, it was for the best. At least Dwoyra was a known ally, unlike the usual bogeymen his brother conjured up in his imagination. "You're probably right," he said encouragingly.

"You don't believe me," Laetu accused him.

Laetu knew him too well. "Look. I don't know what you saw. But whatever it was, it's not here now. Can we go back to sleep?" Pax pushed off against the wall with his feet and swam back toward his brother.

Laetu's face changed as he neared. What had begun as whiny insistence on his own perspective had turned into something else. Shock. Fear. Horror. Quickly, Pax turned around.

There was a face protruding from the wall behind him. He gulped and then choked, having accidentally gasped with his air lungs instead of his gills.

"See? See!" Laetu croaked. "I told you! I told you there was a face!"

Pax coughed, sending bubbles floating toward the surface of the sea—a surface he could not see. "It's real!" he gasped.

"Maybe it's just a nightmare," Laetu stuttered.

"If it is, we're having the same dream," Pax said, trying to regain his composure. "Come on!" He turned and swam toward the face.

Laetu followed him. Pax had known he would. Laetu was frightened of the face, but he was more frightened of the face taking Pax away and leaving him alone.

Light reflected off the face as it blinked and examined them. It was a young face, Pax decided, despite its lined appearance. It was like the face of a person, he decided, but unlike at the same time. Something was wrong about the nose. It was too small, too wide, too flat. The ears were too flat, and the plane of the face was oddly rounded, freakishly so. Short, dark hair floated about a hand's breadth above the face, framing it and beautifying it in its own way.

As they got closer, Pax could see that the creature had hands. It was clinging to the rock, peering through an orifice. The fingers had extensive tala connecting them, and each finger was tipped by a thick, fierce-looking claw.

Pax slowed as he neared the creature. It did not back away, but continued to look at him, blinking slowly, curiously. Laetu caught up to Pax and positioned himself behind his older brother, staring at the face that was staring back at them.

Pax reached out a hand toward the creature. The creature reached out as well. There was no malice in her eyes, Pax decided. Although the hand was decorated with frightful claws, the thick ends were blunt. They were useful, he decided, but not for ripping flesh.

"Don't," Laetu whispered into his gills.

Pax ignored him.

At the precise moment when their hands should have touched, something yanked the face, the body backwards, withdrawing it from his presence. There was a bang and a rush of water, and Pax understood that the door between the creature and their prison had slammed shut.

"What was it?" he asked.

"I don't know," Laetu whispered.

Chapter 8: Camilly

They all crammed themselves onto Torcalon's largest boat. The rain was falling steadily, as was necessary for the primitive style of boat Torcalon still piloted. The innovations of the Garradh Gannoir, the materials and technology that allowed boats to float on an acid sea, had not yet reached the Rhosen where Torcalon lived. The boat was built to hold a maximum of four people, and now the six of them were packed tightly aboard along with Torcalon, who stood atop a platform in the back of the boat, his withered body swathed in a clinging goatskin coat.

"Do you want me to row?" Widman asked.

Camilly looked up, catching the raindrops on her inner eyelids as she squinted at the red light of the convenalations above her, the cracks in the fiery rock at the center of her world. They'd left as soon as Torcalon had come for them, Camilly, her mother Finnan, Kari's father Widman, the Triads, Sadi and Unaleah, and Pax's Gulot brother Byid. Despite her discomfort, Camilly was antsy with anticipation of her mission. She had to find her brother and Pax. She had to find Kari.

Kari was the girl closest in age to Camilly, and the two were best friends as well as sisters. She had no doubt their search would be successful. They wouldn't stop looking until they found them.

"I'll row," Torcalon rasped.

"The boat's heavier than usual," Widman argued. "Please, father. Let me."

Torcalon squinted through the rain toward his destination, still an invisible shore in the distance. Then he looked at Widman, stuffed onto a bench beside Camilly and Byid. Widman was a large man, not fat, but solid and wide. Although Camilly and Byid were the smallest of the six passengers, they barely fit on the bench beside Widman.

"All right," Torcalon said. "You row. I'll sit."

Widman stood, and the boat rocked. Seawater splashed into the boat. Byid shrieked.

"It's okay," Camilly said. "It's the middle of the night. It's more than half water by now. It won't burn you."

"I know," Byid protested. "I was just startled."

"Sit in the middle," Camilly ordered.

Byid scooted closer to Camilly and Torcalon took the seat Byid had vacated. Widman dragged the oars through the water, accelerating noticeably from Torcalon's much slower pace.

Torcalon gazed at him. "Better slow up," he advised. "They're used to seeing my boat out here. If they see you speeding through the water, they'll know something's up."

Widman nodded and adjusted his pace.

"I wish we'd been able to stay until the baby was born," Unaleah mourned.

"Me too," Sadi admitted. "I'm not as much of a baby-lover as you are, but I really wanted to know what was going to happen when the baby came. You know, whether Mailu was going to wake up, or come back to life."

"I want to know if the baby is Mayim, Gulot, Esh, or Triad," Byid announced.

"Or none of the above," Finnan added. "After all, if Gelu is the father, then the baby is half deadblood."

Byid shook his head. "The baby won't be deadblood. Even if Gelu is its father. Mailu is Siann Dha. The baby couldn't help being one of us."

"Especially after the way everything happened," Camilly added. "Mailu's dead, but the baby is alive. It must be something special, not just a regular deadblood."

"Don't say 'deadblood,' " Widman instructed them. "It's rude."

"What are we supposed to call them?" Byid asked. "That's what they are."

"Their blood can't make light," Widman grunted as he powerfully drew the oars through the water, "but they're not dead. They're as much alive as we are. Their blood is their life . . . their kind of life anyhow."

"Do you really think the baby might be deadbl—I mean—uncasted? Not Siann Dha?" Camilly asked.

"Nope!" Byid answered immediately.

"I agree with Byid," Finnan told her daughter. "It's too much to believe that an uncasted one could be born from a dead girl. There is something in the child's blood that contains life at another level. It will either be Siann Dha or . . . something more."

"Like us?" Sadi asked.

"Maybe," Finnan said. "Or maybe not."

"What else is there?" Byid asked.

"Maybe it's something new," Unaleah suggested. "Maybe the baby is going to go one step beyond us Triads in its abilities."

"That'll be awesome," Byid replied.

"And dangerous," Widman noted. "That's why Cudth Deorth is the best place for Mailu and the baby. Especially while it's small and we don't have a full understanding of its powers yet."

Camilly nodded, pondering a baby that had even more powers than the Triads. She herself was only Mayim, water caste. The Triads were three-in-one. Only three castes existed. What else could there be? She was a little afraid to find out. Suddenly she felt more than just glad to be looking for Pax, Laetu, and Kari. She was glad to be going away from Cudth Deorth, away from Mailu and the baby. She shivered.

They rowed in silence for a long time until finally Camilly could see the shores of Rhosen Faide where Torcalon's home was. Widman docked the boat against the shallow clatry and tied it onto the lattice-like structure.

Gratefully, the six passengers climbed out of the boat and stretched, glad to be ashore and free again. Ieska emerged from Torcalon's house and greeted them. They followed her into the house and gratefully sat down to the breakfast she had prepared, even though it was still several hours until firstlight. Breakfast was fish cakes, halas bread, and gwynant, a whipped sea-tree oil that was served as a topping for bread. Fruits and vegetables were rare in the Rhosen, where most of the agriculture was in the form of fish farms.

"The situation has grown more urgent," Ieska explained as they ate. Her black eyes flashed at them, and Camilly understood that she was angry. "They're blaming Xylo for the death of Kleibald—for all the deaths that occurred when the skyboulder crashed, in fact. They're saying that he deliberately engineered the collision to wrest his grandchildren from the influence of Kleibald, Ardanach, and the elders. The fact that Talag is now living with him strengthens their case against him."

"That's bad, but what does that have to do with us?" Sadi asked her mother.

Ieska pressed her lips together. They all knew Ieska and Xylo were to be married as soon as . . . well, as soon as they were able. Camilly thought Sadi's question was callous and unfeeling. Of course, Ieska was upset. Ieska's eyes glittered. "They're closing the passage between Luca and Garradh Gannoir," she told them. "All traffic will be checked to make sure their reason for travel is approved. It may be only during the next day or two that anyone will be able to travel freely."

"So we have to go quickly," Widman said.

Ieska nodded. "We can't have the elders looking too closely at the Triads."

"Should we be going at all?" Finnan asked, her fear palpable in her tone.

"It's impossible to predict how long the roadblocks will last," Ieska answered. "If war breaks out . . ."

"War!" Unaleah exclaimed. "How could war break out? War between whom? Luca and Garradh Gannoir?"

Ieska nodded. "It's a possibility. With Xylo leading the people of Garradh Gannoir and Nadim and Gelu directing Luca . . . it could happen."

"But that's not likely, right?" Widman asked. "They'll figure out that Xylo isn't to blame, and they'll give up on the whole thing eventually."

Camilly felt frazzled and torn. War? Roadblocks? Inspections? "It doesn't matter about the roadblocks," she stated baldly. "We have to go. We have to find Laetu and Pax and Kari." She looked at Ieska. "You agree, or you wouldn't have called for us to come to Rhosen Faide."

A smile raised the corners of Ieska's lips. "Yes. I agree. But I want you all to know what you're facing. It's dangerous. And things could get worse."

Camilly lifted a forkful of fish cake into her mouth. It was delicious. "How soon can we leave?"

"Should we go at all? Really?" Unaleah asked, her voice quavering.

"Don't be a scaredy," Byid snorted. "Our brothers and sister are missing. We have to go."

"I'm with Byid," Sadi announced, tossing her black hair. "We're all going. Even you, Unaleah."

Unaleah nodded. "You're right, of course. We have to try."

"What's the worst the guards can do? Tell us to go home?" Camilly asked.

Sadi held up her hand and flashed her finger tala at Camilly. "We've still got to hide that we're Triad."

"It'll work," Camilly said staunchly.

"It has to," Ieska added grimly.

By the end of the day, the group, led by Ieska, could see the passage to Garradh Gannoir in the distance. Much to Camilly's disappointment, they hadn't needed to go through the heart of the city to get there. She'd wanted to see the gleaming skyscrapers of Lucedth. The passage, however, was located on the Orbokth, not on the Lucedth clatry, or any of the other clatries.

"We're too late," Widman said, staring across the water at the road that led into the hills of the Orbokth.

"I think you're right," Ieska agreed. "The guards are already in place."

"We can pass," Sadi protested. She held her fingers tightly together to hide her finger tala. "We have to try."

"It's too dangerous," Ieska told her. "If the elders find out that Methiant Migas's children exist and have the powers of the Triad, they'll take you, use you, make you work for them. We can't risk it."

"I'm not Triad," Camilly interrupted. "I'm going to go."

"We should stay together," Unaleah said quietly. "It'll be safer."

"Ieska can take you and Sadi back," Camilly argued. "The rest of us can keep going. We're not Triad."

Camilly saw the look in her mother's eyes change from despair to hope. "We could keep going," Finnan said. "Widman, Camilly, Byid, and I—we can pretend to be a family going on a sightseeing trip to the other side of the Orbokth. The guards have no reason to detain us. We're not Triad."

"I want find my brothers and sister," Byid agreed. "Let Sadi and Unaleah go home. The rest of us can go to Garradh Gannoir."

Ieska frowned. She stroked her long, gray braid. "It will still be dangerous," she said.

"I'd rather try than not," Finnan told her.

"Me too," Widman said.

"Please, Ieska," Camilly begged. She knew that the decision rested with the older woman. Ieska and Bridima had consistently maintained their unquestioned authority over the colony on Cudth Deorth.

"I still want to try to pass," Sadi said. "We should all go forward."

"No," Ieska said.

Camilly's heart sank. She thought of her brothers and her sister and best friend, lost somewhere on the other side of the Orbokth. How could Ieska deny them the right to search?

"Sadi and Unaleah will go back to Cudth Deorth," Ieska continued. "It's too dangerous. More is at stake than you realize."

Finnan took hold of Camilly's hand. "So the four of us . . . we can keep going?"

"Yes," Ieska said. "It will still be dangerous, but only to you, not to all Gannoir. If something happens to you—if you're captured or hurt—we will still have the Triads on our side. You're taking a personal risk. And each of you has a right to make that kind of decision for yourself." She looked at each of the four non-triads in turn. "All of you want to continue on?"

They all nodded.

Ieska turned to look at the heavily guarded path on the other shore of the sea. "Go, then. But wait until evening nears. I know you won't betray us."

Chapter 9: Tass

Tass slowly floated from her dreamlike sleep to the subtle sound of bells. Hovering in the realm between sleep and waking, she strained her ears—the ears of the body and the ears of her soul—toward the sound. Not bells, she decided finally. Not a physical sound at all, she thought, but a soulish one. It inhabited the same realm as the voices of darkness that had been her constant companions since . . . since . . .

Looking back, she thought it was likely that they'd been with her always. She'd never been without her inner torment, her sense that she was worthless and unloved, the very refrain the voices impelled her to hear, to internalize, and to sing to herself. This high-pitched ringing was different somehow. It was joyful. It was tiny instead of overwhelming. It was . . . polite.

She tried to lift her arm, to reach out in the direction from which her mind told her the sounds were coming, but nothing happened. Her arm remained the possession of the darkness. So much darkness. It pressed her down, held her captive, inhabited every inch of her body. She wondered if it would ever leave. She wondered if she wanted it to.

Her arm tingled with pain, and she withdrew the mental impulse to make it move. Better to let it lie. The feeling of nothingness was preferable to the feeling of pain.

As Tass slid back into sleep, she thought she heard shouting, but she was already too far from the surface of consciousness to respond to it or even to wonder what it was. The darkness took over once again.

Chapter 10: Xylo

Xylo didn't waste any time. There was none to waste. He had to get back to Garradh Gannoir before the roadblocks were established. It was likely, he thought, that the elders would have the guards watching for him. He decided it would be best to head for the farthest reaches of the clatry before paying to be ferried across the sea to the Orbokth.

Xylo pushed through a seaweed curtain and entered the bottom floor of a five-story high rise, hoping it contained a restaurant. He needed to refuel before leaving the clatry. He found not only one restaurant, but two. The first served seafood and the second, food from the heights. Xylo hesitated and then chose the restaurant that served food from the heights. It would bring back memories of his days as a soil miner. Life had been hard, but he'd been happy raising his two children, Case and Yasamina, with his wife Chwerta. How he missed her!

Xylo slid open the metal panel door of the restaurant and entered. It was a bright space. Chunks of rock had been used for décor, to represent the Orbokth, he supposed. He settled down at a table, and a young man brought him a menu. As he was pondering his options, he heard someone call his name.

"Xylo? Is that you?"

He looked up, his heart racing. To his relief, he saw that it wasn't the henchmen of the elders calling him, but two of the Triads. His relief turned to confusion. What were the Triads doing here? He looked around for Ieska. He knew she was planning to bring them to Garradh Gannoir. When he didn't see her, he wondered if perhaps she was in the restroom or outside the building tending to whatever needed tending.

The girls approached his table.

"Sadi! Unaleah! What are you doing here?" he asked. "Where's Ieska?"

"She took the ferry with the others," Sadi said with a frown.

"With Gudall and Ninach?" Xylo asked. He assumed that was what the girl meant, since Ieska had purposed to bring the four remaining Triads through the Orbokth.

Sadi shook her head. "They didn't come. Gudall's still too sick and Ninach's . . . well . . . Ninach."

"The roadblocks were already in place," Unaleah told him, looking at him with serious blue eyes. "It was too dangerous for us to attempt a crossing. They'd notice that we had dual tala. We couldn't take the risk. The others aren't Triad, so they could keep going."

Xylo looked from one girl to the other. It was apparent that they were sisters. They looked alike with their black hair, blue eyes, and Esh-tala. But where Unaleah's face looked quiet and worried, Sadi's was aflame with indignation. No one would ever mistake Unaleah for Sadi or vice versa.

"I want to go anyhow," Sadi grumbled. "But Mom wouldn't let us. She said it was too dangerous."

"She's right," Unaleah told her younger half-sister. "I want to go too, but we can't take the risk."

"Kari, Pax, and Laetu are missing." Sadi's eyes flashed. "We should be there helping."

"Who are the ones Ieska took on the ferry?" Xylo asked, cutting to the heart of the matter.

"Widman, Finnan, Byid, and Camilly," Unaleah told him. "They're not Triad, so there wasn't as much risk."

"They're going to pretend to be a family going on holiday to Garradh Gannoir," Sadi told him.

Xylo looked at the girls quizzically. "What are you doing here in Tienged?" he asked.

"Waiting," Sadi grumbled. "My mom told us to rent a room for the night. She'll be back late, and then we can all go back to Cudth Deorth together in the morning."

"It'll be nice to be home when Mailu's baby comes," Unaleah said comfortingly.

"The baby will be fine without us," Sadi complained. "We would be of more use looking for the three that are missing."

"That's probably true," Unaleah admitted. "But we have no choice. We can't go to Garradh Gannoir. Not with the roadblocks. At least we can look on the bright side. There's Mailu and the baby. There's Tass. Maybe there's something we can do to help her recover."

Sadi shook her head. "I don't have much hope that Tass will recover. You know how black her skin is. She's more than just unconscious. She's . . . I don't even know."

"You've seen no change in Tass since you got her to Cudth Deorth?" Xylo asked.

Sadi shook her head again, but Unaleah interrupted her. "She twitches. Sometimes it seems like it's deliberate. Like she's trying to wake up. And she moans. She's alive. There's still hope."

"Join me?" Xylo asked, gesturing at the other seats at the small table he occupied.

The girls sat down.

"What would you recommend?" Unaleah asked. "This is our first time eating Esh-qadar food."

Xylo pointed out various items on the menu, explaining their origin and usage. "I'll even spring for a full order of rucloce," he offered. "It's my favorite. Large white berries, each with a different color and flavor at the heart, and each flavor more delicious than the last."

As they ate and chatted, Xylo pondered the situation. If the roadblocks were in place, he, like the girls, was stuck in Luca. He could follow them back to Cudth Deorth. He wasn't sure what other options he had. Then something occurred to him with a startling clarity. He didn't have any other options, but Sadi and Unaleah had. He looked at them intently, wondering if he should mention his idea.

"What?" Sadi asked, pausing with a rucloce berry halfway to her mouth.

"You could go to Garradh Gannoir," Xylo told them.

Unaleah shook her head. "It's impossible. We'd be seen."

Xylo shook his head. "The roadblocks are only on the land passage, right?"

"It's the only passage to Garradh Gannoir that exists," Sadi pointed out.

"It's not," Xylo contradicted her. "Tass and Igracio didn't get to Garradh Gannoir by going through the Orbokth. They swam. There's got to be an underwater passage as well." He had misgivings about suggesting it. He didn't know exactly where the passageway to the other side of the Orbokth was—only that it was underwater. He knew he could be sending the two girls on a fruitless and frustrating mission. But if they could find it, they could join the search for their missing siblings. And they could bring knowledge of the underwater passageway back with them. The knowledge would be useful if things got as bad as war. They would need another link to Luca. He watched Sadi and Unaleah, trying to gauge their reactions to this bit of information.

Sadi's eyes lit up. "An underwater passageway? I should have thought of that! I knew that Tass showed up on the other side of the Orbokth on her own, but I never thought about how she got there. We could do this!" She looked at her sister.

Unaleah looked worried. "Do you know where the passageway is? The sea is large. We could swim for weeks just looking for it. And we'd have to come to land to eat and sleep. Someone would see us and report people with Esh-tala swimming in the sea. Word would get out."

Sadi grimaced at her sister. "You just said you thought we would be more useful looking for Kari, Pax, and Laetu than sitting around waiting for a dead girl to give birth. What are you scared of?"

"I'm not scared. I'm reasonable," Unaleah replied.

"You can both breathe while you're swimming," Xylo pointed out. "There's no reason you can't eat and sleep in the sea."

Unaleah gave him a doubtful look. "I've never stayed down for more than a few hours."

"We can do this!" Sadi exclaimed. "We can eat on the way. We can graze like the fishes do! There's food down there. You cook. You know the sea is full of plant food we can eat."

"And if you can breathe, you can sleep," Xylo added. He wondered whether Ieska was going to be angry with him for dispatching the girls without her approval. Sadi was her daughter, after all.

Sadi popped a rucloce berry into her mouth and bit down. "Think we can get an order of these to go?" She grinned.

"I'll stay here and wait for Ieska," Xylo volunteered. "I'll explain. She'll be glad that we've found a way. And if you can't find the passageway, you can always swim back to Cudth Deorth."

"That's true," Unaleah said. "We have nothing to lose."

Sadi's eyes flashed at Xylo mischievously. "You're just trying to get a night alone with Mom."

The thought had crossed his mind. "That's not why I made the suggestion," he told the girl. "And we're not married yet. I wouldn't . . ."

Blushing, Unaleah said, "We know you wouldn't. Sadi was just joking."

"So are we doing this?" Sadi asked her sister.

Unaleah nodded slowly. "It's the right thing to do. I'm worried, but I can see that we have to try."

"We can give it a week. If we can't find the passageway, we'll go back to Cudth Deorth. We'll be back in time for the baby's birth," Sadi promised.

When Ieska returned last that evening and asked at the hotel she and the girls had agreed upon before her departure, she found Xylo waiting for her in the lobby.

"Sign here," he ordered. "It's a marriage license."

Ieska shook her head. "It'll put our mission in danger to have my name associated with yours. You know I want to marry you, but we have to consider the timing."

Xylo smiled. "Something occurred to me. When I was a soil miner, I was legally registered under my father-in-law's name. It's a valid legal identity still. I don't know why I didn't think of it before.

You won't be marrying Adam Xalantaka. You'll be marrying Xylo Athayer Sapor."

Ieska frowned. "That makes no sense. Case and Yasamina both bear the name Xalantaka, not Sapor."

"I went by my real name familiarly," he told her. "And that's the name I gave to my children. But on my legal registration for work, I was Xylo Athayer Sapor, son-in-law of Athayer Sapor. Marry me, Ieska."

"Xylo Athayer Sapor . . ." she said, trying out the words as though she were trying on a garment she was thinking about purchasing.

"The elders know me as Xylo Xalantaka. Xylo is a common enough nickname. They could connect me to Xylo Athayer Sapor if they did their homework, but I don't think that will happen. I haven't used that name in four years now. Please, Ieska. Marry me."

Ieska's black eyes flashed at him. "All right." She took the pen from his hand and signed the papers. "You'll file these in the morning?"

He took her in his arms. "I'll file them right now," he promised, kissing her.

Chapter 11: Pax

There was no more sleep for Pax and Laetu that night. They were full of speculations about what they'd seen.

"That must be how we got in here," Pax concluded. "There's a door between this cell and the sea outside it."

"They trapped us," Laetu said mournfully. "We're their prisoners."

"Maybe they're scared of us," Pax suggested. "After all, we thought that the girl who peeked through the doorway was scary looking. Her people probably think we're just as weird."

"Maybe," Laetu said. "But who are they? Are they people? Are they Mayim?"

Pax shrugged and pushed himself through the water toward the now-sealed doorway. "If they weren't people—if they weren't rational—they wouldn't have locked us up. And if they're in the water they must be Mayim."

"Mayim don't have claws," Laetu pointed out.

Frowning, Pax had to admit his brother was correct. Mayim didn't have claws.

"Her head was weird, too," Laetu added with a grimace. "She was shaped almost like a fish or something. It wasn't like our heads."

"I've gotta admit you're right there," Pax said, remembering the skewed visage of their visitor. "But maybe she's deformed or something. There could be a group of Mayim living under the water. We only just found out about the deadbloods living in Garradh Gannoir. What if hundreds of years ago, some Mayim colonized the sea."

"Someone would have found them by now," Laetu said. "The Mayim explore the sea all the time. It's not like the Gulot on the land or the Esh on the heights. They do their work and that's all."

"You know that's not true," Pax contracted. "The Mayim spend most of their time working too. And the Gulot and Esh do sometimes explore. We wouldn't know about Garradh Gannoir if they didn't."

"I think they're monsters," Laetu said with a shudder. "They're probably keeping us here so they can fatten us up and eat us."

Pax snorted and bubbles rose from his gills. "We're not going to get fat eating sea plants," he pointed out. "If they're monsters, they're pretty stupid ones." He banged at the door that, an hour ago, he hadn't known existed. He watched as Laetu plucked a handful of fungal sea-growth off the rocky wall of their prison and ate it. When he finished, Laetu patted his belly, pushing it out so Pax would note how "fat" he'd become. Pax sighed.

"I don't think they're monsters," Pax insisted. He banged on the door and pried at its edges with his fingernails. "Now that we know where the door is, we can work on getting out of here."

Laetu plucked another handful of fungus and munched it stoically.

"Don't you want to get out of here?"

Laetu looked at him solemnly. "I'm scared," he admitted.

"Of what?"

Laetu blinked his outer eyelids. "Bad stuff happened. You felt the quake same as I did. What if we get out and everybody's dead? I'm not sure I want to know what happened. At least here we can pretend everyone else is okay."

"We still need to know. Even if we're scared," Pax said.

"It's different for you," Laetu complained. "You have less to lose. Your mother is dead. You haven't seen your father since you were three. And Byid was safe in Cudth Deorth at the time of the boom. My parents and my sister were right there in Garradh Gannoir when it happened."

Wounded to the core, Pax snarled at his half-brother. "You know better than that. We're all a family. All of us from Cudth Deorth. Your parents are my parents. Your sister is my sister. I would suffer the same as you. I'm just brave enough to want to know what happened. I'm brave enough to want to go on, no matter what. You're so cowardly you are content to spend your life penned up in a cage." He scowled at Laetu.

"I'm not!" Laetu protested.

"Then help me out!" Pax grunted as he used a piece of rock to pry at the edges of the closed door.

Pressing his lips together, Laetu swam to his brother. Together they banged, chipped, and pried at the edges of the door, not knowing whether success would bring them happiness or heartbreak.

Chapter 12: Camilly

Camilly kept her hands balled in fists at her sides. They had decided it would be best for Camilly and Finnan to pretend to be Gulot—rock, instead of Mayim—water, despite their finger tala.

"You know Mayim from the city don't have long hair," Finnan had argued. "We're trying to be inconspicuous."

"You look typical for the Gulot," Widman had added. "Even with the red hair. But your mother's right. Mayim don't have long hair. It's either cut your hair or hide your hands."

And that was that, Camilly reflected. She wasn't going to cut her hair to fit in. Lots of the Gulot had vestigial finger tala. Even if someone noticed, it wouldn't be a big deal. But a Mayim with long hair would stand out.

They chose to wait until evening to approach the guarded part of the road. The light would be dim and the mist in the air would be at its thickest. Camilly wasn't particularly afraid of the guards. None of them had lived on the clatry in more than ten years. There was no chance they would be recognized. It was Xylo they were looking for. The guards could have no way of knowing of the association of makeshift family with the "criminal" they'd been engaged to track.

"Name and caste?" the burly Gulot guard requested.

Widman spoke for the group. They'd agreed to use Widman's real name for their family. If they were looking for verification of identity, it existed, even if Widman hadn't conducted business in any of the cities in sixteen years. "Widman Xunisso Ansidla and family. Gulot," he told the man.

"Their names?"

"My wife, Finnan. My stepdaughter, Camilly, and my son, Byid."

The guard looked at them skeptically. "Do you have identification papers?"

Widman shook his head. "We've been farming on the Orbokth for over ten years. Haven't been to the city. I didn't know I needed to bring my papers."

The guard looked at them uneasily. "No papers?"

"There should be a record of my employment from before I left, if you want to investigate," Widman said, keeping his tone humble.

Camilly clutched the sides of her tunic firmly in her fists, hoping the guard didn't ask for proof of her caste. She wondered whether it would have mattered. The guard hardly looked at her. He was staring at her mother, however.

Finnan smiled at the guard and twirled a bit of her long red hair around her finger. "You're going to let us go, aren't you? We've been planning this trip ever since we heard about Garradh Gannoir," she said. "I'm longing to see the trees!"

"What is your full name?" the man asked her, his eyes softening.

"Finnan Ansidla," she answered promptly. She used only Widman's surname instead of revealing her own second and third names, the surnames of her parents.

The guard smiled at her, clearly dazzled by her looks. Camilly had to force herself not to roll her eyes. She knew her mother was pretty, but she'd never imagined any man other than her father looking at her mother like that. And this one was supposed to be guarding the road.

"How long do you plan to stay in Garradh Gannoir?" the guard asked.

"Three days," Byid piped up. "And three nights! In a hotel by the seashore!" He bounced a little to convey his excitement. Camilly was impressed.

Relaxing, the guard waved them on. "Go ahead. I can tell you're not the person we're looking for."

Finnan waved sweetly to the guard as they passed. Then at the look of surprise on his face, she blushed. "It's vestigial tala," she told him, tucking her hand into the folds of her tunic."

"Hey—no one is perfect," the guard retorted with a wave.

None of them relaxed until they were far enough into the tunnel that they couldn't see the guard anymore.

The two-mile journey in relative darkness was uneventful, although Camilly enjoyed seeing the phosphorescent algae that lined the walls of the passage through the rocky cliffs. The air inside was cold and damp—colder than the nighttime temperature in the city and far, far colder than the tropical warmth of Cudth Deorth. Camilly was too keyed up to feel the chill, however. They walked quickly and quietly, not wanting to give themselves away should anyone hear them.

They weren't the only ones traveling. Garradh Gannoir had become a popular destination for the people of Luca, and vice versa. Twice, they overtook other groups in the tunnels, and four times, they encountered the uncasted people of Garradh Gannoir. There was danger there. No one from Luca would recognize them, but Finnan and Camilly had been part of the rescue efforts that freed the inhabitants of the skyboulder. They were known to many of the people of Obumbro, the main city in Garradh Gannoir. No flicker of recognition met their eyes as they passed the deadbloods in the passageway, however.

When they passed the final bend into the room that led outside of the passageway, Camilly sighed with relief. She could see the dark red glow of the rainy sky outside, and the undulating reflection of the convenalations on the sea. She wanted to dive off the cliff into the water, to begin her search for Kari, Pax, and Laetu immediately, but she knew she couldn't. Someone might see. And besides, they were a team, all of them. They had to make a plan, to consult with Ceres about her own explorations, before they could be effective in their own search.

"How far is it to the caves of the Dynroc?" Widman asked as they climbed down the staircase to the beach far below them.

Finnan pointed. "It's just past that outcropping there. There is an entrance at sea level, so we won't need to climb back into the heights before entering."

"Just after," Camilly grinned.

Finnan smiled ruefully. "She's right there. Most of the occupied rooms are near the heights. But I'll feel better once we're inside."

"Aren't we safe here?" Byid asked. "The guards were at the other end of the passageway, not this one."

Camilly had been wondering the same thing.

"We still have to be cautious," Finnan replied. "Ieska mentioned war. War doesn't happen without a lot of internal unrest. It's never the work of a single man or woman."

Camilly shrugged. "They worship us here. We're the Siann Dha. They won't do anything to us."

"If things are as bad as Ieska suspects, then being Siann Dha won't be any protection," Widman said. "The elders want to arrest Xylo for his part in everything that happened with the skyboulder. You two,"—he looked at Camilly and Finnan—"were part of that rescue as well. And we know the elders have allies among the leadership of Garradh Gannoir." He shook his head. "We should be careful."

Chapter 13: Xylo

The golden light of the Ghalon streamed through the window of the high rise where Xylo and Ieska had spent the night. *I'm an old man,* Xylo thought. *I've been through happy times, sad times, and horrible times.* He looked at Ieska who was still curled up in their bed. *I never thought I'd been happy like this again.* He let bliss wash over him as he gazed at his wife, ignoring, for the time, the danger he knew awaited them. Their happiness might not last. At his age—and at Ieska's—it couldn't last much longer. But for now, it was enough.

They packed quickly after eating the breakfast they had brought with them to the room. Ieska combed and braided her long gray hair, smiling to herself as she did so.

"I think we ought to try to reach Garradh Gannoir," Xylo said.

Ieska started to object, but Xylo held up a hand to stay her comments.

"I know what you're going to say. And I know we can't go by means of the passageway. The guards are looking for me."

Ieska fastened the end of her braid with a length of rubbery sea ribbon and looked at her husband questioningly. "How then?"

"Over the top," he replied. "Over the Orbokth."

Ieska shook her head. "It can't be done. The Orbokth is too high. Near the top, the rock is nearly liquid from the heat of the Ghalon. We'd never make it."

"We're Esh. We can do it."

"We're Esh, but we're not immortal," Ieska pointed out.

"There has to be a way," Xylo retorted. "We can't give up."

"It's not giving up to admit that something is impossible."

"We can't know until we try."

Ieska smiled. "I'm a mathematician and a scientist. I've done the math. It's impossible. No one could survive a trip over the top of the Orbokth. It's too hot."

Xylo frowned. "I need to go back."

"Badly enough to wait for the right time?" his bride asked.

Pressing his lips together, Xylo answered, "By that time, it may be too late."

"Do you have any choice?" Ieska asked. "I mean, any choice that doesn't involve incinerating yourself?"

Xylo winced at her use of "yourself." Somehow, she had made the "us" into "you." "I don't know," he said heavily. "I just don't know what to do. I don't want to make a habit of running away. I still believe in justice. I still believe that Gelu and Nadim need to pay for their part in the plot against Gannoir. I believe in my obligation to the people of Garradh Gannoir. I'm acting Dynroc. I'm their leader. I have to be the one to train Talag, to bring him up to his responsibilities. If I can't get back there, I've failed."

"The roads won't be blocked and guarded forever," Ieska replied. "How long do you think they'll keep it up? A week? A month? Once they're gone, we'll go back to Garradh Gannoir. Talag is safe. He's with Case and Ceres. And Widman and Finnan will be there to help soon. Maybe they're there already. Garradh Gannoir will be fine. Not only that, justice will be better served if you're not dead or imprisoned."

"So what do you suggest?" Xylo asked. "Where should I go?" His heart ached at the thought of going into hiding without his bride of less than a day.

"That's easy enough," Ieska told him. "You'll go to Cudth Deorth. And so will I, for a time. I still need to be going to work in the city. The elders might get suspicious if I skip out on my job. But you'll be safe there. And I'll come often."

By evening that day, Ieska and Xylo were safely inside the hidden hollow that was Cudth Deorth.

"You'll stay in Widman's home, of course," Bridima decided. "He's in Garradh Gannoir, so only Ninach's living there now. And she can come stay with me while you're here. You'll want privacy." Her eyes twinkled at the newlyweds.

"Will Ninach be okay with that?" Ieska asked.

Bridima shook her head. "Ninach's never okay lately. I'm not sure what to do."

"She's never had a sunny disposition," Ieska commented.

"It's more than that," Bridima said, running a hand through her white hair. "She's angry. Bitter."

"Maybe she regrets not being part of the mission to bring the skyboulder back?" Xylo suggested.

"Maybe," Bridima answered.

"How's Dynny?" Xylo asked.

"The same as always," Bridima told him. "He's a fine man. He takes good care of Tass and Mailu."

"Any change in their condition?" Ieska said.

Bridima shook her head. "Tass is the same. She lives, but never wakes. Mailu's belly continues to grow, but there are no other signs that she's alive. Dynny keeps a close watch on them both. I'd trust him with my life."

Xylo nodded. "Caring is what he does best." He thought of Afa and how Dynny had kept her alive after her fall into the acid sea. Even Dynny's power hadn't been enough to save her in the end. And now, both of Afa's daughters, Tass and Mailu, were hovering near death themselves. Dynny, he thought, was their only hope. And they couldn't have a better one.

He looked around at the blues and greens of the broad hollow of Cudth Deorth. It seemed quiet with so many of its inhabitants gone. He thought back to his first visit, when the cool colors had seemed so foreign to him after a life lived in a world of golds and reds. Only the sea was blue outside of Cudth Deorth. And even then, it reflected much of the gold and red from the sky. It wasn't the same. There was no place on Gannoir like Cudth Deorth.

In the distance he could see Gudall slowly working on his hut. Rhyder was helping him. Dynny and his patients were in a cliffside cavern, and Ninach was nowhere to be seen. And that was all. The six other Triads were gone, and so were Finnan and Widman.

Xylo cringed at the thought that it had been his own visit that had changed things so much for the inhabitants of the isolated paradise. They'd lived in happy seclusion for years . . . until he had come with his plea for help, with his plea for their blood to save the world. Now they were scattered. He wondered what would have happened if he'd just let things be, if he'd never tried to bring the skyboulder back, if he'd never tried to prevent the destruction of Gannoir. Would Kleibald and Gelu have succeeded in destroying the world? Or would they have died of starvation aboard their rocky skyship? Had it been necessary to recruit the Triads at all? He would never know.

Ieska seemed to sense his turmoil. She took hold of his hand, and together they climbed the grassy cliffs to the cave where Dynny was keeping watch over Tass and Mailu.

It took a minute for Xylo's eyes to adjust to the dim light inside. Finally, he saw that Mailu's coffin had been placed against the wall of the cavern to his left, and Tass's cot to his right. A cot for Dynny occupied the back wall, but the little man wasn't in it. He hovered over Tass, massaging her blackened hands in his own ancient, gnarled ones. Xylo wondered how old Dynny was. He'd never thought to ask, though he assumed Dynny had attained more than his own sixty-five years.

"How's she doing?" Xylo asked softly.

"Better," Dynny said decidedly. "She bends better now."

Xylo peered at Tass, thinking of her fiery spirit. Tass was bitter and angry, but she had always been so alive, so sure of herself, even at twelve. That now the best that could be said of her was that she was more bendy was heartbreaking. "Has she been awake?" he asked.

Dynny shook his head. "But she's not dead. She's not dead. Not like poor Mailu." Xylo could hear the little sob in Dynny's voice.

"You've taken good care of Mailu," Ieska said. "It's hard to look after a dead girl."

This was certainly true, Xylo reflected. "No one could have done it better," he added.

He walked across the tiny room and leaned over the glass-topped coffin. Mailu's placid, scarred face was still pale and dead. But he was startled to find that her belly was touching the glass of the lid. Even though everyone had told him that the baby was alive and growing, there was a part of him that hadn't believed it, that had attributed it to wishful thinking. Now he could see for himself. It made him feel uneasy. How could a dead girl give birth? How could her body nourish a child? What if it wasn't a child in there? He took a deep breath and released it slowly, hoping the others wouldn't notice his discomfiture.

"Have you seen the baby moving in her belly?" Ieska asked Dynny.

He nodded. "I can see it kicking and squirming. Her baby is coming soon."

"You and Rhyder have a plan ready for opening the coffin?"

Dynny bobbled his gray, wrinkled head. "Rhyder knows what to do. He and Gudall are going to take the glass off very, very carefully." He laid a hand on top of the glass over Mailu's swollen belly protectively.

"And Bridima will deliver the baby?" Ieska said.

"And me. I'll take care of the baby once it comes out." Dynny smiled proudly.

"Caring is what you do best," Xylo said respectfully. He took Ieska's hand, and they walked to the exit of the little cave that used to be the storage space for the colony on Cudth Deorth.

Once they were far enough away, Xylo asked, "Do you think the baby can be alive? The girl is clearly dead."

"Dynny said he's seen it moving," Ieska answered.

"What if it's not a baby?"

"What else would it be?"

"I'm not sure I want to guess," Xylo said with a frown.

They were awakened in the middle of the night by frantic shouts that carried across the water.

"The baby!" Ieska gasped. Hurriedly she put on a tunic and robe and rushed outside. The rain was falling lightly—it was nearing morning—as she and Xylo hurried toward the cave. Rhyder and Gudall were already inside, prying at the glass that sealed Mailu in her airtight tomb. Xylo, Ieska, Bridima, and Ninach crowded around at the doorway. Dynny hovered between the doorway and the coffin fretfully. The space was lit by a pale-yellow glow that seemed to be coming from the sarcophagus.

"I can't watch!" Ninach shrieked. She hid her face in Bridima's shoulder.

"Pull harder," Rhyder grunted.

"It's not working," Gudall panted. "What did they use to affix the glass to the stone?"

"It doesn't matter," Rhyder retorted. "What matters is that we get it open. We'll break the glass if we have to, but it would be better if it didn't come to that."

Xylo and Ieska rushed forward and began to pry at the glass lid with the others. Peering into the coffin, Xylo could see that the glow was emanating from a pale liquid that now filled the space to a fingertip's depth. Mailu's rounded stomach was taut, and he could see the dark, bruised appearance of her skin through her white gown. He wondered how the child they were striving to free would survive such a birth.

"Ow!" Ieska exclaimed, putting her hand in her mouth. A smear of blood glistened on the glass and stone she'd been trying to separate.

A whistling noise filled the air. Xylo, Rhyder, and Gudall stopped prying in astonishment.

"You broke the seal!" Gudall exclaimed.

"More blood! More blood!" Xylo cried. "The blood's the key!"

"Let me," Gudall offered. "I'm Triad. My blood is more powerful, right?" He quickly moved into Ieska's place and pushed on the glass where a tiny chip had sliced Ieska's hand. Gudall's blood flowed into the seal between glass and stone. There was a popping sound.

"Now!" Rhyder shouted.

Xylo, Rhyder, Ieska, and Gudall lifted the lid of the coffin.

Chapter 14: Tass

Tass opened her eyes. Her fingers and toes were burning with pain and her stomach hurt. The tormenting voices in her mind had quieted, but a raucous din of noise seemed to throw itself at her, assaulting her ears without speaking any meaning into her mind.

Turning her head from one side to the other, she was able to discern that she was lying on a bed next to a wall and that the room was full of people. Taking a gasping breath, she drew in the damp air. It flooded her lungs with cool relief, blessed relief. She tried to move her limbs and found that, for the first time in forever, she could. It still hurt. The blanket chafed her skin as though it were covered with thorns. She wondered what sort of people had tucked her into this bed of torture.

The cacophony increased and decreased in volume but was still unintelligible. Tass moaned. How everything hurt! Her body was stiff. She could wiggle her hands and feet, but only just.

With every ounce of willpower she could muster, she pushed at the blanket, trying to free her body from its torturous texture. She succeeded in freeing her arms. Glancing down she noticed that her arms were a funny color—too dark—but maybe it was the dim light of the room. She wondered where she was. Her last waking memory was of the violet seawater around her as she rode the insect-like giant dga. After that, it had been darkness, pain, and the inner torment of the voices. Had the voices brought her here? Was she injured? Was she awake even now, or was it just a trick of the darkness, meant to plunge her into further despair?

She blinked, first with just her outer eyelids, and then with both pair, trying to coordinate their movements in the way that was usually automatic for her. Her eyes were dry and itchy. Turning away from the wall and toward the bustling chaos, she found she could discern the movements of other people, lots of them. They all had their backs to her, and there was an electricity in the atmosphere that confused her. It was dark, and she noticed after a while that the space was enclosed and lit only by the blue light of an ymolenegth lamp on a short table near her bed.

"Hold him back!" someone yelled, and one of the figures took a staggering step toward her, still facing in the opposite direction.

Someone was wailing. Maybe she wasn't awake. Maybe it was a nightmare. It was certainly unlike any waking reality she'd experienced before. Her thoughts started to become more coherent as she listened to the sounds around her. Blink. Wiggle fingers. Wiggle toes. Ouch. Awake.

"Don't hurt her!" a voice cried.

Tass wondered if the voice was talking about herself. She hurt.

"Is it breathing?" someone else said.

"Girl or boy?"

"Casted or deadblood?"

There was a frail warble—the cry of a baby. The baby was the focus of the attention in the room.

"It's bleeding! You must have cut it when you slit Mailu's belly!"

Mailu! Tass groaned again. Her sister was there! And the baby was hers? She was going to see her sister again! Warmth flooded Tass's senses as she relaxed into the hope of having her sister-protector, the one person who had loved her even as her mother had rejected her. Mailu!

"Hand it here," a woman's voice said.

There was a shuffling of the players in the room and the small, wailing baby was handed to a wizened dwarf of a man, who cuddled it close and soothed its anxious fretting.

"Do we sew her back up?" someone asked.

"Not much point," another person said with a bitterness that stung Tass's throat.

"She's dead then? All dead?"

"Never drew a breath. And her blood's not making ymolenegth. I tested some of it in Dynny's water cup. She's gone. Has been for a long time."

"Miracle baby," someone murmured.

"Casted?"

"I'm testing the blood now."

A stillness settled on the room and Tass felt herself drawn into the aura of anticipation.

The light in the room grew brighter and the silence more intense.

"Son of a vauzigk!" someone swore.

Chapter 15: Unaleah

Unaleah wriggled uncomfortably. She'd never slept underwater before, and although she could breathe easily, she couldn't get comfortable. Her own weightlessness in the water caused her body to rock with the waves, even when she tucked herself as tightly as she could against the underside of the Orbokth. Sadi seemed to be having no trouble. She'd fallen asleep easily.

The two girls had spent the day exploring the outskirts of Luca, looking for any obvious passageway to the other side of the Orbokth. Sadi had wanted to swim to Lucedth first and begin their search there, but Unaleah's calm rationality had prevailed. They'd begun their search where they were, by the Orbokth near Tienged. It would waste less time, Unaleah had argued, if they began where they were and systematically explored the ring of rocky land that surrounded the Great Sea. It also made sense that there might be a passageway under the sea near Tienged, since the overland passageway was there. Sadi had finally agreed to Unaleah's plan, more out of a drive to begin their search than because she agreed.

Unaleah wasn't sure how large the Great Sea was. It hadn't even been called the Great Sea until the discovery of Garradh Gannoir.

Before then, the Great Sea had been the "sea," the only region of water that existed. Having been raised in the seclusion of Cudth Deorth, Unaleah found the vast open spaces of Luca overwhelming. It was going to take more than a week to explore, she was sure of it. Of course, as Sadi had optimistically pointed out, they only needed to go halfway around the sea, as they knew in what direction Garradh Gannoir was located. Unaleah supposed her sister was correct, but she was still worried. She wasn't sure if she was hoping they would succeed, find an underwater passageway to the other side of the Orbokth, and be able to begin their search for their missing younger siblings, or whether she wanted to fail quickly and go home to Cudth Deorth to help with Mailu, Tass, and the baby.

Maybe, she reflected ruefully, that was part of why she couldn't sleep. Maybe it wasn't just the rocking motion of the sea.

When Unaleah groggily woke after a fitful night of cycling from sleep to waking and back again, Sadi was full of energy and ready to go.

"Eat," she urged her sister. "Maybe today's the day we'll find the way."

Her words were garbled, as neither of the girls was used to speaking regularly in their gill-voices. Unaleah grabbed some sea plants and began to munch. Idly, she wondered how it would be possible to cook under the sea. She'd eaten this variety of vegetation before, but always cooked, seasoned, and in combination with other foodstuffs so that it was a delicious part of a balanced meal, not just a rubbery plant plucked from the side of a rock.

After she'd eaten what she thought was probably a meal's-worth of the plantstuff, she reached into her knapsack and pulled out a handful of rucloce berries they'd brought from the restaurant. She handed two to Sadi and kept two for herself. Her knapsack was by no means waterproof, but in a world dominated by the sea and where rain fell all night every night and mist filled the air in the day, it didn't make much difference. The waxy white exterior of the berries sealed the flavor inside.

She bit into the berry, covering the bite-mark with her thumb to keep the juices from floating away. A sweet and tangy flavor filled her mouth. Xylo had introduced the Triads to rucloce, and Unaleah loved it. They all did. She finished the first berry and then bit into the second. This one was sweeter, almost like the honey produced by the melilla shrimp.

"Ready?" Sadi asked.

Unaleah nodded, and they dove through the rainbow layers of the sea. The passageway, the girls had agreed, would be located below the yellow zone. Otherwise Garradh Gannoir would have been discovered much earlier. The Mayim frequented the blue and green zones and only rarely descended into the cold yellow layer. Anything below that was off limits to them due to the extreme cold and the uncomfortably stinging acidity of the liquid of the sea at that level. It didn't bother Unaleah. The stinging sensation felt good on her skin, and she supposed her sister felt the same way. They explored the rocky Orbokth with their hands, looking for openings that would lead them out of the Great Sea of Luca and into the world of the Others.

Twice they came to openings. They spent hours pushing themselves through narrow cracks in the rock, going further and further into the submerged cave system. Strange creatures dwelt there in the depths. Unaleah saw one animal appended to the rock above her head. It had projections that looked like smooth blubbery fingers. Each tip ended in what she took to be an eye, from the way it was looking at her. She couldn't tell its true color because of the orange glow of the ymolenegth around her, but it was pale with dark eyes ringed with an even lighter color. She was unsure if it was a plant or an animal or something in between. In her mind she christened it a finger-eye coral, although it was not exactly like fingers or eyes or coral. Sadi poked at it, and it recoiled from her touch.

Fish swam around them of a multitude of colors and shapes. There were crawling things, too, that came out of cracks in the rock to look at them. Unaleah wondered if she was the first person to see those creatures ever—she and Sadi. The underwater caverns would be a rich trove for research, if the Mayim could come down this far. She thought of the skyboulder and wondered if it would be possible to build ships that could penetrate the caustic waters to enable scientists to come.

After hours of exploration, they decided the cave system was only a series of dead-ends. Swimming back to the main part of the sea, Unaleah sighed with her gills, and bubbles rose from the sides of her head. They ascended near the surface and lunched on sea vegetables and salt oranges plucked from bushes with their roots in the sea and their branches in the air above. It was tastier than the vegetation she'd eaten for breakfast but not very filling.

"There's always sarxworms," Sadi pointed out when Unaleah expressed her dissatisfaction with the meal.

Unaleah grimaced. "Not raw. I couldn't."

Sadi grinned. "I almost think I could. I need some meat."

"Maybe by tomorrow I'll be hungry enough for that," Unaleah said. "But not today. Biting off their heads is disgusting."

"How far do you think we've come?" Sadi asked. She'd poked her head out of the sea to look around at the Orbokth fringing their pocket of the world.

Unaleah pointed off in the distance. "That clatry there is Tienged," she noted. "We're not even as far as Lucedth."

"Told you we should have started on the far side of Lucedth," Sadi commented.

Unaleah shook her head. "We would only have had to come back around to this area in the end."

"Not if we found the passageway."

"I think this is going to take more than a week," Unaleah sighed.

Sadi twirled her hair so that it was all in one wet rope down her back. "Depends if we find anything."

"Are you still planning to go home to Cudth Deorth at the end of the week?" Unaleah asked.

Sadi shook her head. "I'm going to find Kari, Pax, and Laetu. We have to try. I'm going to keep looking until we find a way to get to Garradh Gannoir."

"I thought you'd say that." Unaleah frowned.

"You know it's the right thing to do."

"There is more than just one right path."

Sadi shook her head. "The baby has plenty of people to look after it, if it even gets born anytime soon. You've seen how big the sea is. Kari, Pax, and Laetu could be anywhere. It's going to take all of us working together to find them."

"Let's go then," Unaleah said. She ducked her head under the water and pushed her body down through the colorful layers of the sea.

Chapter 16: Pax

"I think I've got it!" Pax shouted. "Come help me!"

Laetu crammed his fingers into the gap Pax had opened in the doorway in the rock.

"Pull!"

"I'm trying," Laetu grunted.

The rough rock scraped at their fingers, and the water in the gap began to glow.

"I'm bleeding," Laetu mourned.

"Me too. It's a small price to pay," Pax shot back. Even after so many weeks under the water, his gill-voice sounded strange in his ears. He braced his feet against the wall beneath the gap and pulled. "It's working!"

Laetu balled up his hand into a fist and shoved it in the gap.

Pax, following his younger half-brother's lead, shoved in first a fist and then a foot. "Pull your fist out," he ordered. "Then give the door a good hard kick."

Laetu obeyed. The rock cracked.

"Again!" Pax said.

Laetu kicked the door again and the rock gave way. The doorway was open. Both boys reoriented themselves and then pushed their bodies through the narrow opening.

"I'm scared," Laetu whimpered.

"Me too," Pax admitted.

The turquoise glow of the sea around them told them they weren't far from the surface of the sea, but no lights descended from the Ghalon above. They had not come, as Pax had anticipated, into a wide-open space, but to a system of arches and tunnels, winding doorways that led this way and that, all lit by the sumptuous glow of the ymolenegth. Pax led the way as they explored. Sea creatures scuttled here and there, and in places there was evidence of civilization—netted off caverns full of fish and shrimp, rows of sea plants in patterns too regular to have come about naturally, herds of vauzigk in huge caverns, barred from exiting by metal grates.

"What is this place?" Pax breathed.

"There's a whole world down here," Laetu agreed. "That girl who peeked at us was probably one of them."

"Not probably. Definitely," Pax corrected. "I wonder where she is—where they are."

"Is it day or night?" Laetu wondered.

"I thought it was day, but now I'm not so sure," Pax said. "Living underwater, it's hard to tell."

"Are they all asleep?"

"Maybe."

A sudden jerk on his ankle told Pax that wasn't the case. He spun around, but the grip was too strong for him to break free.

"How did you two get out?" the man asked.

Pax stared at him. His captor—and Pax's, for the man had a firm grip on Pax's ankle as well—looked like the girl they'd seen. His face was oddly protuberant, his nose, short and wide. Both his fingers and his toes had the same extensive tala and blunted claws that they'd seen on the girl. This man's hair had been braided into hundreds of tiny rows on his head, and all the braids had been gathered into a rope that went halfway down his back, including his beard hairs. He wore an apron-like coverall of thick, woven, rubbery sea string that covered him front and back. His feet and hands were oddly elongated, so that the tala that connected his digits became more like a fish's fins and less like the tala of the Mayim. The man was large, muscular, and frightening.

"Don't hurt us!" Laetu cried.

"Please," Pax added.

"How did you get out?" the man repeated slowly and ominously.

"We broke the door down," Pax told him.

The man flinched. "Broke the door down?" He released their ankles and sped through the meandering passageways toward their former prison. When he arrived, he found the piece of rock that had split from the door and put it back in the doorway. Then he took a chisel from the pocket of his apron and chipped away at the Orbokth a few feet from the doorway. He filled the crack with gravel, balancing it expertly until the gap was sealed. Pax and Laetu watched him in amazement.

"What are you doing?" Pax asked.

"Protecting my people," the man grunted harshly. "Now come with me. When the time of rest is over, I'll take you to our leadership. Until then, I'll take you home."

"Home?" Laetu squeaked.

"He means his home, not ours," Pax noted.

"They said you were dangerous, but you don't look dangerous to me," the man said, looking them over critically. "You look kind of puny. And you're definitely not Tehom."

"Tehom? What's that?" Laetu asked, his curiosity finally overwhelming his fear.

"We're Tehom. The water people."

"Are you related to the Mayim?" Pax wondered.

"You know of the Mayim?" the man asked, surprised. "But then, I suppose the legends are the same all over Gannoir. After all, we speak the same language."

"The Mayim aren't a legend," Pax told him. "They're one of the three castes of our people."

The man looked at them warily. "Who are you?"

"I'm Pax, and that's my brother, Laetu. Who are you?"

The man made a face. "I'm Ged," the man said. "But that wasn't what I meant. Where did you come from? How did you get here?"

"We were exploring the heights around Garradh Gannoir," Laetu told him. "We saw a lake and decided to swim. Before we knew it, we were trapped. We've been in that cave for . . . I don't know how long."

"You're from the land?" the man asked.

Pax shrugged. "I guess. We were far from home when we went exploring. We live on the other side of the Orbokth. Near Luca."

The man blinked his eyes and whistled through his gills. "Luca? You're from Luca? Are you Mayim yourselves? You're in the sea, and you don't look like your skin is blistering."

"We're kind of . . ." Laetu began, but Pax motioned for him to be quiet.

"We're not really Mayim," Pax said. "We can just, I don't know, swim for some reason." He shrugged and tried to look innocent.

"But you know the Mayim? Not just know of the Mayim. You know them yourselves?"

Laetu nodded. "My mom and my sister are Mayim."

"By the wings of the vervol!" the man exclaimed excitedly.

Pax slugged Laetu. "You shouldn't have said anything."

"This is so exciting!" the man was saying. "We thought we were the only race of Siann Dha left! To find that there are Mayim still living! I changed my mind. I'm not going to take you home. I'm going to take you straight to the leaders. They would be angry if they knew you were not brought to them immediately."

"There are Gulot and Esh still living too," Laetu informed the man. "My father—step-father—is Gulot."

Ged shook his head in disbelief. "Mayim, Gulot, and Esh. Together with us, the Tehom, that means that four of the seven original castes of the Siann Dha yet live! Glory be!"

Pax digested this statement. He wondered what Ged meant by "seven original castes." He had only ever heard of three: Esh, Mayim, and Gulot, although the Esh-caste was divided into Esh-qadar and Esh-maor. Maybe the other castes were originally divided as well. If the Mayim and Gulot each counted as two castes, that would make seven when the Tehom were added.

"How come we haven't heard about you, when you've heard about us?" Laetu asked.

Ged shook his head. "The legends talk about all the castes. They also say that when the seven castes are united, Tel-Maor will come to us in the flesh."

"Tel-Maor is real?" Pax asked. He wasn't sure what he believed about the mysterious creator of their world.

Ged shrugged. "No one knows for sure. None of us has ever seen him. All we have is the written legends."

Pax frowned. "You have books down here?"

"What's a book?" Ged asked.

Laetu began a lengthy explanation about how paper was made from sea plants and then started on a history of the alphabet and writing. Ged listened intently and then shook his head. "It is not how we do it here. Such material is too flimsy. Don't your legends rot away with time if they're only written on plant fiber? No wonder you've never heard of us."

"We have old books," Pax objected. "They've been copied over and over again. We have legends going back to the beginning of time."

"But no Tehom peoples come into your mythology?" Ged asked. They were swimming now, heading, Pax assumed, for the home of the leaders or for some other meeting place.

"We're not educated," Laetu said. "Not really. The Esh-maor have all the old texts. They're taught in the college on Nozoffi."

"Not all the old texts," Pax said slowly. "Remember? There are some in the caves of the Dynroc in Garradh Gannoir."

"That's right," Laetu agreed. "Xylo did say that there were ancient manuscripts in the caves of the Dynroc. He hadn't had time to read much, he said, last time we were there."

"Maybe the stories about the Tehom are in the Dynroc's cave."

"Maybe," Laetu said.

"What is this Garradh Gannoir?" Ged asked.

"It's where the deadbloods live," Laetu answered. "They're not Siann Dha. Their blood isn't like ours. It doesn't make ymolenegth."

"These people I know," Ged nodded. "We thought that they were all that was left. No more Siann Dha. No more ymolenegth except among the Tehom. Of course there's always a bit from the animals, but it's not like the blood of the Siann Dha. It's much less powerful."

The trio passed through archway after archway, tunnel after tunnel, as Ged led them forward. The underwater world slowly became an obvious city, albeit an uninhabited one.

"Is that where your people live?" Pax asked, pointing to a solid column of rock that looked anything but natural.

"It's one of the places," Ged said. "You can see the doorways."

"That's why I thought it might be a house," Pax said. "We do the same on land, making homes in the rock."

"Not just in rock," Laetu objected. "The caves in the rock are the back ends of the houses, but the front ends are huts made of reeds."

Ged pointed. "Like those?" he asked.

Far below them where the water was a brilliant lime color, Pax could see rows of huts with woven roofs.

"Yes," Laetu said. Pax noticed that his gill-speech was improving.

Ged swam down low and passed through an archway into the city. The columns of rock abounded here. They could see other people too, people who looked like Ged, with protruding faces and elongated hands and feet.

"Does your blood make the ymolenegth?" Pax asked.

"Yes," Ged told them. "We offer blood regularly to keep the light going in Sorbel."

"They do the same in Lucedth," Pax told him. "That's the main city in Luca."

"You live in dwellings in the Orbokth there?" Ged asked. He turned and swam backwards so he could face them as they answered.

"We do, where we live," Laetu told him. "But in Luca they live on the clatries."

"What are clatries?" Ged asked.

Laetu turned a shocked face toward Pax and then looked back at Ged. "Everyone knows about the clatries!"

"They're like webs of rock floating on the sea," Pax said. "Kleibald ordered tall cities built on them so people wouldn't have to stay on the Orbokth in primitive huts and caves."

Ged swam into an opening in one of the large columns of rock. Pax and Laetu followed him. Pax's initial apprehension had turned into raging curiosity. Another caste of Siann Dha? One of what had originally been seven? He was eager to talk to the leaders to find out more about their legends.

"Is this where your leaders live?" Laetu asked.

Ged swam up through a channel in the middle of the column. Pax could see doorways on either side of the structure. Homes, he guessed. The water grew warmer as they ascended. The ymolenegth there, too, was very bright and pale. It was almost not blue at all anymore. Pax squinted through his outer eyelids, trying to block out some of the light.

"Benjo!" Ged hollered through a thick woven curtain door. "Wake up!"

A woman came to the door and peered out. "What do you want?" she asked. She sounded irritated, Pax noted.

"Visitors from Luca!" Ged exclaimed excitedly. "I've brought visitors from Luca!"

The woman's eyes widened. She was wearing a short garment, and Pax could see her legs. He gulped in surprise as he realized she had scales like a fish. He looked at Ged to see if he, too, had scales, but Ged's lower body was covered. His bare arms looked normal, if slightly hairy. "By the wings of the vervol!" the woman swore.

"You see why I broke protocol and came directly here?" Ged asked.

She nodded. "I'll get Benjo." She disappeared into the interior of the dwelling.

"That's Benjo's wife," Ged told the boys.

"Is she a leader too?" Pax asked.

"She's female," Ged replied, as though that explained something.

"So, is she a leader?" Laetu repeated.

Ged looked at them in puzzlement. "Women don't lead."

Laetu snorted and drew water into his air-lungs. He coughed. "Don't tell that to Ieska and Bridima," he advised the Tehom man.

Ged shook his head. "I don't know anyone by those names."

Before they could continue the conversation, a large man came to the door. "Brenina said you brought visitors from Luca?"

"The prisoners. The ones by vent four. They escaped. I found them and patched up the door to the hydrolock. While I was talking to them, I learned they were from Luca. I knew you'd want to see them."

Benjo narrowed his eyes and examined the boys. "And you believed them?"

Ged shifted uncomfortably in the water. "I . . . yes . . ."

"Where are you really from," Benjo asked.

"Luca," Pax answered promptly.

"Cudth Deorth," Laetu said at the same time.

Benjo gave Ged a knowing look. "See what I mean? They can't even keep their story straight. Take them back and lock them up."

"They broke down the door," Ged protested.

"Fix it," Benjo ordered.

"They're from Luca," Ged stuttered. "That one"—he pointed at Laetu—"said his mother and sister are Mayim."

Benjo leaned close to Laetu. "Your mother and sister and Mayim?"

Laetu shrank back but nodded. "They're Mayim. They swim. My stepfather is Gulot."

"See?" Ged said hopefully.

Benjo looked at the boys doubtfully.

"They can't be from the lands above," Ged argued. "Those people can't tolerate the chemicals in the sea. And they can't breathe in the water. These boys can."

"Gills," Pax said, pointing at the side of his head.

"You're Mayim?" Benjo asked. Pax thought it seemed like he was starting to believe them.

Laetu shook his head. "We're not really one thing or another," he said. He held out his arm and pushed up the sleeve of his loose tunic to reveal his body tala. "See?"

Benjo looked sharply at Ged. "What is the meaning of this? Why wasn't I told weeks ago when they were first trapped in the hydrolock?"

Ged shook his head. "I didn't see the body tala. Their clothing hides it well, especially in the water. I knew they could swim, but it never occurred to me that they were Siann Dha. It wasn't possible. But then I talked to them and . . ."

Benjo pushed the seagrass curtain aside. "Come in. I want to hear all about it."

Chapter 17: Camilly

"It's been too long," Widman said shortly. "Someone should have come by now."

Finnan frowned. "Case, Ceres, and Talag. I would have thought Ceres would be here, at least."

"Xylo said she'd been exploring the sea," Camilly noted. "Maybe she's spending the night underwater."

Byid shivered. "That's crazy."

"She's Mayim. She can breathe in the water. It's not so crazy." Camilly couldn't let herself believe that something bad had happened to the others. They had been in the caves of the Dynroc for hours and hours and hours and there had been no sign of Case, Ceres, or Talag.

"Maybe they went wherever Pax and Laetu went," Byid suggested with a darkness that was uncharacteristic of him.

Camilly's heart filled with hope. "Maybe they found Pax and Laetu!" she exclaimed. "That would explain why they're not here."

Finnan looked at her daughter lovingly, trying not to let her heart hope. "I hope that's true."

"We'll give them until morning," Widman decided. "Then we'll go out looking."

****

Morning came, and there still had been no sign of the others.

"I'm worried," Finnan confessed over a meager breakfast of halas bread and gwynant. "With the leaders of Luca hunting for Xylo, there's bound to be unrest everywhere. Do you think the leaders of Garradh Gannoir are looking for him too?"

Camilly shook her head. "Xylo **is** the leader of Garradh Gannoir. He's the Dynroc. The people here listen to him. They love him. They practically worship him."

"We can't take anything for granted," Widman said. "We must be careful. Especially with Case, Ceres, and Talag missing."

"You think we should stay here?" Finnan asked, tucking her long red hair into a braid and fastening the end with a sea-string-fiber tie.

"That'd be dumber than anything," twelve-year-old Byid criticized. He put on a mocking falsetto. "Everyone is missing. We'll probably find them if we hide in the caves and do nothing."

Camilly laughed and Byid laughed with her.

"We have to try," Widman said. "I was just saying we ought to be careful."

"Camilly and I will take to the water," Finnan said. "There shouldn't be any danger for us there. None of the deadbloods can swim."

"There could be Mayim here," Camilly pointed out. "Lots of people are traveling back and forth now."

Finnan shook her head. "I still think it's safer in the water. The Mayim in Garradh Gannoir are tourists, not agents of the elders."

"Byid and I will work on the land," Widman said.

"Duh," Camilly giggled. "How soon can we leave?" She looked at her mother.

"After breakfast. Finish eating," Finnan scolded lightly.

Once they were ready, Finnan and Camilly headed down through the passageways that had brought them up to the residential areas of the Dynroc's caves. There was an exit at sea level. The glow of the Ghalon lit the land with a clear, golden light. The mist was sparse, as it usually was early in the morning before the heat of the day had a chance to suck much of the water into the air. Camilly could see far out to sea. A few fishing boats floated in the distance, but the sea was entirely devoid of clatry.

"It is beautiful here, isn't it?" Camilly sighed contentedly.

Finnan tightened the straps of her cross-body satchel. "Let's go. The less time we spend on land, the better."

"Are you worried about Widman and Byid?" Camilly asked.

"Your brother and Pax disappeared over a month ago," Finnan reminded her. "There's clearly more going on than we understand."

A pang of guilt stabbed through Camilly. Of course, she knew that there was danger, but the boys had to be okay. They would find them. The whole thing with Xylo and the elders would resolve itself. Still, she felt bad that she had made her mother sad. "We'll find them," Camilly said encouragingly. "Pax and Laetu and the others."

Finnan quickly walked into the sea and dove under. Camilly followed more slowly. She wasn't used to the feel of the sand under her toes. In Luca, the shoreline was only rock. Of course, the sand was made of rock as well, but it acted more like a liquid—a solid liquid. She bent down and ran her fingers through the sand under the water, watching it cascade, diffusing in the water so that the sea looked murky. She wondered what made Garradh Gannoir have sand when Luca and Cudth Deorth had none.

Finnan poked her head above the surface of the water. She was so far out to sea that Camilly had to imagine the expression on her face. "What are you waiting for?" Her voice carried across the water.

Camilly rinsed the fine grains of sand off her hands, rubbing them to get the grit out of the folds of her finger-tala. She stood up and looked toward the spot where she'd last seen her mother's tiny, bobbing head. "I'm coming," she shouted, knowing that Finnan couldn't hear her under the water.

She lifted her arms over her head and bent her knees, ready to propel herself into the sea.

Someone caught her from behind just as her feet left the shore. Camilly hovered in the air for a second, winded with surprise and fear. She kicked backward at her attacker, trying to free herself, but it was no use.

"Mother!" she screamed. "Finnan!"

Chapter 18: Xylo

"You ever see anything like that?" Bridima asked.

Ieska shook her head. "Even the Triads' blood doesn't make ymolenegth like that." She held up the lamp and peered at the fluid inside it. "Has Dynny been able to make the bleeding stop?" she asked.

"Yes," Xylo told her. "The wound was small. It just bled a lot. He's bandaged her tiny leg."

"Has he fed her?"

"Mhowis goat milk in a bottle," Ninach reported from across the room. "The baby is taking it easily."

Xylo's whole body buzzed with emotion. Mailu was dead—all dead, now that the baby had been born. Her daughter was thriving so far. The room, crowded with people, was warmer than it should have been, but the heat was comfortable for Xylo. As an Esh, he naturally needed more heat.

"Maaaaa . . ." someone croaked.

"Was that the baby?" Gudall asked in surprise.

Dynny lifted his face to look at the others. "Not the baby," he said. "She's still eating."

"It was her," Ninach whispered.

A hush descended on the room as everyone turned to look at Tass.

Tass blinked her eyes and looked back at them.

Xylo's eyes burned with the potential of tears. Tass was alive.

Bridima moved toward Tass's cot. "Good morning, honey," she said. She reached down to smooth Tass's forehead but stopped before she touched the girl. Tass's skin was still a rotten brown color that spoke more of death than life. Bridima pulled her hand back.

"Mai . . . lu . . ." Tass groaned.

Xylo knelt by her bedside. "Mailu is dead," he said gently. "She's been dead for a long time. Somehow her body was able to feed her baby until it could be born, but now that the sarcophagus has been opened, we know for sure that she's gone. I'm sorry."

Tass closed her eyes as though the effort hurt her.

"Stay with us, Tass," Xylo pleaded. "We want to help you get well."

Tass pulled her knees up to her chest and wrapped her arms around them, burying her face.

"We're going to be your family now," Bridima told her. "It's a lot to process. You almost died in the sea. You're still quite sick. But we're here to take care of you."

"We love you, Tass," Gudall noted. "You're my little sister."

"And mine," Ninach added gruffly.

"And you're an aunt!" Dynny exclaimed happily as he cuddled the baby girl.

Tass's body went slack, and Xylo looked up in alarm.

Bridima bent to check Tass's pulse. "She's all right. Probably just fainted from pain and exhaustion."

"You don't think she's gone from us again?" Xylo asked.

Bridima shook her head. "I don't think so. I don't know why, but I think she's on the mend."

"Do you think the baby's coming had anything to do with Tass's waking?" Xylo wondered. It seemed far-fetched to think it was a coincidence.

Ieska reached into the open sarcophagus, careful to avoid the jagged bits of glass still embedded in the rock. "It's dry," she reported. "She may have breathed in the amniotic fluid as it evaporated."

"So?" Ninach asked.

"The baby was born alive," Xylo breathed. "There must have been something . . . other . . . something supernatural . . . about the conditions in the womb. Never before has a dead girl given birth."

"Woman," Ninach corrected him.

"Woman," Xylo repeated. He turned to his wife. "Is there any precedence for amniotic fluid having special powers?"

Ieska frowned. "Not like this, but who knows? There's no precedent for any of this."

"We should clear out of here," Bridima said. "Let Dynny have his space back."

"Will he be able to care for both Tass and the baby?" Rhyder asked, his dark eyes filled with concern and compassion.

"I'll stay with him for a bit," Bridima offered. "It would be better to let the air clear."

"What about the coffin and the . . . Mailu?" Gudall asked.

Xylo's eyes moved over the body of the dead girl. Even in death and covered with scars, she was still beautiful. Afa must have resembled her in her youth, he thought, before life twisted her soul into the mangled wreck of a woman she became—the woman who had abandoned four-year-old Tass.

"Get the sarcophagus out to the shore," Ieska ordered. "We'll have a proper ceremony at dawn."

Rhyder, Gudall, Xylo, and Ninach shared the burden of the sarcophagus on the uneven walk from the cave in the Orbokth down to the rocky shore that surrounded the sea of Cudth Deorth. Ieska followed.

"Are you sure we ought to . . . you know?" Xylo asked. "Shouldn't we keep the . . . Mailu . . . her body . . . for testing? You said yourself that nothing like this has happened before. If we consign her to the fires, there will never be an opportunity for us to learn from her."

Ieska shook her head. "It wouldn't do any good. She's been gone for a long time. There's no life left in her. If anything is going to give us clues about what happened and why, it's going to come from the baby. From her daughter."

"Do you think the baby is Triad?" Xylo asked.

"You said Gelu fathered the child?"

"Yes."

Ieska frowned and fingered her long, gray braid. "I don't see how she could be Triad. Half of her genetic material would be deadblood. It's a miracle that she's casted at all."

"You saw the glow," Xylo reminded his wife. "The baby is more than just casted."

"There was no tala," Ieska said. "The Triads have finger-tala and body-tala."

"You think the baby's Gulot?"

"I don't know," Ieska admitted. "It may be. Or it may be something else. Something new. After all, this is the first time that a child has been born of the union of a Siann Dha and a deadblood."

"What are we going to name her?" Xylo asked. He already thought of the child as family, a granddaughter of a sort.

"We should give it time," Ieska said. "Find out who she is."

"Her surnames will be Harreg Pagos," Xylo said. "Mailu Elisus Harreg and Gelu Pagos."

"Are you sure Gelu is the father?" Ieska frowned.

Xylo bit his lip. "There's a possibility that Mailu was Triad," he said. "We don't know for sure that Afa's Triad child was Tass. It may have been Mailu."

"There's another possibility," Ieska said slowly.

"What?"

"I'm a scientist. I know more about the biology of casteing than anyone else except those who worked directly with me on the Methiant Migas project," Ieska said.

Xylo could see the pain in her eyes. The Methiant Migas experiments had been a harrowing violation of justice, even if the victim had been a criminal. He knew the burden Ieska bore as a result of having participated in the project, even though she'd been under orders from Kleibald.

Ieska continued. "It's possible that experiments were performed on Mailu before she conceived or even after."

"You're saying the baby could be Triad because of something Gelu did?"

"Gelu or scientists under his command," Ieska nodded.

Xylo felt a sick wave of realization wash over him. Kleibald and Gelu had been working together long before he had discovered an "other side of the Orbokth" existed. If Kleibald's scientists had been working on creating a Triad in Luca, wasn't it possible that Gelu's scientists had been trying the same thing in Obumbro? Maybe their desire to obtain a Gulot, Esh, and Mayim had been motivated not just by a desire to reverse the gogyvehr and turn Gannoir inside out, but by a desire for their blood for experimentation. "Case might know," he said hoarsely. "He was there. He would be able to tell us if they took his blood at any time."

Ieska looked up sharply. "You think the child may be Case's?"

Xylo sighed heavily. "Who knows? Talag said Gelu spoke of Mailu's baby as his son who was going to rule the new world. Gelu obviously believed the child was his. But if they were experimenting on Mailu and using Case's blood—and Ceres'—it's possible that they concocted a genetic hybrid of Gulot—Mailu—as well as Esh from Case and Mayim from Ceres."

Ieska pressed her lips together grimly. "And deadblood from Gelu. It's theoretically possible. But I didn't think science had advanced so far among the deadbloods. It's cutting-edge theory even here in Luca."

"The child could be my granddaughter," Xylo realized.

"That I can test in the lab," Ieska said. "I'll take a blood sample when I go back to work."

"You think it's safe to go back to the university?"

"Safer than not going," Ieska told him. "After all, no one knows we're married. As far as the elders know, I'm still working for them."

"We can't let the elders know about the baby," Xylo said.

"You think I don't know that?"

"I love you."

Ieska smiled. "I know."

"I'm going back to Garradh Gannoir," Xylo told her. "I'm leaving in the morning."

"Xylo," Ieska's face was anguished.

"I have to try," Xylo said. "I'm going to go over the top of the Orbokth."

"We talked about this before," Ieska said. "You'll burn up."

"I'll make it," Xylo promised. "I have to find out what's going on in Garradh Gannoir. I have to talk to Case about what happened while he was a prisoner."

"I'll come as soon as I can," Ieska told him.

Chapter 19: Tass

Tass turned her head to look across the small room at the cradle. The sides were mesh, and she could see the silhouette of the baby sleeping in it. Mailu's baby.

"Your niece," the voices pointed out. "You should be glad."

I'm not glad, Tass thought angrily. *My sister is dead. If someone had to die, why couldn't it have been the baby?*

There's a reason no one has ever loved you, the voices mocked. *You can't even love a newborn girl-child. You're unlovable . . . worthless . . .*

It was the same refrain they always sung. Every thought Tass had got twisted by the voices that consumed her. She'd invited them into herself, but it had all been for nothing. Mailu was dead. And her ugly, wretched, orphaned baby lived.

The baby started to squall, and Dynny shuffled over to it, making a clicking sound with his tongue.

"I'm coming, love. I'm coming," he crooned. He lifted the baby gently and held it against his shoulder. Tass could see its wide, staring, startled eyes looking at her.

The baby was ugly. Its skin was an oddly mottled mess of light and dark tones. Its nose stuck out too far for a newborn. And it had no tala at all. Tass wondered if it was Gulot, like Mailu, or if it was a deadblood. She'd gathered from the conversation that had swirled around her for the last three days that Gelu was baby's father, but she could see no resemblance. Of course, Gelu probably hadn't looked like Gelu at three days old either.

Dynny settled into a low-slung chair and gave the baby a bottle of milk. Tass was disgusted. Mhowis goats were filthy animals. And her niece was being nourished by its secretions. She wondered if the baby had always been so ugly, or if it was because of the foreign milk. Tass shut her eyes. Her head hurt. Her everything hurt. She had thought herself ugly before, but now, with her blackened, rotten skin, she was horrific. She sensed the revulsion the others had when they looked at her. It wasn't just the voices who told her she was unlovable. She could see it for herself.

I don't care, she told herself. *Nobody's ever loved me, and I've been fine.*

You want to be loved, but it will never happen, the voices commented.

I don't want to be loved, Tass thought stubbornly. *All I ever got from love was pain. Mailu loved me, but now she's gone. Igracio loved me enough that he died trying to save me. And now he's gone too.*

You kill everything you touch, the voices trilled.

Tass was startled out of her mental conversation by a loud burp.

"That's a good one, it is," Dynny crooned. He wiped at the baby's tiny mouth and then carried the child over to Tass's cot. "Come see your auntie," he offered. He held the baby toward Tass.

The atmosphere in Tass's mind cleared, like wind blowing rainclouds away. She opened her eyes but immediately closed them when she saw the ugly child. "Go away, Dynny," she rasped.

"I'll tend you in a minute," Dynny said. He took the baby back to its bed and covered it with the layered woven cloths that kept it warm.

The clouds moved in on Tass's soul again.

Dynny dragged a bucketful of water from under a low table and began to smooth Tass's skin with a smaller and damper version of the baby blanket. "You're Mayim, so you need to keep your skin wet," he said knowingly.

The water felt good. Tass longed for the sea, but she wasn't yet strong enough to get out of bed.

"I'm not the Dynroc anymore," he said sadly, "but I'm still a good carer."

"Go away, Dynny," Tass requested.

"Not until your skin is all wet," he said. "I have to make you wet so you can get better." He shook his head. "I wish the water could wash off the darkness. But it's not working."

Tass grimaced. "The darkness is inside me," she told him. "You can't fix it that way." She looked at the elderly gnome who was ministering to her. "It's all for nothing, Dynny. Don't you know that yet?"

"Xylo said your soul was sick," Dynny retorted. "He said that's why you're so grumpy."

"I'm not grumpy," Tass shot back. "I'm realistic."

"And grumpy," Dynny added.

"Well, what do you think?" Tass cried loudly. Her throat spasmed with the effort. "My mother is dead. My sister is dead. My father is a rapist. My best friend is gone. And I can't move. Wouldn't you be grumpy?" She closed her eyes again.

So unlovable! the voices taunted her.

Dynny continued to wet her skin and her clothing. "You'll feel better soon. I'm a good carer."

Tass was going to make a sharp, contradictory remark, but refrained. A part of her liked the intellectually disabled old man and didn't want to hurt him.

A rustle told her someone had entered the room. Tass looked up and found that Ninach had entered. Ninach. Her sister. The notion gave her pain. Mailu was her sister. Her only sister. They had explained the whole thing to her, how her father was a man named Methiant Migas—or Mantais Nayro—she didn't see what difference it made. How he had violated her mother, and she was the result. And because of his medical condition, all his offspring were different. Tricasted. Tass thought of her glowing fingertips. It was proof, wasn't it, that she also was a Triad? Her fingertips didn't glow anymore. The darkness inside her had seen to that. But it had betrayed her, nonetheless. Now she was stuck in the secret outpost of Cudth Deorth living apart from society with her half-siblings, only two of whom were present. Mentally, she recited the names she had learned in order from oldest to youngest: Unaleah, Gudall, Sadi, Ninach, Kari, Pax, and Laetu. And Igracio. Igracio had also been Triad. Her very own brother.

"Time to take you outside," Ninach said mechanically.

"Don't wanna go," Tass mumbled.

"And I don't want to take you, so we're even," Ninach spat.

"Then why are you?"

"What Bridima says, goes," Ninach replied. "She says you're to be outside for an hour in the morning and an hour in the afternoon. And it's my day to do sister duty."

Tass made a face. "Don't bother," she said hoarsely.

Ninach ignored Tass's protests and lifted the immobile girl in her arms. Ninach was tall and strong. Tass tried to resist, but she didn't have the strength. She wondered why she was so weak, but there didn't seem to be any answers. None that anyone would tell her anyhow.

Tass's eyes yowled in protest when Ninach carried her into the golden morning light on the shore. Even with both sets of eyelids shut, the brilliance was still painful. Ninach settled her into a long, reclined chair by the sea. Rhyder had built the chair for her. He was the stepfather of one of her half-siblings, she had been told. It was all very confusing. She couldn't remember which sibling Rhyder parented, only that he lived in Cudth Deorth with the rest of the misfits.

Misfits like you, the voices reminded her. *You aren't good enough to live in the city. You're too low even for the Calix. You should never have been there in the first place. Worthless . . . weak . . . useless . . . unlovable . . .*

Tass muttered the words after the voices. *Worthless . . . weak . . . useless . . . unlovable . . .*

Ninach scowled down at her. Tass could feel it even though her eyes were shut. "Stop being so self-absorbed," Ninach spat, tossing her shoulder-length brown hair over her shoulder. "You're not the only one of us who was abandoned because of caste. Gudall and I were both foundlings. If it hadn't been for Bridima and Ieska we'd probably be dead."

Tass tried to shut her mind against the onslaught of Ninach's words. It didn't matter. Ninach had been living with her siblings since she was four. She remembered that much from what Bridima had said to her. Tass had been on her own since she was four. There was a difference.

You didn't deserve anyone's love, the voices told her.

They were right.

"Go away," Tass ordered as loud as she could.

Ninach snorted. "Suit yourself." And she left.

Chapter 20: Unaleah

"It's been three days," Unaleah noted. "I think we should turn around."

"We can't go home," Sadi protested. "We have to find Pax and Laetu."

Unaleah popped her head out of the sea and looked around. She pointed to a gleaming group of skyscrapers. "That's the Lucedth clatry way back there. We've passed Zafir too. We're all the way on the opposite end of Luca." She pointed again. "See the darkness of the sea there? It's from the soil mining operations on the Orbokth."

"So?" Sadi asked.

"So Garradh Gannoir is beyond the west side of Luca," she said. "The passageway must be under the Orbokth on the west. If we keep going, we're going to pass the meridian. Then we'll be on the east side of Luca."

Sadi looked around. "You're probably right," she admitted reluctantly. "But what if there's a passageway from the east side through to the west. We won't find it if we go back."

"We haven't finished searching the west side," Unaleah complained.

Sadi shook her head. "We'll waste time if we go all the way back to Tienged. It's taken us three days to get this far."

"Three days of searching. We could do it more quickly if we went directly there."

"You only promised me a week of searching," Sadi complained. "Maybe if you were willing to stay underwater for an extra week, I'd be willing to waste a couple days swimming back over an area we've already searched . . ." She let the sentence dangle, trying to tempt her sister to give herself up to the hunt.

Unaleah sighed and looked at the sleek head of her lookalike sister. "However many days it takes us to get back to Tienged, I'll stay down for that many extra days."

"Really?" Sadi asked. "I thought you wanted to get back to Cudth Deorth to see the baby."

"We don't even know if the baby's been born," Unaleah said. "Besides, I just promised. I'll do it."

A cloud marred Sadi's jaunty expression. "You'd do anything to find Pax and Kari and Laetu, just like I would," she said.

Unaleah nodded slowly. "I would. I just . . . I just don't think there's much hope. You remember what happened. We were all bleeding. We were all injured. Gudall almost died. Kari was down there with us. If she were alive, we'd have found her by now."

Unaleah watched as Sadi's face crinkled up in agony.

"I know," Sadi said.

"You agree with me, don't you?" Unaleah said softly. "There's no hope for Kari."

"Not none," Sadi protested weakly.

"Minimal hope, then. It's Pax and Laetu we're trying to find."

"And they could be anywhere," Sadi noted. "And it's still worth it. Even without Kari, it would still be worth a couple weeks' travel underwater if we can find them."

Unaleah frowned. It wasn't that she disagreed with Sadi. Finding her little brothers was of utmost importance to her. *I'm scared*, she admitted to herself. *Scared we'll find their bodies. Scared we'll find whatever it was that killed them. Scared that we'll be killed too. Scared that whatever we're doing is just going to end up causing more grief in the end.* Her face felt hot.

"You'll keep looking with me, won't you?" Sadi asked.

"Yes," Unaleah said quietly.

It took them two days to swim back to the area of the sea near Tienged. They had agreed to keep searching for the passageway as they swam. Occasionally surfacing to get their bearings, they could see that the guard was still posted at the tunnel that led to Garradh Gannoir.

"Do you think the underwater tunnel could be right under the land tunnel?" Unaleah asked. Her underwater gill-speech was improving.

"It makes as much sense as anything," Sadi said. She had grown surly over the two fruitless days of searching. Sadi, Unaleah reflected, was used to getting what she wanted. Unaleah herself was used to giving up before she could discover how little she could change anything.

Unaleah felt along the underside of the Orbokth, looking for openings that could lead them to Garradh Gannoir. She hadn't realized how shallowly the Orbokth was planted in the sea. In her mind's eye she had pictured the Orbokth extending quite far—even being anchored to the Bec, the rind of Gannoir. This was by no means the case. The Orbokth barely descended to the orange layer of the caustic liquid sea. The stability she had imagined for her world did not exist. It was all floating on the sea. It was too cold for her and Sadi to swim down in the red layer. Otherwise, it would have proved a surefire way to arrive in Garradh Gannoir. She looked up again, pondering the rocky cliffs over her head. She wondered what the underside of Cudth Deorth looked like. Probably the same as the underside of the Orbokth nearer Luca, she told herself.

A colony of ribbon snails above her head distracted her from her thoughts. Their tentacles, longer than her hands, dangled from the Orbokth above her and waved in the shifting current of the sea. She wondered what color they really were. The yellow light of the deep ymolenegth obscured their true hue. She thought they might be brown or orange, but it was hard to tell. They could be lavender. She wondered how their appearance would change at different sea levels. Just past the ribbon snails, she and Sadi came to an opening overhead. The blue light of the sea shone down from above her and Unaleah pushed toward it, hoping it might prove to be the two-mile tunnel they were seeking.

When her head broke the surface of the water she was surprised. She'd thought of the Orbokth as a solid roof over her head in this place. That there was air to be had was startling. She gasped for breath for a second as she switched from her gills to her air-lungs to breathe.

Sadi's head popped up next to hers. "What is this place?" she asked, looking around in amazement.

Unaleah shook her head. "I don't know. A pocket of air?"

"I got that much," Sadi shot back sarcastically.

Unaleah sighed and shook her head violently, trying to get the water out of her ears. She hadn't figured on pining so much to be dry. Idly, she wondered what effect it would have on her hair.

"Why is it glowing?" Sadi asked.

"Remember? Ieska said there were bioluminescent algae growing on the walls inside the Orbokth. Kind of like natural lighting to get people where they're going."

"I never thought it would look like this!" Sadi exclaimed.

"What?"

"Beautiful."

It was that. A rainbow of color lit the rock over their heads in gentle patterns of lime green, yellow, red, and magenta. Unaleah found that her eyes kept trying to decipher regular patterns in the growth of the algae, but as soon as she thought she saw the rhythm, something interrupted it.

"How tall do you think this chamber is?" Sadi asked.

Unaleah shook her head. "Tall. Several stories at least."

"Think there's any value in getting out of the water?"

"Out of the water?"

"Yes. To explore."

Unaleah looked around. The roof of the cavern that had opened over their heads was dome shaped. There wasn't anything she would have called a shore for them to climb out on. "How?" she asked.

"Come on," Sadi said. "Follow me." She ducked back under the water and swam around the edge of the oval fissure, feeling the rock of the Orbokth as she did so. Near the opposite side of the chamber, Sadi found a place she could get a toehold, and she ooched herself up onto the rock. Unaleah followed. Standing on a ledge, both girls were only in waist-deep water. The walls were difficult to hold, however, as they were slimy with the glowing algae.

"Think this stuff is edible?" Sadi asked, pointing a glowing finger at a particularly thick patch of lime-green moss.

"No," Unaleah said without bothering with analytical thought. She was not by any means going to eat glowing algae.

"I'm going to try some," Sadi noted.

"Don't," Unaleah advised her. "Light is life and light comes from blood. Who knows whose blood makes those things glow."

Sadi looked repulsed for a minute, but then she grinned. "Pax would have tried it."

"Maybe Pax did," Unaleah shot back darkly.

Sadi scraped off some of the algae and put it in her mouth. Unaleah watched, waiting pessimistically for her sister to drop dead. Finally, she asked, "Is it good?"

Sadi frowned. "Not really." She jammed her fingers into a crack in the rock above her head and pulled her body further out of the water. "I think I see another ledge up there," she said.

With difficulty, the girls made their way up to the damp ledge a body's length higher than the surface of the sea. Unaleah sat down to rest, glad to finally stop swimming. The constant movement of the water had made her slightly sick at first. She was days and days past that now, but she still felt like she was floating. Sadi sat down beside her. Unaleah wrung the seawater out of her hair and clothes. "I'm tired of being wet."

"Me too," Sadi admitted. She opened her cross-body satchel and took out a lump of what had been dried fish. It was now rehydrated and limp. "Want some?"

Unaleah grimaced. "All right," she said, taking a piece of the damp fish. She put it in her mouth. "It could be worse."

Sadi pushed herself to her feet.

"Where are you going?" Unaleah asked.

"I see something," Sadi answered. "Up there."

Unaleah looked. "What? That dark thing?"

"It could be a tunnel," Sadi said.

"Doesn't matter. There's no way to get there," Unaleah said.

"What time is it?"

"How should I know?" Unaleah asked.

"It was midmorning when we started under this section of the Orbokth," Sadi said. "It can't be evening yet."

"Probably not," Unaleah agreed.

"I think I know how to get up there."

"How?"

"We wait."

"Wait?"

"When the rain begins, the sea will fill up. The water will rise. It will lift us up to the tunnel."

"You think it will rise that much?" Unaleah asked, squinting up at the tunnel several body-lengths above their heads. "I don't think the sea levels change that much at night."

"Not out there," Sadi admitted. "But in an enclosed space? It's possible."

Unaleah shrugged. "I'm okay with waiting. I don't think you're right, but it's worth a try."

***

When night came, Sadi and Unaleah were asleep on the ledge, propped against each other. The water woke them, lapping gently at their feet. Unaleah opened her eyes and poked her sister. "Sadi!" she whispered.

Sadi woke up. "What?" she mumbled.

"The water's rising," Unaleah pointed out.

Sadi climbed to her feet. "This is it."

Unaleah joined her. "If it's going to happen, it's going to be soon."

And it was. Due to the narrowing of the dome as it got higher, the water rose with increasing speed. Soon Unaleah found herself knee deep in the sea—and then submerged. She took Sadi's hand. Sadi pointed toward the tunnel, which was, just as Sadi had hoped, submerged. They swam into the narrow opening. Unaleah had to let go of her sister's hand as they half-swam, half-crawled through the passageway.

It's probably a dead-end, Unaleah told herself. *It's narrowing even more. It's going to go nowhere.* But they swam on and on and on. The tunnel jagged first to the right and then to the left, leaving Unaleah disoriented and lost. She wasn't even sure she was going in the direction of Garradh Gannoir anymore. Finally, after hours of pulling themselves through the watery passageway, the tide began to ebb. Rather quickly once it had started, the tunnel became dry.

"We did it!" Sadi whispered.

Unaleah held up hands that were coated in bits of rock. "Ouch," she commented. Then, "Can we rest now?"

Sadi sighed. "We've been up all night. I'd say we deserve a rest." They ate some of the soggy dried fish as well as some sea vegetables, which were far less offensive in their damp state. Then, leaning back-to-back with the roof just above their heads, the sisters fell asleep.

Chapter 21: Pax

At Benjo's command, Pax and Laetu explained the world of Luca to the Tehom. He listened with rapt attention, trying not to let his incredulity show on his face. He was a leader. These were young boys.

"So in Luca, you have Mayim, Gulot, and Esh? Three castes?"

"The Esh are a split caste," Laetu told him. "Esh-qadar are the soil miners who work in the heights. Esh-maor are the leaders."

"A split caste," Benjo mused. "They can go in the fire and on the land?"

Pax wrinkled his nose. "I don't know if you'd call it 'in the fire'," he said. "The Esh can go on the heights nearer the Orbokth than the other castes, but I think even they wouldn't survive actual fire." He turned to Laetu. "What do you think?"

"Yeah," Laetu agreed. "They don't get so near to the Ghalon that they would burn up."

"Then they're Gulot," Benjo noted. "Just very warm ones."

Pax and Laetu both denied this vigorously.

"They're not Gulot," Pax said. "They have body-tala." He held out his arm and pointed. "Like this. Gulot don't have any tala at all."

"They're not deadbloods," Laetu interjected. "Their blood makes ymolenegth."

Benjo frowned. "Half castes . . . impure castes . . . much has been lost . . ."

"Tell us about it," Pax encouraged him. He wanted to know and understand. The idea that there were seven castes instead of the three he'd known all his life was the most intriguing thing he'd ever heard.

"We are Tehom," Benjo explained. "We can only live in water. We have gills, not lungs."

"And scales," Laetu interrupted. "I saw it on your wife's legs. Do you all have scales?"

Pax smacked him. "That's not polite."

"But I want to know," Laetu said. "He asked us all sorts of questions."

"We do have scales," Benjo confirmed. "Do your Mayim not have any?"

"The skin of the Mayim is different from the skin of the Gulot and the Esh," Pax told him. "The water doesn't burn them like it does the others. But it's not scales." He looked down at his own unscarred legs and wondered about them.

"Originally," Benjo said, "there were four pure castes—Water, Fire, Land, and Spirit."

"Like in Luca," Laetu interrupted. "Water, fire, land. It's the same as now."

Benjo shook his head, and his long hair floated around his head like an eerie mane. "It's not the same. These were pure castes like the Tehom. The Tehom can only live in water. Your Mayim . . . they can live on land or in the water, right?"

Pax nodded. "They have gills and air-lungs. So do we."

"But you're not Mayim?" Benjo asked.

"We're . . . a mishmash," Pax offered.

"The Gulot is a pure caste," Laetu said. "Land only."

"He gets it," Benjo said. "Your Gulot is the only pure caste in Luca if what you're saying is accurate."

"I don't get it," Pax said. "Gulot is land, Mayim is water, Esh is fire. Three castes."

"Gulot is land," Benjo confirmed. "But Mayim is land-water. Esh is land-fire. Tehom is pure water."

"You're saying there is a pure fire as well?" Pax asked, impressed.

Benjo nodded. "Beings only able to withstand the fires."

"Did that caste have a name?" Pax asked.

"The were the Pihr."

"Are they still around somewhere?" Laetu wondered. "Like up in the Ghalon?"

"Possibly," Benjo said.

"They must be," Brenina interrupted from the far corner of the room where she had been sitting quietly.

Benjo shot his wife a derisive glance. "She knows nothing," he apologized to the boys.

"Why does she think they must be there?" Laetu asked.

"She's female. A fool," Benjo said.

Pax was scandalized. He'd been raised on Cudth Deorth with Bridima and Ieska as the matriarchs. The notion that "female" equaled "fool" was nonsensical to him. Still, he understood that contradicting the leader of his captors would be stupid. He kept his mouth shut.

"But how would you know?" pressed Laetu, seemingly uninhibited by Benjo.

"We can't know," Benjo pointed out. "That's why she's a fool."

Laetu blinked and looked over at Pax. Pax held up his hand and motioned for Laetu to be quiet. His fingers were glowing nervously. "So . . ." he said, "Mayim, Gulot, Esh, Tehom, and Pihr. That's five. What were the other two castes?"

"Our writings speak of a fire-water caste," Benjo said, "and a case of pure spirit, the Maor."

"Esh-maor. Tel-maor. Maor!" Pax said excitedly.

Benjo nodded. "You know the word. That is to be expected if you have ancient literature. None of us are anything without the Maor."

"And the fire-water caste," Laetu said. "What were they called?"

"Fossa," Benjo told them. He stood abruptly, strode across the room, and then looked back at the boys. "I've said too much. You're strangers, and we have no way of knowing if your story is true."

Pax shook his head indignantly. "It is true. We're from Luca. We're multi-casted. It's all the truth."

Brenina gasped from her corner.

Benjo's eyes narrowed. "Multi-casted? How did that come about?"

Pax and Laetu exchanged a glance.

"I'm not sure we should say any more," Pax told the scaly fish-man.

"Suit yourself," Benjo said abruptly. He beckoned and Ged came back into the room. "Take them back to the hydrolock. Shut them in until they're ready to speak."

"But . . ." Ged protested.

"Now," Benjo ordered.

"No!" Laetu cried. "We'll tell you whatever you want to know. Just don't lock us up again!"

"What are you doing?" Pax hissed.

"I want to go home eventually," Laetu said. "They're our best chance."

"What if they're not on our side?" Pax said softly.

"The only side that counts is the one that wants us to go home," Laetu pointed out.

Pax shook his head. "That's not right. We came to Garradh Gannoir to fight the darkness. How do we know he's not with them?"

"Speak up or be quiet!" Benjo thundered. The volume he was able to create underwater was impressive.

"We . . ." Laetu began as loudly as he could.

Pax shoved him. "Lock us up."

Chapter 22: Camilly

"Shut up!" someone ordered.

Camilly clamped her mouth shut. Her kidnappers wouldn't tell her anything. She was angry. At least if they were going to kidnap her, they should tell her why. But they wouldn't. They wouldn't even let her ask.

She'd been blindfolded until they'd reached their destination, a house carved out of the rock of the Orbokth in what she assumed was Obumbro. She'd felt the smooth pavement of the streets as they'd marched her toward it. They'd walked up a staircase of twenty-two steps before arriving in a little room. There, they'd removed her blindfold and tied her to a chair. At least she was facing the window, she mused with a smidgeon of her usual optimism. She tried to discern her location from the view through the window, but it was impossible. Golden mist filled the air, obscuring any landmarks she might have seen.

She looked at her captors, a man and a woman, probably deadblood, as they had no tala and she was, after all, in Garradh Gannoir. The man was pale and red-haired with a narrow face and beady eyes. The woman was as unlike him as could be. She was plump and dark and seemed anxious.

The woman set a bowl of food on a table near Camilly and shoved it toward her. "Eat up," she advised. "We won't be back for a while."

Camilly rocked on the chair. "You'll have to untie me if you want me to eat," she pointed out.

The woman looked at the man questioningly.

"Untie her. We can tie her up again before we leave."

The woman complied.

Camilly contemplated making a break for it once her arms were free, but her legs were still anchored to the chair, and even if she could get away, it seemed wiser to eat first. She reached for the bowl. "What is it?" she asked, looking at the grayish mush in the bowl.

"Mush," the woman said. "Fish and halas. You'll get no better here."

Camilly grimaced but ate. It wasn't good. She wondered how many weeks the fish had been dead before it had been cooked and ground into the paste in the bowl. It was disgusting. The man and woman were talking softly in a corner of the large, low-ceilinged room. Camilly strained her ears to listen.

". . . others. Why separate them?" the man said.

The woman replied, but Camilly could only catch individual words here and there. Her voice was lower than the man's. ". . . Siann Dha . . . all of them . . . can't tell . . ."

"How are we going to get the others? How many are there?" His voice grew louder. "Now that the passageway is open, there are too many of them. It's impossible."

"So you're going to give up?" the woman retorted angrily. "Garradh Gannoir belongs to us, not to them. You know what will happen."

Although their anger worried Camilly, she was grateful that their volume had risen.

"I'm not giving up, Estraya, dear. I'm just pointing out the facts. They are many. According to their leaders their population is at least as large as that of Garradh Gannoir."

"You are giving up. I should never have married you, Lefty. You've always been one who takes the easy way out."

"You're being impractical," the man, Lefty, said.

"And you're being short-sighted," Estraya snorted loudly.

Camilly slurped the last of her fish paste. She'd been wiggling her legs throughout the meal, and she thought she'd be able, if not to break the cords that held her legs, at least slip the chair legs out of the loops. She would have to be quick. She glanced down at her feet, hoping Lefty and Estraya didn't pick up on her intent.

Despite their annoyance with each other, they had both been careful to watch her as she ate. She hadn't felt she could risk reaching down to work on the knots that bound her legs. Her quick glance revealed that she had, in fact, stretched the sea-string ropes enough that there was a gap the size of two of her fingers between each of her legs and the chair's legs. If she stood quickly and lifted the chair, she could pull the chair out of the loops, freeing herself.

This is it, she said to herself. She pretended to take another bite. Lefty and Estraya went back to arguing.

Quickly, she stood, lifted the chair and pulled it through the loops. Instead of attempting to duck behind her captors into the stairwell, she leapt for the window. They wouldn't be expecting that, she reasoned. Catapulting her body through the small space, she found herself tumbling down a rough section of the Orbokth. Her legs were still loosely bound together, which didn't help her coordination. Scrabbling at the rock to stop her fall, she managed to slide to a halt, bloodied and bruised.

"Get her!" Lefty's shrill voice resounded through the mist.

Camilly reached down and extricated her feet from the rope. With relief, she noted that she was on the side of a cliff that dropped off sharply toward the sea. She stood up shakily on the rocky, near-vertical wall and leaped.

By the time Lefty and Estraya reached the place where the ropes adorned the cliff, Camilly was gone, the only sign of her exit, the glowing patch of ymolenegth where she'd hit the water.

Chapter 23: Xylo

He had expected the heat, but he hadn't expected the wind.

Higher than he'd ever been before, Xylo continued to ascend toward the Ghalon. The journey thus far had taken him longer than he had hoped by several times over. He had been forced to throw himself off the cliffs multiple times, using his Esh-tala to glide back down. He had figured on heat being a problem, as well as his own stamina—he was, after all, an old man. But what he hadn't expected was that the farthest reaches of Luca where he'd begun his trek, though largely uninhabited by the people of Luca, were thoroughly populated by animals. The mhowis goats had been annoying, headbutting him in order to protect their young, but Xylo wasn't afraid of them. He'd adjusted his route to circumvent the scattered flocks, and they had ceased to bother him. It was the packs of yovod that were the real problem.

Although Xylo had worked on the heights for years and years, he had never seen more than a single yovod at a time. The big cats were beautiful, and he relished the sight of them, with their coats of red, gold, and black arranged in intricate patterns of spots and dashes and their noiseless footfall. He hadn't known they hunted in packs.

The first time he'd spied one, he had simply kept his distance, hoping it would see him as a poor dinner prospect. He'd soon realized seven or eight of the stealthy creatures had surrounded him, intent on hunting him into oblivion. He'd thrown himself from the cliff, gliding down on his tala until he couldn't see them above him. They'd followed on foot but thankfully had lost sight of him as he disappeared in the mist.

Resolving to leap at the first sight of a yovod, Xylo continued. He speculated that the yovod, with their thick fur, were not equipped to live above a certain elevation. They were built for the heights, but not for the extreme heat nearest the Ghalon. Once he passed the level at which they could survive, he would be safe, assuming he could endure the temperature.

Relentlessly he trekked on, hiding himself in narrow crevices when he needed to stop to sleep. He did most of his traveling at night and in the early morning. The yovod seemed disinclined to hunt during the dark hours when the rain fell incessantly. Though they became active again once the Ghalon turned its face toward the land, the morning mists were thin, and he could see them coming from a long distance. There was time to tuck himself into a crack in the rock too small for the yovod to enter. They were roughly twice as large as he, he estimated. And that was the smaller ones.

After two days of pushing toward the highest heights, he was exhausted. His feet were burning, and he felt sure that his hair and skin were scorched, despite his Esh-defenses. He reflected on the peculiar qualities that made it possible for the Esh to endure the heat. He'd learned some of it in school, but Ieska, with her background in science, had been telling him more about the marvel that was Esh-skin. The chemistry of Esh-skin was particularly conducive to a certain genus of microorganism that thickly populated the entire body of the Esh. Xylo looked at his skin in the dim light of the glowing algae in the tiny cave into which he'd tucked himself for the daylight hours. It glowed faintly with the rainbow sheen called iridis, the result of the interaction between their own bodily offal—sweat, oils, skin cells—and the waste of the microorganisms. It was because of the coating of microorganisms and iridis that the Esh were able to endure the fire. Despite Ieska's attempts to explain the science behind it, Xylo still couldn't grasp the exact mechanism by which they did this. But he was glad they did. He was going to put his skin and its tiny parasites to the test once night fell. He was going straight up toward the fire.

The rainfall of night woke him up, and he slithered out of the cave and gripped the rock around him. He'd chosen this night to go up because here, the cliff face looked scalable. He could do this. And once he was out of range of the yovod, he could relax and travel more efficiently. He didn't have to stay in the heights for long, he reasoned. Just long enough to go over the top. He could glide down on the other side into Garradh Gannoir. He reached down to pluck some fuuegn for a snack as he climbed, reflecting that his taste for the bland, fungus-like organism had grown during his trek. He hadn't packed much in the way of provisions, knowing that he could sustain himself by what he found growing on the heights.

The water that fell on him grew hotter as he ascended. It hovered near the border between deliciously hot and painfully scalding. He set his jaw determinedly. Painfully scalding was what he wanted. The yovod could endure delicious heat. But they wouldn't be likely to put up with actual injury for the sake of a dried-up old morsel like himself.

Xylo could see the Ghalon far above his head, fiercely glowing through the rain with its fissures of red light—the convenalations. They grew distorted as he went higher and higher, closer and closer to the fiery ball at the heart of his world. The heat was intense. Looking at his hands as they gripped the rock and pulled him forward and upward, he could see that his iridis was glowing white-hot, in contrast to its usual lavender and rainbow hue. He wondered if Ieska had been right, if, in fact, he was attempting the impossible.

No, he told himself. He could do this. He had to. He had to get back to Garradh Gannoir. He had work to do there. He raised his eyes to the heights, hoping to see the peaks above him. The rain washed the air of mist, but it also obscured his vision. The rain itself seemed to glow red as he climbed. Even as a soil miner, he had never been so high, so near to the Ghalon.

Something hit his face—a burning ember, maybe. It was followed by more and more stinging hot slaps. He reached up to touch his face, to see what was hitting him. They were hitting his hands as well, and his tunic and boots. He kept his inner eyelids shut, as he had throughout most of his journey. Now, however, as he plucked one of the tiny bits of fire off his hand, he opened both sets of eyelids for a better view of the tiny object. It wriggled in his grasp, tiny and offended.

Xylo whistled in amazement at what he saw. The slender worm in his hand, not much longer than his fingernail and thin as a sea-string, wriggled and flapped tiny membranous wings. It looked at him with glowing red eyes. A glance told him that he was covered with the tiny creatures. Pauluvervol, he reflected. Miniature flying worms. Fire creatures. He'd learned about them in school, but they were thought to be either extinct or mythical. They were, he thought ruefully, neither. Their burning skin scorched his clothing, leaving tiny, ashy holes. They stung his skin but did not have the same destructive effect. He wondered if he could take one back down the mountain to show Case, Ceres, and Talag. They'd want to see it, he knew. He slid his hand into his pocket and scraped his fingers against the fabric, trying to knock a few of the tiny creatures off. It might work. Or they would burn holes in his pocket and escape. Xylo was filled with a delicious sense of wonder and discovery that he hadn't experienced since he had discovered that there was, in fact, an "other side of the Orbokth." But Kleibald had found that first. This, he thought, was his own discovery. After this, Ieska would want to explore the heights with him. He wished she were there with him.

Climbing higher, he found to his relief that the storm of tiny creatures abated. He no longer needed to fear the pauluvervol, but because of the heat of the Ghalon, he still chose to travel during the dark, rainy hours. At daybreak, just as the golden crescent of Ghalon slid into view, he tucked himself into a crevice in the rock and curled up just inside to wait out the day.

Chapter 24: Tass

"Time to go back," Ninach said shortly as she approached Tass.

Tass glared at her half-sister, although she really felt relieved that her "outside time" was over. She just wanted to sleep.

Ninach hefted Tass into her arms and carried her gently back inside. Dynny shuffled over as soon as Ninach laid Tass on the cot and tucked her in. The baby wailed.

Tass frowned. "What's wrong with her?"

"Probably just hungry. Or wet," Dynny said cheerfully. "I'm a good carer. I'll make the baby feel better."

Tass hated the baby. It had sucked all the life out of her sister to feed its ugly self. And now it was taking time Dynny could have been using to take care of her.

Ninach glanced away from Tass toward the squalling baby. "It's an ugly little thing," she said with a relish.

You're uglier than the baby, the voices pointed out to Tass.

It was true, Tass reflected. At least the baby was new and undamaged. She was like rotten fruit. Rotten at the core. She closed her eyes and turned her face to the wall.

The baby's cries quieted into slurping sounds as Dynny fed her. Tass heard Ninach leave through the curtain that hung in the doorway. She wasn't sure what she thought of Ninach. She was certainly no Mailu. Mailu had loved her. Ninach never would, she felt sure. Ninach was nasty.

Just like you, the voices said.

Tass felt the darkness filling her being to her very fingertips. She wished she'd never invited the darkness in. She hadn't gotten what she wanted. All she'd accomplished was losing herself.

Tass awoke later to a rising din outside the cave. Voices. A lot of voices. Then someone pushed their way into the room. Tass rolled over (she could do that much on her own now) and opened her eyes.

Ninach, Bridima, Gudall, Rhyder, and of course, Dynny, were huddled around the tiny girl, as well as a man she didn't remember. What was going on? She listened.

"He's looking for her," the stranger said anxiously.

Bridima shook her head. "He won't find her here. No one knows about Cudth Deorth."

"She's his daughter. Maybe we should just give her to him," Ninach suggested.

There were murmurs of disapproval. Tass thought she heard Dynny gasp. She hadn't realized Ninach hated the baby as much as she did.

"We can't give her to Gelu," Bridima said firmly. "She's different. She's one of us. She belongs here in Cudth Deorth."

The stranger nodded sagely. "He's a bad man. He was a part of everything Kleibald did, even the destruction of my son. It's unfortunate that he's the father of Mailu's child, but we must protect her."

"You think he'll look far enough to discover our settlement here?" Gudall asked sharply.

Dynny hugged the baby girl tightly. "Gelu's bad. Gelu killed Arros."

"We won't let Gelu have the baby," Bridima reassured the little old man.

"I'll take care of her," Dynny promised.

"She may not be Gelu's child at all," Bridima noted. "If the same sorts of experiments were happening in Obumbro that were happening in Lucedth, it's possible that she bears no trace of Gelu in her body at all. Ieska was explaining it to me before she left."

"Who, then?" Rhyder asked. "Who is the father?"

"Ieska didn't know. They may have been splicing genes, hoping to create a Triad. It could be why her blood is so powerful. You all saw the ymolenegth. It was more than even a Triad's blood would engender."

"Nonetheless, she's one of us," Gudall said staunchly. "She's a misfit and an experiment, just like we are. She belongs with us."

"I'm afraid this may be what's behind the plot to arrest Xylo," Bridima said. "They're going to come for us. They'll find us if they look hard enough."

"The baby is ruining everything," Ninach said sourly. "We should give her to Gelu and protect ourselves. They won't come looking for Cudth Deorth if they have the baby."

It sounded good to Tass. The baby had taken her sister away. She would be glad if she never saw it again.

"I'm surprised at you, Ninach," Bridima said. "The baby is innocent. We need to protect her."

"We owe the baby nothing. Or Mailu. Mailu did nothing to help us. She was dead before we met her. The baby's not one of us.

She's going to get us all killed. Make us all objects of experimentation. You're too soft-hearted," Ninach objected.

Tass looked over at the group gathered around the baby. The small ugly thing was the center of attention. And except for Ninach, she was the center of everyone's love. A ripple of dark laughter flooded through Tass. The baby was loved unconditionally. She, Tass, had given her blood to save the world, had been the instrument by which the skyboulder was brought home, and had lost her entire family and her best friend. If anyone deserved to be the center of affection, it was she, not some detestable science-experiment brat who had ended Mailu's life. Her expression grew even more bitter. Ninach understood. Ninach was the only one thinking rationally about justice and common sense. The baby had to go.

Dynny clutched the baby so tightly that it yelped. Bridima patted his shoulder, and he relaxed his grip.

"We'll take care of the baby," Bridima said. "There will be no more arguments." She looked pointedly at Ninach, who tossed her mousy brown hair defiantly.

"I'm a good carer," Dynny pointed out.

"I'll start enlarging the cave system," Rhyder offered. "We can make a hiding place. Somewhere we can put Dynny and the baby if they end up coming here to look for her."

"I'll help," Gudall said. "Building my own house can wait."

"Lot of help that'll be," Ninach snorted.

"Ninach!" Bridima chastised her. "Gudall is injured. He doesn't need you discouraging him."

"Where are *we* going to hide, Bridima?" Ninach spat. "We're hiding here too. The seven of us, though it's only Gudall and I now. Why are we here if it's only the baby who needs a hiding place?"

Tass again thought Ninach was making sense. She didn't want to fall into the hands of Gelu and Nadim. If only someone would think about something but Mailu's baby! "She's right," Tass croaked.

She and Ninach exchanged a glance of solidarity, the first positive communication that had happened between the half-sisters.

"We'll make it big enough," Rhyder promised. "Big enough for all seven of the Triads, plus Tass, Dynny, and the baby."

"I'll take good care of the baby," Dynny said. "Protect her from Gelu." He stroked the baby's sparse hair.

Tass rolled over and closed her eyes as the others filed out of the room. She remembered who the stranger was now. Torcalon. Her grandfather, so they said. The father of her mother's violator. The grandfather of all the Triads, even Igracio. Even her own grandfather didn't love her. He loved Mailu's baby, who was no relation to him, and not Tass.

Chapter 25: Unaleah

"It's a dead end," Unaleah said in despair.

"There were other passages," Sadi reminded her sister. "Tass got from Luca to Garradh Gannoir through the sea. There must be a way."

"It could be anywhere," Unaleah answered. "We could spend the rest of our lives looking and still not find it."

Sadi shook her head. "I have a feeling about this place. It means something."

"It means we're fools. We should go home."

"You promised me two extra days of searching," Sadi reminded her sister.

"That means we have one day left, and after that, we're going home. This isn't doing any good."

The girls crawled back through the passageway. Twice they explored the narrow fissures running off the main passageway, and twice they were disappointed. Unaleah was tired, body and soul. She felt in her heart that Kari was gone. Probably Pax and Laetu as well.

The rough stone of the Orbokth scraped at Unaleah's hands and knees as she pressed into a third tunnel. One more day. One more day and, Sadi had agreed, they could go home. She tried to focus her thoughts on the baby. Perhaps he had been born already. Perhaps he was dead.

Think positive, she coached herself. The baby would be there, waiting, when she got home, a balm to ease the loss of her siblings.

The tunnel widened as she crawled. She still couldn't stand, but she could stretch and turn around. The rock here was damp, something she hadn't observed since they'd begun exploring the passageways. She called ahead to Sadi. "Why's it wet in here?"

Sadi shrugged. "We descended some. Maybe there are cracks in the rock where the sea gets in when the tide is high."

Unaleah paused to lean back on her heels. She wiped miniscule particles of rock off her hands, listening for any sounds of dripping water. There was nothing.

Suddenly she heard a gasp from Sadi, who had continued to trek toward the inevitable third dead end.

"What is it?" she called.

"Something!" Sadi exclaimed.

Unaleah sighed. It was typical of Sadi to be excited about "something." For herself, she wanted to know what it was before she celebrated.

"Come here," Sadi requested.

Unaleah complied.

"Well? What do you think?"

"What?"

"The floor of the tunnel! You didn't notice?" Sadi backed up so that Unaleah could see what she was talking about.

A circle of perfectly smooth rock in the floor denoted the end of the tunnel.

Unaleah blinked. "Why is that exciting?"

"This couldn't have happened by itself. Someone smoothed this out." Sadi ran her fingers along the smooth circle almost lovingly.

"Does it matter?" Unaleah asked. "Someone came here before we did. Big deal. It could have happened any time in the past thousand years."

Sadi shook her head and pointed to the walls of the cave. "The algae coating is thick in this tunnel. It's thick everywhere. The circle on the floor is bare."

"Most of the floor is bare," Unaleah pointed out. "That doesn't prove anything."

Sadi was pressing on the circle, squatting on the circle, jumping on the circle—or approximating jumping in the truncated space.

"What are you doing?" Unaleah asked.

"I think it's a door," Sadi said. She pointed to the edge of the circle. "It's not attached to the rest of the rock. It's like it wasn't carved out of the same stuff as the ground. Feel it."

Unaleah touched the smooth rock and scraped her fingernail against the join between circle and floor. "That's weird," she said, her heart beating faster. "I think you're right about it being a door. There's something crammed between the circle and the rock." She dug at her fingernail. "It's waxy. Not like rock at all."

Sadi jumped again. "Come on! Help me!"

Unaleah took Sadi's hands and placed her feet on the circle with her sister's. Clinging together, they rocked and bounced. Unaleah could hear the stone circle groaning beneath them.

"Harder!" Sadi cried.

The girls bent and unbent their knees.

"Push your back against the roof," Unaleah said. "Then press down with your feet. It'll give us some leverage."

Clinging to each other's waists with their heads bent low, the girls jammed their bodies between ceiling and floor and pushed.

There was a popping sound, and the floor went out from under their feet.

Chapter 26: Pax

Benjo sighed. "I don't want to have to lock you up. I want to know how you came to be tri-casted. It's important to us. It's important to all Gannoir."

"What do you mean, 'important to all Gannoir'?" Pax asked.

"Prophecies," Benjo told them succinctly. "When the seven castes come together again as they were in the beginning, Gannoir will be restored. It's in the ancient writings."

"See?" Laetu said. "They're on our side. They want Gannoir to be restored."

"Gelu and Kleibald said the same thing," Pax reminded his brother. He turned to Benjo. "What do you mean by 'restored'? And what do you mean by the seven castes coming together? How can a pure fire caste and a pure water caste come together? They can't ever meet."

Benjo nodded. "We've been pondering both of those questions for our entire history. What will the restoration bring? No one knows. What does it mean for castes to come together? We think we know." He paused. "We thought we knew. The idea that someone can be multi-casted is a new one to us. To me. We believed that the castes could come together, so to speak, if they were all working in cooperation. Tehom can only communicate with Mayim and Fossa, as those are the only castes that can come down to us in the water. But the Mayim can communicate with Esh and Gulot. The Fossa can communicate with the Pihr and the Esh. See what I mean? But now, with this idea that someone can belong to more than a single caste . . . It's revolutionary. It's a whole new way of looking at the idea of the castes coming together. Three castes—or so you say—came together in you." He looked at the boy, his eyes blazing with purpose.

"The leaders of Luca and Garradh Gannoir, the land of the deadbloods, also thought of a restoration," Laetu told him. "Their idea of a restoration was a reversal of the gogyvehr. An inversion of Gannoir to bring it back to its original state, with the fire on the outside and the ice at its core. They thought if they made a hole in the Bec, the icy outer shell of Gannoir, that they could cause the inversion to happen."

Pax shifted uncomfortably. He wasn't sure whether telling Benjo was prudent.

"And did they succeed?" Benjo asked.

Laetu shook his head. "You'd know if they had. The whole sea would have been sucked into the chaos. The Ghalon would have ripped through every bit of the world."

"Everyone would have died," Pax pointed out.

"Why didn't it happen?" Benjo asked.

"Igracio . . ." Laetu began.

Pax kicked him.

"The holes in the Bec let in some of the darkness—the evil—from the chaos outside Gannoir. We are on a mission to find a way to close the holes and prevent more evil from leaking into Gannoir."

"And to bring back the skyboulder," Laetu added. "Xylo wants to bring the skyboulder back. Justice must be served."

"Skyboulder?" Benjo asked. "I don't know what this means."

Pax sighed. Then he coughed and choked. His ability to speak under the water had grown astronomically, but the act of sighing still seemed to require his air-lungs. He took a deep breath and tried again. "The leader of Luca, Kleibald the Reformer, and the leader of Garradh Gannoir, Gelu, built a stone ship that was supposed to survive the inversion of the world. Even though the inversion didn't happen, the skyboulder, with forty people on board, slipped out through the hole they'd been digging in the Bec. It's out there in the chaos somewhere."

"Forty people? In a rock in the chaos?" Benjo shook his head. "How is this possible?"

"It was his blood. Igracio's. It made a spinning of the water and the wind. The skyboulder passed through the center of it and went out the hole. And Igracio's blood sealed up the gap. But the darkness still got in. And the skyboulder still got out," Laetu said.

Pax winced. He hadn't wanted to tell Benjo about Igracio.

"Who is this Igracio?" Benjo asked.

"He was Triad, like us," Laetu proclaimed.

Pax groaned. "He's dead. Let's not talk about Igracio."

"It causes you pain? He was your brother?" Benjo asked.

"Yes," Pax said quickly. "Please, let's talk of something else."

"I'm sorry," Benjo said. He seemed sincere. "We know the Bec well. He's a protector and friend."

"He? Friend?" Pax repeated incredulously. "The Bec's alive?"

Benjo looked at them quizzically. "I assumed you knew. The Bec has maor. It's a soul. A person."

Pax digested this. It made the whole concept of the holes in the Bec more hideous. Not only were Gelu and Kleibald digging in the outer layer of the world, attempting destruction, they were digging at something that was alive.

"You mean like Dwoyra and Gaoth!" Laetu exclaimed. "They have different bodies too, but they're people."

"We know Dwoyra well," Benjo nodded. "But who is Gaoth?"

"The wind," Pax explained. Then, in case the water people didn't know of wind, he clarified, "The rational air."

"Are Dwoyra and Gaoth and the Bec casted?" Laetu wanted to know.

Benjo shook his head. "They are other. Not like us. Their bodies are different."

"Do the Pihr have bodies like ours?" Laetu asked.

"We believe so, although it's only speculation," Benjo told him.

Pax was about to ask about the stories in the ancient literature concerning the Pihr, the pure fire people, when a man burst through the waving curtain that served as a door.

Benjo looked up. "What is it, Gelihr?"

This man had miniature blond braids covering his head. The tails extended to his fingertips. He was muscular, and Pax could see the scales covering his forearms and legs. Pax was starting to get used to the protruding faces of the Tehom.

"Intruders," Gelihr replied. "Hydrolock seventy-three."

Benjo raised his eyebrows—nearly to the center of the top of his misshapen head, Pax noticed. "Seventy-three? Are they deadbloods?"

"We're still investigating. I sent a crew to take them into custody."

"If they're deadbloods they'll be dead by the time you get there. They can't breathe in the water. Remember what happened last time."

"You want us to leave them in there?" Gelihr asked. His eyes flicked nervously toward Pax and Laetu. Pax wondered if his flat face looked as eerie to the Tehom as their pointy faces did to him.

Benjo looked at Pax and Laetu and then back at Gelihr. "Things are beginning to happen," he said slowly. "It's possible that this is something new. We can't speak with deadbloods. They only breathe air, and we only breathe in the sea. We can't learn their motives for entering our world. But," he paused and gestured toward the boys, "we have a new weapon in our arsenal."

Pax shivered. He didn't want to be Benjo's new weapon. He wanted to go home.

"We'll go talk to them," Laetu volunteered eagerly.

"Yes, you will," Benjo replied. "Let's all go."

Chapter 27: Camilly

Camilly propelled her body through the water with all the speed she could muster. She wanted to put as much distance between herself and her kidnappers as she could, although she had noticed their lack of finger tala—indicating they couldn't swim—and she knew she ought not fear being followed.

Mom. I've got to find Mom, she thought. *She'll be looking for me, too. Stay in the water, Mom*, she thought at her mother, wherever she was. *There's danger on land.* She wondered if Pax and Laetu, wandering on land, had been taken by the kidnappers just like she'd been. It was an idea. Her kidnappers had spoken of "others." She would find her mother. She would tell her. It gave her new ideas about where to look for her missing brothers. As scared as she still felt, she was full of new hope and direction.

Ymolenegth lit the water behind her as she swam—she was still bleeding. Even if the deadbloods couldn't swim, they had boats that could float on the chemical sea at any time of day. They'd be able to track her. She dove deeper, hoping the cold of the sea would slow her bleeding. The worst cut was one on her elbow. The smaller scrapes and bruises were nothing, but her elbow, which she'd cut on a rock when she'd thrown herself out the window, was deeply gashed. She pressed a hand over the wound and continued to kick through the lemon-yellow sea. Glowing lumalauae swirled around her as if to bring her comfort. It helped, but it also made her worry. What if the warmer temperatures made her arm bleed more?

She sighed and tried to enjoy the beautiful golden creatures, with their phosphorescent appendages. Settling into the beauty and warmth, Camilly relaxed. She was safe. The lumalauae wouldn't let the kidnappers take her, she realized. They weren't just sea creatures. They were protecters. Perhaps they'd even been sent by Dwoyra.

"Mom?" she called as loudly as she could in her gill-voice. "Mom? Finnan?"

She wondered where she was. She knew she couldn't be impossibly far from where she'd attempted to enter the water earlier. Her mother would be looking for her, too. Taking her hand off her injured elbow, she checked to see if the bleeding was slowing. A brilliant yellow glow surrounded her arm when she did so, but it was a diffuse light, not the bright bloody streak that she'd seen before. It was working, she decided, clamping her hand over her wound again. Once it stopped bleeding she would go to the surface and see if she could tell where she was.

The current grew wild around Camilly as she swam. She wondered if a storm was about to happen. She fought through the waves to the surface and stuck her head out. "Mom? Finnan?" she called.

The water curled around her feet and yanked her beneath the surface.

Dwoyra.

Camilly spun around and looked. She always expected to see something when Dwoyra was near. A shift in the colors of the water. A shape. Anything. But, as usual, there was nothing to see. The fingers of water grabbed her again, pulling her down.

Camilly dove back into the yellow layer of the sea, following the current, which she now understood was Dwoyra's friendly nudges.

"Dwoyra, I need to find my mom," she said in her gill-voice.

Dwoyra didn't answer, but she kept leading Camilly onward. The watery creature and the girl ducked under the Orbokth. Small fish schooled around them, each bearing a small smudge of darkness. A ripple of fear shuddered through Camilly at the sight. This was what they had to fight. It was everywhere.

They passed the school of fish. Dwoyra led her up inside the Orbokth. The sea changed from yellow to green to turquoise. When Camilly found herself at the surface, she held her breaths and pushed her head through the water. She was in a round cleft in the Orbokth, and it was open to the sky above her. She could see the Ghalon through the mists over her head. It was not unlike Cudth Deorth, where she had been raised, but it was far smaller. If Cudth Deorth were the size of a town, this would be a neighborhood, and a small one at that.

Through the golden mist she could see the rocky shore. Camilly pulled herself out of the water and looked around. "Mom?" she called hesitantly. Her words bounced off the tall rocks that surrounded her on all sides. "Mom? Finnan?" she tried again. Her elbow ached. Looking at it, she saw that the bleeding had stopped. The wound still gaped. "Mom?"

"Camilly!" a voice cried from above.

Camilly looked up.

Finnan was climbing down from the rocks toward her. "Oh, Camilly! I was so worried! How did you get here?"

"Dwoyra brought me," Camilly said. Her teeth started to chatter despite the warm air. All the fear she had endured caught up with her as she relaxed into her mother's arms. She took a deep breath and then coughed, finding she was unable to stop shaking.

"Are you all right?" Finnan asked. She pushed Camilly away from her and inspected her from top to toe.

"I'm banged up pretty good," Camilly said. "But the only bad cut is on my elbow." She held up her arm so Finnan could see. "I was lucky this was all I got." She looked into her mother's eyes. "They kidnapped me, Mom."

Finnan nodded. "Dwoyra suspected as much. Who was it? Do you know?"

"A man and a woman. Deadbloods," Camilly said, putting as much vitriol into the pejorative as she felt it warranted. "A man named Lefty and a woman, Estraya."

"I know those names," Finnan exclaimed. She flicked her long red braid behind her. "They were on the list of survivors from the crash of the skyboulder. They're Gelu's people."

Camilly digested this. Then, disheartened, she answered her mother. "I thought maybe they had Pax, Laetu, and Kari. They spoke of 'others.' But Pax and Laetu disappeared before the skyboulder came back." She shook her head. "Whoever they were talking about, it must have been someone else."

Finnan reached out to stroke her daughter's wet red head. "I'm sorry."

"Yeah. Me too," Camilly said. "I really hoped it was a clue."

"It might be a clue," Finnan said. "Just not a clue about the boys and Kari."

"What do you mean?"

"If the kidnappers have some of the Siann Dha, that may be the reason we haven't seen Case, Ceres, and Talag."

Camilly's eyes widened. She hadn't thought of that. She nodded slowly. "That makes sense." She paused. "That's bad."

Finnan nodded. "Much worse than if they were just out foraging for food and decided to spend the night. But at least now we have a clue where they might be."

"How did you find this place," Camilly asked. "Why did you stop here?"

"Dwoyra brought me," Finnan said. "She couldn't explain—or she didn't want to. I thought maybe she brought me here to look for Kari and the boys. I've been climbing the rocks looking for any sign that they may have come this way."

"Did you find anything?"

Finnan shook her head. "Nothing. But I've only searched about a third of the shoreline."

"And then Dwoyra brought me to you," Camilly said.

"Yes."

Camilly stretched and then winced as the wound on her elbow split open and began to bleed again. She clapped a hand over it.

Finnan tore a strip off the bottom of her tunic and bound Camilly's wounded arm. "That should help," she said.

"Thanks, Mom," Camilly said. "Now let's look for the others."

Chapter 28: Xylo

Xylo woke suddenly. He was sweating profusely, something that rarely happened to him. The crevice into which he'd tucked himself for the night was searingly hot. He suspected morning had arrived. With the turn of its fiery face to the land, the Ghalon was heating up the tiny cave like an oven. Xylo reached a hand toward the opening of the crevice, hoping to find relief in the thin mists of morning.

The air was dry and hot outside the hollow. When he pulled his hand back inside, it was glowing painfully. He shook his head. He would have to wait for nightfall before he could continue his journey. He wondered why he'd woken. Had it been the intense heat or something else?

A scratching sound coming from somewhere behind him made him think it was the latter. Xylo pushed his body as far into the crevice as he could. It was cooler the deeper he went. When he'd tucked himself in to sleep, he'd thought the crevice only extended a few feet, but now he saw that was an illusion. A slender crack in the rock at the back of the crevice wasn't a crack at all, but overlapping rocks that concealed a passageway. By the glow of his iridis and the light of the luminescent algae, Xylo squeezed through the fissure into a magical world. Beyond the surface crevice, the cave opened wide. The Orbokth here was hollow. He wondered how high the ceiling went. The dim light did not allow him to see its end. It was cooler here, but not by much.

As his eyes adjusted to the darker chamber, Xylo opened both sets of eyelids and looked around. His body grew still with shock. This was no natural cave. The walls had been smoothed—carved, he thought—by someone who knew what they were doing. Serpentine patterns wound over the algae-coated walls, rivulets of stone that went on as far as his eye could see. His eyes traced the undulating pattern, following it to its end. Again, his eyes widened in surprise. The vaguely eel-like shapes ended with a coiled tail, complete with fins. Whatever doubts he'd had about the intelligence of the carvers melted away completely. What had he found?

Before he could move forward to investigate the intricately carved tail, he felt a hot wind descend on him from above. The scratching noise that had led him to find the cave grew louder. He looked up.

Curled above him, nestled against the roof of the cavern, he could see the outline of another carving. This elongated creature was just as large as the one that occupied the walls of the cave, but its body was segmented, and it had thousands of short, hairy legs. He thought he could see the faint outline of six membranous wings outlined against the rock, worn away through the passage of time. It was magnificent. Even in the darkness he noted the breathtaking realism of the sculpture.

The image of the thing grew brighter, and Xylo thought his eyes were making another incremental adjustment to the dim lighting. The creature seemed to glow with golden light. Then, suddenly, fire poured forth from the mouth of the thing.

It was magnificent. How, Xylo wondered, had the ancients managed to create a sculpture that directed the light from the Ghalon in such a breathtakingly realistic way?

It was only when the creature reared back its head that he realized the truth.

This was no sculpture.

It was alive.

Xylo's eyes widened in terror.

As the creature readied itself to strike, Xylo scrambled quickly back into the fissure through which he'd entered the cavern. He heard the creature slam its body against the rock of the Orbokth. A river of gravel showered down on him. He had to choose—face the heat outside, or the horrors within.

He chose the heat.

He knew the dangers of the heat.

The creature was an unknown.

And it looked hungry.

Xylo tightened the straps of his crossbody bag and threw himself into the blazing heat of the Ghalon. The morning mists had not yet risen to the level of the heights, and the fire scorched his skin. Xylo pulled himself higher and higher, scrambling for the pass between the peaks of the Orbokth where he could get through to the other side and begin his descent.

He had just reached the top, his iridis now shining a fiery red, when he saw the long body of the creature silhouetted against the Ghalon. It was coming for him. As it grew closer and closer, he could see its small, hairy legs and its face of prickly, pinching jaws and too many beady eyes. He knew now what it was. He'd read about them— the giant scolopendrae, mythical creatures of the heights.

Instinctively Xylo threw out his arms, stretching his tala to its fullest extent. He threw his body off the Orbokth toward the sea below, toward Garradh Gannoir. If, somehow, the creature didn't get him, he had done it. He had done the impossible.

If.

Chapter 29: Tass

Tass lifted her arm and examined her skin. It was closer to its normal, yellowish color. The color of rejection. The color of a slave. The color of a Mayim. She shook her head. Bridima had tried to explain tri-casteing to Tass, had tried to explain that she wasn't Mayim at all, she was one of them—a Triad—but Tass hadn't bought it. She was Mayim through and through, no matter what her fingers did. And her fingers hadn't done it since the darkness had invaded her body. No more glowing. No more confusion. No more . . .

She looked up. Ninach was coming toward her. She didn't like Ninach, but she understood her. Ninach was like Tass. She was a loner. She was angry. She had clarity. Tass looked away, further down the shoreline of Cudth Deorth toward the huts that extended from the Orbokth. Bridima and Dynny were laughing together, tickling the baby and trying to make her laugh.

Ninach drew near. "It's disgusting, isn't it?"

Tass looked at her. "What? The baby or the fuss they're making over it?"

"Both," Ninach grunted. "All that fuss over a deadblood."

"They say she's not a deadblood," Tass argued listlessly. She could hear the faint ringing laughter of the voices of the darkness in her head.

Ninach shook her head. "She was fathered by Gelu, leader of the deadbloods. Even if your sister was her mother, that doesn't make her one of us."

Tass nodded. "Too bad we can't get rid of it. It's ugly and disgusting. Too many lives have been sacrificed for it already. How many more people will it hurt?" It gave her pleasure to call the baby girl "it" instead of "she." The baby, she thought, had been the death of her sister. Mailu had given every last drop of her lifeblood to form and grow the child. There had been nothing left for Mailu. And nothing left of Mailu for Tass.

Evil . . . spawn of darkness . . . the voices laughed in her head. She could feel her resentment tingling all the way to her fingertips.

"Keeping the baby here is dangerous for all of us."

"Then why are they doing it?" Tass asked.

Ninach shrugged. "They're soft and weak," she said.

Tass nodded. The voices had been telling her much the same thing. She wondered if Ninach heard the voices too, if the darkness also talked to her sister.

Ask her, the voices whispered. Tass felt an electric energy, an impulse to act. It was like coming back to life.

"Do you . . ." she ventured.

Do it! the voices screamed in her head. *Be useful for once!*

Tass swallowed hard. "Do you hear them too?" she squeaked. She wished she'd been able to speak with more authority.

"Hear what?" Ninach asked suspiciously.

Tass bit her lip. "The voices. The darkness. It talks to me. It insults me. It spurs me on to be better, to do what needs to be done."

"Are they talking to you right now?" Ninach asked.

Tass nodded. "They're inside me now. They're part of me. It's why my skin looks like this," she said, holding how her now faintly blackened limbs.

"I thought your skin was burned."

"No. It's the darkness. I thought maybe you heard it too. It . . . it talks like you talk. Soft and weak, it's been saying, just like you said. Did you hear that from them?"

"I don't know about voices and darkness," Ninach said. "But my own thoughts are dark. Soft and weak is what they are. It's the truth. The baby is ugly and useless. She's a danger to us all. We have to do something."

Tass nodded. "That's what I was thinking too. But how can we fix this?"

The voices hooted and howled. Tass heard the answer clearly.

Ninach's voice echoed the shouts of the darkness. "We have to get the baby to Gelu."

Tass nodded. "You're right. But how?" She lifted her arms weakly. "I have no strength. I couldn't lift the child, much less travel to Luca to find Gelu."

"I can lift a baby. I can go to Luca. But I'll need to distract the others from the baby. That's going to be the hard part. That's where you come in."

"Okay," she agreed. "Let's do it."

Chapter 30: Unaleah

Unaleah looked around her in shock. She and Sadi had fallen into a sort of prison. The door, which had given way under them, had slammed shut, trapping them in a small chamber. She swam, frantically pushing against the walls trying to figure out how to get out. She could reach the walls on all four sides without doing more than extending her body lengthwise. She clung to Sadi. "Where are we?" she asked.

Sadi pushed her off. "Breathe. It's going to be okay. Use your gills. Nothing has changed."

"We're trapped," Unaleah noted frantically.

"We're safe. We just have to think. We got in here, and we can get out of here," Sadi said. "There are two doors above us. Look up. One of them must open. Either the one we came through or the other one."

Unaleah looked up. Sadi was right. Two circles were apparent over her head. Two doors. "Which one did we come through?" she asked.

Sadi frowned. "I'm not sure."

"This is bad," Unaleah noted.

"Or good," Sadi suggested. "We could be near to solving the mystery of our missing brothers and sister. Remember why we came here? It wasn't so we could be safe. It was to explore unknown regions in order to find Pax, Kari, and Laetu."

Unaleah nodded. "You're right." She breathed heavily, trying to calm herself.

A sudden current drew the two girls upward as a door above their heads opened. Sadi, who was situated most directly under the door, slipped through it easily. Unaleah slammed into the Orbokth, scraping her arms and bruising her back. Then she followed her sister through the doorway in the ceiling.

Chapter 31: Pax

Pax stood back as Benjo opened the hydrolock. He wondered who he would find on the other side of the door. Deadbloods? Siann Dha? It could be anyone from Luca. Vacationing Mayim? Elders?

"I'm scared," Laetu whimpered.

"We don't have any choice," Pax hissed. "Whoever it is, we'll deal with it."

"What if it's someone from the elders?"

"The elders are Esh," Pax pointed out. "It can't be one of the elders. They can't breathe under the sea."

"Well, Mayim on a mission for the elders, then," Laetu worried.

"Don't borrow trouble," Pax shot back. "We have no choice, so we might as well not worry."

When the first form shot through the hydrolock, he couldn't see much more than dark hair and a girl's body. The girl coiled her body and kicked against the water. Pax drew in his breath. "Sadi!" he cried. "Oh, Sadi!" He pushed himself through the water toward his sister.

Minutes later he saw his brother hugging Unaleah.

"We thought you were dead," Unaleah sobbed.

"We thought you might be dead," Pax told her. "We felt the earthquake."

"Is Kari here too?" Sadi asked. She looked around and noticed Benjo. "Who's that?" She gave him a curious stare.

Benjo came forward. "You know these people, I presume," he said.

"These are our sisters," Pax said.

"We were looking for them," Unaleah told Benjo. "When the skyboulder came back it caused a lot of destruction. We thought sure they were hurt or dead."

"The skyboulder came back?" Pax asked in surprise. "Was that what the earthquake was about?"

Sadi nodded. "We went down with Rhyder's fire pouches in our mouths. We had to unite the fire, the sea, and our blood." She showed her brother her scars. There were only the four of us—me, Unaleah, Gudall, Kari—with Triad blood. Tass was . . . well, she was working for the other side. She was digging a hole in the Bec."

"Digging a hole in the Bec?" Laetu squawked in horror. "Tass was digging a hole in the Bec?"

"With a shovel?" Pax asked, confused.

"With the help of a giant dga," Unaleah said. "The combination of Tass's hole, our blood, the fire, and the sea somehow brought the skyboulder back. As far as we can tell, the pressure from the skyboulder lodging in it made the fissures in the Bec close. No more darkness can get it."

"But the darkness that seeped through before that happened is trapped inside Gannoir. It's bad," Sadi told them.

"What about Xylo?" Pax asked. "Did he get his family back safely? And were Kleibald and Gelu brought to trial?"

"Xylo's grandchildren made it back safely," Sadi said. "His son and daughter died, along with half the people on the skyboulder, Kleibald included."

"Kleibald is dead?" Laetu repeated in astonishment. "Who's the Esh-Maor now?"

"His son-in-law, Nadim," Unaleah said. "And Gelu's working with him."

"So there was no justice for Gelu? They didn't do anything to him for trying to blow up the world?" Laetu asked.

"Blow in the world," Pax corrected. "It would have imploded, not exploded."

"Not only was there no justice, they're blaming the deaths in the crash on Xylo. The elders are looking for him. They want to arrest him," Unaleah told the boys.

"And Tass? And Mailu?" Pax asked.

"Tass survived, but she was in bad shape. They took her and Mailu to Cudth Deorth. Bridima and Dynny are taking care of them. Mailu's going to have a baby," Sadi told them.

"She may have had it already," said Unaleah wistfully.

"Wow," Pax breathed. "We missed it all."

Benjo had watched the exchange without interrupting until this point. Then he swam toward the foursome. He pushed his protuberant nose into the conversation. "I think we all need to talk. We need to understand what has happened. I need to gather my council to hear your testimony."

Unaleah seemed to notice Benjo for the first time. "Who is this?" she asked.

"I'm Benjo, leader of the Tehom," he said, nodding to the girls.

"What's a Tehom?" Unaleah asked.

"Are you a friend or an enemy?" Sadi demanded.

Benjo looked at her in disgusted surprise. "That is not how a female should address a male," he reprimanded her.

Sadi raised her eyebrows. "That is how any person would address a possible enemy," she told him.

Pax nudged her. "They don't make much of females among the Tehom. Just go with it."

"I won't," Sadi spat.

"Try to get along," Unaleah urged her sister nervously.

"I asked if you were a friend or an enemy," a now-furious Sadi addressed Benjo.

He frowned at her. "That," he said, "remains to be seen."

Chapter 32: Camilly

Camilly pushed her body through the sea. She was tired but not unhappy. She and Finnan had left the secluded cave where Dwoyra had reunited them. They'd been swimming for hours, trying to systematically explore the perimeter of the sea in Garradh Gannoir.

"Kari was with the others when it happened," Finnan noted. "If she's injured, she would have tucked herself into a hollow in the Orbokth to wait for help. She's a smart girl."

"We'll find her," Camilly answered. "Maybe we should look closer to the skyboulder."

"I was thinking the same thing," Finnan said. "Although it's possible that the impact of the skyboulder hitting Gannoir propelled her far from the landing site."

"The others made their way back quickly," Camilly argued. "She can't be far from the skyboulder."

"We already searched the underside of the Orbokth near the landing site," Finnan said. "She wasn't there."

"We should still go back. We may have missed something."

"You're probably right."

"Maybe she's not clinging to the Orbokth," Camilly suggested. "Maybe she tucked herself into the skyboulder."

Finnan shook her head, and her red braid floated from side to side. "It's too cold at the bottom of the sea. She wouldn't do that."

"But what if she did? What if she was so cold she couldn't think straight?"

"You're not going to let this go until we look, are you?" Finnan said.

Camilly grinned. "Nope!"

The duo swam through the sea and under the deepest section of the Orbokth. The water grew colder as Camilly propelled herself through the layers of colored liquid. Green. Yellow. Orange. She felt her fingers grow numb. When the sea around them turned red, Camilly and Finnan swam huddled together for warmth.

"You still want to do this?" Finnan said, her words thick and slow.

"Yes." Camilly's voice sounded faint, even to herself.

The waters in the mine were largely uninhabited nearest the surface, but once they passed the yellow layer, sea creatures began to abound. Camilly saw a school of milky white fish swim past her, and then a long line of tiny dga, each sporting a blotch of malignant darkness. Larger creatures frolicked there too—lumalauae and vauzigk among them. Camilly reached toward the lumalauae. A vauzigk, with its fatty body, would offer more protection against the cold, but the lumalauae seemed more intelligent, more likely to perceive her difficulty and act on it. She thought she might be able to summon a lumalaua. Only Dwoyra could make the vauzigk obey.

Camilly's fingers glowed a pale yellow in the red sea as she stretched her hands out. Finnan noticed what she was doing and added her efforts to Camilly's. They mimicked the motions of the lengthy creature flipping and spiraling in the water. The lumalaua, attracted by their dance, began to circle around them.

The water grew warmer.

"Keep it up," Finnan said. "It's working."

Together they danced lower and lower, closer and closer to the bottom of the sea. The water turned magenta. In the distance, Camilly could see the pulsing of the icy purple flames of the Bec.

Finally she saw it—a gargantuan blotch of darkness against the glow of the Bec. They'd found the skyboulder. Being careful to maintain the dance that kept them warm enough to continue, she and Finnan approached the giant rock.

As her eyes adjusted to the darkness, Camilly noticed something near one edge of the skyboulder—a pattern of faintly glowing orange spots. Five, and then five again. She put a hand on the rock.

"Mom," she said quickly, "come this way. I think I see something."

Camilly and Finnan danced with the lumalaua—danced toward the ten bits of light. Camilly held up her hand. Excitement made her fingers blaze with light—enough that she could see the reason for the glowing orange spots. Fingers. Ten glowing fingers.

"Ceres!" she cried. "Oh, Ceres!"

Ceres it was. Her eyes were closed, and her face was frozen in an expression of intense concentration.

Camilly grew still. "Is she dead?" she whispered.

A rush of cold washed over her. The lumalaua was leaving.

"Keep dancing," Finnan ordered.

Immediately Camilly resumed the dance. The lumalaua swirled around them joyfully, its glowing tentacles further lighting the scene. The water warmed.

Finnan touched Ceres.

Slowly, Ceres opened her eyes.

"She's alive!" Camilly breathed.

"What's she doing down here?" Finnan wondered aloud. Being careful to keep dancing with the lumalaua, she pressed her body close to Ceres.

Ceres shuddered but did not move.

"Dance, Camilly," her mother commanded. "I've got to warm her up. It's up to you to keep the lumalaua with us until we can get her out of the depths."

Finnan pried at Ceres' hands, trying to make her let go of the skyboulder.

Consternation loosened Ceres' tongue. "No . . ." she croaked.

"You have to come with us," Finnan said. "It's too cold here. Let us help you."

"No . . ."

Finnan continued to tug at Ceres, trying to loosen her grip. Camilly, dancing all the while, saw what Finnan did not. "No, Mom! No!"

"What?" Finnan said, turning toward her daughter.

Camilly shook her head. "She can't move. Look at the cracks in the skyboulder. Ceres is holding it together. She's keeping it from breaking up. If it loses a single chunk, it will create a hole through to the chaos. Gannoir could be destroyed!"

"Son of a vauzigk!" Finnan swore.

"What are we going to do?" Camilly asked.

Finnan shook her head. She rubbed Camilly's shoulders and arms, trying to warm her up. "Keep dancing. Just keep dancing."

Chapter 33: Xylo

Xylo lay on his cot in the caves of the Dynroc. He had expected to find the others there, coming in and out as they went about their business. He had arrived in the morning. It was now afternoon, and he'd neither seen nor heard anyone. He had searched every part of the cave system to no avail. His son Case was nowhere. Ceres was missing. Even young Talag was gone. Of the party that had gone ahead of him, Widman, Finnan, Camilly, and Byid, there was no sign. Knowing he needed to rest, he'd decided to sleep.

Sleep did not come.

His mind was too full of what he had seen. The thing that shocked him most was not the discovery that giant scolopendrae were alive and well, though that fact was surprising enough. What occupied his thoughts was the fact of the intricately sculptured walls of the scolopendra's cave. Who had carved the interior of the Orbokth? Legends in Luca told of no previous civilizations, even ancient ones, who lived inside the fiery heights of the Orbokth. Who could live there? Yet whoever had carved the walls was clearly intelligent. Had it been a single person? Or group of people isolating themselves from the rest of Luca? He shook his head. No one could inhabit the caves where he had been. It was too hot. Even his brief visit had told him that. He was Esh, the fire caste, and he could not bear the heat. Maybe in times past, the temperatures had been milder. He had to find out more. He would go back, he decided. The sculptures did not look ancient. There was no weathering on them, no blackening of the rock where melted bits had dripped down during the daylight hours.

Maybe, he thought, the giant scolopendra itself had carved the walls of its home. He squeezed his eyes together as he tried to imagine the ferocious creature endowed with a rational mind. Could it be so? Could scolopendrae have intelligent maor? Could they have souls? Dwoyra and Gaoth had rational maor, yet their bodies were amorphous, made of water and wind. It was not impossible, but it was a fantastical idea, born of his own exhausted mind, he thought. Still, he wanted to know. His thoughts swirled in circles, denying him the rest he needed.

Where were the others?

What was the nature of the giant scolopendra?

Who had carved the Orbokth?

When would he see his wife again?

How long would it take Gelu and Nadim to hunt him down in Garradh Gannoir?

At long last he fell asleep, only to dream of people with the short, hairy legs of the scolopendra who were armed with hammers and chisels. Melted rock oozed from their pores as they worked in the intense heat. He slept fitfully, waking frequently only to slip back into his nightmare.

"Xylo! Xylo!"

Xylo thought the voices were part of his dream, that the alien beings had seen him, that he was no longer a passive observer of their activities, but an active participant in the scene.

"Xylo!"

Xylo opened his eyes, still feeling fuddled and disoriented.

"He's awake!" a voice cried with relief.

Xylo ran a hand through his white hair, causing it to stand up in damp, freakish ridges.

"Are you all right?" a man's voice asked.

Focusing his eyes, Xylo saw that it was Widman standing over him, asking after his health.

"Yes," he said. "I'm fine. Nightmares." He pushed himself to a sitting position and looked around. He noticed that twelve-year-old Byid was hovering nearby. "You made it here," he said gratefully. "Are Finnan and Camilly here too?"

"They're swimming," Byid said. "Looking for Ceres."

"Looking for Ceres?" Xylo's brain felt thick and slow.

"There has been no sign of Case, Ceres, or Talag," Widman explained. "We waited at first, thinking they had gone into the city for the day, or that they were foraging for food, but they didn't come back. We decided something must have happened and went out to look for them. Finnan and Camilly took to the water. Byid and I went into the heights."

"It's hot up there," Byid complained. "I'm burned." He rubbed his skin, wincing.

"The heights aren't for the Gulot," Widman agreed. "I'm scorched as well. Still, we felt it was imperative to stay together. And since Case and Talag are both Esh, it made sense that if they'd gone somewhere, it would have been into the heights."

"And?" Xylo asked. "No sign of them?"

"Nothing," Widman told him. "And Finnan and Camilly haven't returned."

"How many days has it been?" Xylo asked.

"Too many," Widman said heavily. "Something's wrong."

Chapter 34: Tass

Tass understood her part. She and Ninach had decided that it would be smart if she sported a real injury instead of faking an ailment. It was to be the diversion, the thing that made Dynny turn his attention from his constant care for and adoration of the baby and toward Tass. While he was ministering to Tass's wound, Ninach would slip in and spirit the baby away. She would hide in the caves higher in the Orbokth until Torcalon arrived for his weekly visit. Then, while the others fretted, she would steal out of the heights and row toward Luca in Torcalon's boat.

It had to work.

Tass had decided that opening the wounds on one of her shoulders would be best. Her shoulders ached continually. Further injury was not likely to make them worse, only to continue what had begun months earlier. Tass slipped down to the shore on shaky legs, crawling the last bit of the journey. The farther from the caves she was, the better. It would give Ninach more time to gather the baby and its things.

Her skin looked darker under the dim light of the convenalations. The rain washed her skin with pure water, a feeling that usually brought her pleasure and comfort. Now, however, she was too keyed up for either. The flicker of light from the heights told her Ninach was ready. It was time.

Tass pulled the little knife Ninach had given her out of the pocket in her tunic. She had to make it look like her injury was accidental. Running her fingers over the rocky ground, she found the sharpest bit of rock she could. She lay down on the thick vegetation, so alien to her after a lifetime of water and rock. Little purple flowers lifted exhilarated faces to the rain. Tass wondered what they would think of blood raining down instead.

Quickly she slit the wound on her shoulder, taking care to cut a jagged streak instead of a straight line. She smeared the blood on the sharp rocks under the plants and then tucked the knife back into her pocket. Blood ran out of her shoulder onto the flowers and plants and onto the rocks. It dribbled into the water, which glowed with brilliant teal ymolenegth.

Tass cried out again, louder this time. "Help! Oh help!"

She waited, hoping it would be Dynny who heard her.

"I'm hurt! Help me, please!" she shouted through the thick rain.

The rain diluted her blood, spreading it out and making a satisfactory circle of ymolenegth around Tass.

Footsteps sounded.

The voices in her head laughed in triumph.

Ninach's light flickered in the hills above her. Dynny was coming.

"Help!" Tass cried again, as though the blue light needed something additional to draw the others to her.

Rhyder was the first to arrive, with Gudall on his heels. Dynny came next, scurrying as fast as his loving, pudgy, elderly limbs could carry him. Tass could see Bridima in the distance, making her way toward them.

"Help me! I'm hurt," Tass wailed.

"What happened?" Rhyder asked. He put a hand on Tass's back as she lay face-down on the grass.

"I fell," Tass cried. "I cut my shoulder. Cut it right where it was injured before. It's bad. It's so bad!"

Rhyder and Gudall gently lifted her to a sitting position. By this time, Dynny had arrived carrying a satchel full of healing wares. He knelt beside her and pressed his hand against her bleeding shoulder. Her black and yellow arm was covered in red blood, glowing with blue light.

"Get a bandage out," he said, gesturing toward his satchel.

Rhyder pulled out a length of cloth and held it up.

Dynny nodded and took it from the younger man. He worked clumsily to bandage Tass's shoulder. "Shoulders are hard," he grunted. "Not like arms and legs. Not like heads. I do better with heads," he confided.

"Why were you out in the middle of the night?" Bridima asked sharply.

Tass tried to look pitiful. "I just wanted to feel the water on my skin. I thought I'd come down to the shore. I shouldn't have done it. I know that now. I'm not strong enough to be out by myself. I fell."

"We need to get her inside as soon as possible," Bridima ordered.

"No!" Tass cried. She had to keep them away from Dynny's little hospital as long as possible. If they went back before Ninach had gotten away . . .

"You need medical care," Rhyder explained gently. "We can carry you. We'll be gentle."

"Dynny's the best," Gudall reminded her. "He'll see that you get feeling better as quickly as possible."

"It's just . . . the rain feels so good on my skin. Please. I'm Mayim. It's best for me to be out here in the wet," Tass explained.

Bridima glanced toward the hills, toward Dynny's dwelling.

Tass held her breath.

"You're not Mayim, though," Gudall said. "You're one of us. Our little sister. You're Triad. It won't be bad for you to come out of the rain. Especially with an injury like that." He looked at her shoulder and shuddered.

Bridima turned back toward Tass. "I suppose a little more time in the rain can't hurt," she said gruffly.

Tass tried not to sigh with relief. "Is the bleeding slowing?" she asked, looking at Dynny.

He nodded. "I'm a good carer. You're getting better."

"I'm going back to bed, then," Bridima said. "Midnight excursions might be okay for you young people, but I've got too many years on me to stay out in the night when I don't have to."

"I'll stay with them," Rhyder offered. "I can carry her back to bed in a few."

"I'll stay too," Gudall said.

Rhyder shook his head. "It's not necessary. You're still healing too. Go to bed. Dynny and I've got this."

"If you're sure," Gudall hesitated.

"I'm sure," Rhyder said. "Right, Dynny?"

Dynny nodded vigorously, happily. "I'm a good carer. I can do it."

Gudall smiled. "All right," he agreed.

Tass looked toward the hills. She saw a flicker of light from the highest part of the Orbokth. Ninach had done it. That was the sign. She closed her eyes. "I think it's okay now," she said. "You can carry me back to bed."

Chapter 35: Unaleah

Unaleah shivered despite the warmth of the water. The appearance of the Tehom disturbed her. She wasn't sure what made her more uncomfortable, their clawed digits or their oddly shaped heads. They were people, and yet they weren't. They were something from a nightmare.

To Sadi's disgust, the council had refused to allow them to testify. They would only hear Pax and Laetu—the males. Of course, Unaleah didn't like it either, but her anxious mind was more occupied with keeping Sadi from doing something destructive than with fretting about how she was being treated.

Unaleah hadn't considered how an underwater meeting room would be structured. She had been surprised to find that instead of seats facing a speaker's platform, the Tehom meeting place was a large cavern. The speaker floated in the center, and the listeners lined the walls and ceiling. The sound of the speaker's voice seemed to emanate from all sides of his head, not just from his mouth.

"We are gathered to hear the testimony of the intruders," Benjo addressed the all-male crowd hovering over him. "Things have been happening—things we have sought to understand. These others come bringing answers."

At length, Benjo guided Pax and Laetu through an interview during which they explained the ways of Luca and the Siann Dha as well as the events that preceded the crash of the skyboulder. Pax and Laetu's voices did not have the same encompassing resonance as did the voices of the Tehom, so an interpreter repeated their words after them.

"We know nothing about these people," Sadi hissed. "We can't let the boys betray all our secrets."

"We have no choice," Unaleah soothed. "We're captives, if you hadn't noticed. Their civilization is sealed off from the rest of the sea. There's no going home unless we do as they say."

"They could at least lie to them," Sadi grumbled.

"Shh. Just listen."

"But I can't," Pax was saying. "I was here among you when that happened. You have to ask Sadi or Unaleah."

Wary eyes turned toward Sadi and Unaleah.

"Do they understand enough to give testimony?" Benjo asked.

Laetu nodded. "They're very smart."

"They're the only ones who can tell you what happened," Pax added.

Benjo beckoned to Sadi and Unaleah to join him in the center of the cavern. A scowling Sadi and a terrified Unaleah complied.

"What of this skyboulder," Benjo asked. "What happened?"

Unaleah looked at Sadi, wondering how much she should tell. Sadi was silently glowering.

"Pax already explained how the leaders of Luca and Garradh Gannoir intended to implode the world after making their escape," Unaleah said. "They failed, and in so doing, became trapped outside in the chaos. We don't understand the mechanism, but they were able to return to Gannoir. The skyboulder smashed into the Bec and became lodged there. When it landed, the pressure on the Bec was so great that the fissures that were letting bits of darkness into Gannoir were sealed shut. On board the skyboulder were Gulot, Esh, Mayim, and deadbloods. A great many died, either from the impact or from the seawater. Some, however, lived. We, my family and I, brought them to shore."

Benjo looked at her doubtfully. "We already understood this from what your brothers have told us. What we want to understand is how it happened. How you were able to draw something from the chaos toward Gannoir."

"We don't have to tell you that," Sadi fumed.

A murmuring enveloped Unaleah. That all-encompassing sound seemed to be causing turbulence in the water. She wondered about the physics of the voices of these underwater beings. She put her hands on the sides of her head, covering her ears and gills to shut out the noise.

It didn't work.

"Have you forgotten that you are our prisoners?" Benjo asked. "You must do as we say." His voice was commanding and brutal.

Unaleah felt her throat catch. She wanted to cry. She didn't think they ought to explain about the extraordinary power of their Triad blood, but what could they do? She searched her mind for a believable lie.

"It's the power of the blood!" Laetu exclaimed before Unaleah could reply.

Sadi glared at him. "All of the blood of the Siann Dha has power. It makes the water glow."

Maybe that would satisfy these ugly beings, Unaleah hoped. Maybe it would. She looked around at the expectant faces—expectant and unsatisfied.

Nope, she thought.

Chapter 36: Pax

"Your blood makes the water glow too, doesn't it?" Pax asked. He was worried. Sadi was being too confrontational. Unaleah looked terrified. And Laetu was being a fool, telling too much without thinking about what the consequences might be.

"Take the females away," Benjo ordered. "We have heard all we need to hear from them."

Immediately, Gelihr and another burly male grabbed Unaleah and Sadi and dragged them out of the cavern.

"Where are you taking them?" Laetu asked.

"They'll be safe," Benjo promised. "Gelihr will take them to the area reserved for females. They won't escape."

That, thought Pax, was hardly what he'd been worried about.

"What we have to discuss is not for the ears of females," Benjo continued. "They have little understanding, and their lack of comprehension leads to endless repetition as we try to make them see the most basic of facts. It's better to keep them away from any serious business."

Benjo's logic was sound, but Pax wondered at the premises. Unaleah and Sadi—and all the women he ever known—were intelligent and quick to understand. He wondered if perhaps the Tehom females were different.

"As we explained before, there were originally seven castes on Gannoir. Only when all the castes come together will Gannoir be restored. Only then will Tel-Maor be among us."

The dozens of Tehom nodded from their places on the walls and ceiling.

"Since you have come, we have learned that three of the original seven castes are still alive. Gulot, pure land. Mayim, water-land. Esh, fire-land. With the Tehom, pure water, that makes four castes. We had been under the impression that if we desired restoration and reconciliation with Tel-Maor, that we would have to bioengineer the missing castes. We want to know more about the power of the blood as well as your own efforts to bioengineer the other castes. You say that the Tehom are entirely unknown in your dry world?"

Pax nodded. "I have never heard of the Tehom. Not until we came here."

"Everything I've ever heard says there are only three castes, not seven," Laetu agreed. "Mayim, Gulot, and Esh. It's all there ever were."

"Surely the ancient writings remain," Benjo asserted. "The ancients knew. The castes were all in communication at first. There must be knowledge somewhere, hidden in your literature."

Pax bit his lip. "We have been living in isolation. Only the Esh-maor study the literature."

"Ieska would know," Laetu piped up. "Xylo too. They're both Esh-maor. They've studied at the university."

Pax sighed.

Benjo jumped on this information. "Ieska and Xylo. They are your family members?"

"Ieska's one of our mothers," Laetu said. "Xylo's going to marry her. Then he'll be sorta like family."

"One of your mothers?" Benjo pounced. "How can a boy have two mothers? Did you grow in the wombs of two different women?"

Laetu shook his head. "Finnan's my birth mother," he explained. "She's been with me always. She adopted Pax because his father abandoned him and his brother, Byid, after their mother died. When we moved to Cudth Deorth, Bridima and Ieska took care of us all, even my mom."

Benjo's eyes narrowed. "Cudth Deorth? What is this? Another opening in the Orbokth like Luca? A place of dry air?"

Laetu nodded. "It's where we live. In Luca. We live apart from the others. We didn't want Kleibald and the elders to find us."

Pax's heart sank. Was there no secret Laetu could keep? He poked Laetu in the ribs. "Stop telling them everything," he hissed.

"I'm not going to tell them where it is," Laetu protested. "Besides, they can't come there. Then can't breathe air."

"Why do you live apart? Why are you hiding from your elders?"

The other Tehom pushed their bodies toward the center of the chamber in anticipation.

"Don't!" Pax hissed desperately through his gills.

"Because we're the children of Methiant Migas," Laetu told the Tehom cheerfully. "The elders were trying to make someone who was all the castes. He wasn't any castes by the time they were done with him. He killed himself."

"But not before begetting dozens of children?" Benjo asked.

"Not dozens," Laetu said. "Just nine."

"And now your elders want you. They want your blood," Benjo astutely derived.

Laetu nodded. "So we live apart. So they can't find us."

"And it was your blood, your special blood, that brought the skyboulder home?"

Pax pinched Laetu, hoping to cut off his words. "Our blood is nothing special," he said. "The elders just think it is. And we weren't even there when they brought the skyboulder back. We were here. We have no idea what power caused it to return. There are other powers besides the blood of the Siann Dha, you know."

"Like what?" Benjo's voice sounded hungry.

"Like . . . like . . ." Pax hunted for a plausible answer.

"Like the power of the Dynroc," Laetu answered. "That's another power. And who knows how many other things are out there that we don't know about. No one even knew about Garradh Gannoir until a few months ago. And the power of the Dynroc is the ruling power of Garradh Gannoir. There may be other pockets of civilization. Other places and other peoples, with different powers." His voice grew excited. "Even you, the Tehom. You are another people. No one in Luca or in Garradh Gannoir knows about you. There may be others."

Benjo nodded. "It's true," he said. "There may be others. The Fossa, the Pihr, the Maor—the missing castes—may still be alive on Gannoir." He looked toward a particular individual hovering nearby. "You have questions for these boys, Rannasc?"

A man flicked his body through the water to come hover near Benjo and the boys. He had the typical look of the Tehom, but his hair was thin and white, and his claws were a dull brownish yellow. Pax thought he was probably elderly.

"We want to know more about this Methiant Migas, this man who was the subject of the experiments by your elders. What powers did he acquire? By what means did they effect the changes in his body? Can you tell me these things?"

Pax shook his head. "He was our father, but none of us ever met him. He died when we were small."

"We've never even met the scientists," Laetu said. "Except"—Pax shoved him to no avail—"Ieska."

Pax winced at this betrayal.

"Ieska," Benjo said. "Your mother?"

"One of them," Laetu said blithely. "She was one of the scientists who created Methiant Migas. Then he . . . he . . ." Laetu cringed at the word necessary to finish his thought and then substituted another, "made her have a baby. His baby."

"He raped her," Rannasc said bluntly.

Laetu nodded. "Yes. All of us were made that way. All the Triads."

"All of you are tri-casted?" Rannasc asked.

Laetu nodded again. "All nine of us."

"How can we meet with your Ieska," Rannasc pressed. "She can provide us with vital information for our own research."

Pax shook his head. "You can't. She's Esh. She can't be in the water, and you can't be out of it."

"We'll need emissaries. Translators. Go-betweens," Benjo mused.

Rannasc nodded at Pax and Laetu. "These boys?"

"Perhaps the females as well," Benjo said. "They often provide indirect information by their silly chatterings. We may make much use of them."

Rannasc's eyes seemed to glow with exhilaration. "The sooner we can communicate with this Ieska, the better. Our experiments are on the verge of success. We're close. With the help an experienced biologist can provide, especially one from a realm outside our own, who knows what we can accomplish!"

"She's a female," Benjo frowned.

Rannasc shook his head. "If what these boys say is true, if she was able to create a being that begat tri-casted children, then she is unlike our females. She is intelligent. She can help us with our experiments."

"What experiments?" Laetu asked.

"The Fossa, boy!" Rannasc exclaimed. "We're almost there. Almost to the heights, do you understand?" His eyes blazed. "We've been working for thirty years, tweaking the inner workings of the body of a particular Tehom. Working since the day of her birth, trying to re-caste her as fire-water instead of pure water. And we're close. We're close!"

But not there, Pax realized. The Tehom were working on the same dastardly experiments that had changed his biological father from a common criminal into a deadblooded sociopath. Ieska, he thought, would not approve. He wondered about the woman the Tehom had been using as the subject of their experiments. It would be a woman, he thought. They wouldn't think twice about destroying a woman. His heart swelled with concern for his sisters, prisoners of the Tehom with him, but in far more danger.

"That's why we have the hydrolocks," a dark-haired man said, coming up beside Rannasc. "With the water locked inside Sorbel, we can gradually admit more and more water, pump it in, so that the water will rise to the heights. There are places, you know, where the Orbokth rises nearly to the Ghalon. Places of intense heat. If we can get the water high enough, the appropriate environment for a Fossa might be created. Hot water. Boiling water, part fire part water . . ."

"That's enough, Ayruno. They don't need to know all our secrets," Benjo reprimanded the grim, scaly man.

Ayruno clenched his fists and Pax wondered what it would be like to function with such long talons at the tips of his fingers. He wondered whether Rannasc and Ayruno were evil or merely misguided. Ieska, after all, had participated in the experiments. She had come to regret it. Would these men also come to regret their machinations? He tried not to think of them as evil.

"You will go to your Ieska," Benjo was saying. "You will take messages from us to her. You will bring her words back to us."

The Tehom were going to let them leave. Pax's heart lightened with relief.

"To make sure you return, we will retain your females among us. Once we are satisfied that you have kept faith with us, we will consider letting them leave. Until then, they will remain here."

Pax's heart sank again. For a glorious moment he had seen an end to their captivity.

"We'll do it!" Laetu declared. "For the restoration of Gannoir!"

Pax stared at his brother, dumbfounded. Had Laetu not understood anything of what had been said? The Tehom were conducting experiments on a living person. They were in the wrong. They were kidnappers who were holding their sisters hostage to their desire for information. They were being used. Laetu, it seemed, had been swayed by the desire of the Tehom for the restoration of Gannoir. Would it lead, as it had with Gelu, to a bid for destruction?

He closed his eyes. It wasn't right. It wasn't good. He should have choice in whether to be the emissary of the Tehom. His sisters should be released. There was too much force being applied. The Tehom were doing wrong.

And he had no choice.

"All right," he reluctantly agreed.

He saw no other way out.

Chapter 37: Camilly

Camilly swam. The sea was yellow around her now. She ascended but found no sign of Dwoyra. She had called until her gills ached. Frowning, she kept ascending. The water turned green and then turquoise.

"Dwoyra! Dwoy . . . ra!" she called.

Slipping under the Orbokth, she looked around. Tiny dga covered with blotches of darkness clung to its rocky underside. They scuttled about, which struck Camilly as unusual. Most of the time, dga were slow.

"Dwoyra?" she whispered experimentally.

A coil of water wrapped itself around her.

"Dwoyra!"

The water around her hissed and bubbled. The dga scurried frantically. Dwoyra was harassing the beleaguered dga.

"Darkness . . . go . . . bad . . ." Dwoyra told her.

"Dwoyra," Camilly began, "it's Ceres. She's down with the skyboulder. It's cracking up. It's going to break. Ceres is holding it together, but she can't do it much longer. She's too cold. We need help!"

The water sucked itself into a ball. The relieved dga huddled together, motionless.

"Come on!" Camilly begged. "Come to the skyboulder. Help us! If the skyboulder cracks up, nothing will be plugging the hole in the Bec. You have to help!"

Finally, Dwoyra understood. The current of her movement carried Camilly quickly downward. She saw the color of the sea change at a dizzying pace. Then her blood began to slow as the cold took over.

Dance, she told herself. *Dance!*

She danced and was relieved to find that more lumalauae had come to join the party. As her body grew warmer, she squinted toward the dark blotch marring the twinkling purple lights of the Bec.

"Camilly!" Finnan shouted. "Did you find Dwoyra?"

"She's here!" Camilly called back to her mother. "How's Ceres?"

"Exhausted, but warmer," Finnan reported.

"Go," Dwoyra's voice rang in Camilly's gills. What did she mean? Did she want her to leave?

"Go," Dwoyra said again. "Find . . . help . . ."

"Mom," Camilly said. "Did you hear Dwoyra? She wants us to leave. We've got to find someone who can help us. Ieska or Xylo, maybe. Or even Talag—he's the Dynroc after all. Someone who can actually do something."

"No!" Ceres protested weakly. "If I let go, the skyboulder will break apart. Everything inside Gannoir will seep through to the outside. We'll all die."

"Dwoyra can hold it together," Camilly noted.

"Dwoyra's made of water," Finnan answered wryly. "And her strength is fleeting. She can only exert force for a short time before her molecules grow weary and separate. The skyboulder is a solid. Dwoyra's no match for it."

"She said to leave," Camilly argued. "I trust her."

"I can't," Ceres sobbed. "I have to help."

"Camilly's right," Finnan said quietly. "We have to trust Dwoyra."

"Let go, Ceres," Camilly urged. "We'll get you home. We'll figure something out. Or Dwoyra will."

"Dwoyra told us to get help," Finnan pointed out. "So let's do that." She pried at Ceres' stiff fingers and toes, trying to dislodge them from the skyboulder. It wasn't all stubbornness that kept them there. The water was colder than ice and Ceres had been in the same position for hours, probably days. Even had she wanted to move her body, she couldn't.

Camilly felt the water grow turbulent around her. It was worse than turbulent. It was a nightmare. The lumalauae danced crazily, upsetting the water even more.

"I can't hold on!" Ceres wailed. As her fingers and toes separated from the skyboulder, Camilly felt a strong downward tug. They were being sucked out!

Instantly the current increased. Dwoyra. Lumalauae. Fish. Vauzigk. It was as though all the life in the sea had been sucked down to the skyboulder and the eminent implosion of Gannoir.

"Swim!" Finnan ordered. Her arms were around Ceres.

Camilly swam.

They sat on the shore for a long time after they surfaced. Ceres was too weak to walk, and even Finnan and Camilly were exhausted. It was dark and the light rainfall of early evening had begun.

"Pure water feels good after the sea," Finnan commented.

Camilly nodded, her thoughts never leaving the chaos happening near the Bec. "Are we going to die?"

Finnan shook her head. "Not right now. I've been watching. The sea level is steady. See that stripe of gray along the far shore? The water's been lapping against it for the entire time we've been sitting here. Dwoyra's succeeding. She's keeping the seawater in."

Ceres gave a little sob.

Finnan stroked her short brown hair. "It will be all right," she soothed. "Let's see if we can get you home."

"Do you think the others will have returned by now?" Camilly asked.

"I'm sure of it," Finnan answered.

The journey from the shore to the caves of the Dynroc took twice as long as it usually did due to Ceres' weakened condition. The woman barely spoke during the trek, as though she needed every ounce of strength she possessed just to put one foot in front of the other.

Their hopes were justified, however. Xylo, Widman, and Byid were at the Dynroc's caves. They had just come back from finding food for dinner. Ceres had been immediately escorted to a cot to rest, but they brought her food and sweet methyglyn, and her frightening pallor and weakness seemed to ascend into something akin to a normal tiredness and hunger. She slept with her hands cradling her belly, as though she could protect her unborn child from everything that had happened to her.

Back in the sitting room, Camilly fretted. "Do you think Ceres' baby is okay?"

"Time will tell," Finnan answered shortly. Camilly could tell that her mother was worried too.

"The baby will live," Xylo said firmly.

Camilly smiled at him, not sure whether to believe him or not. After all, the baby was his grandchild. It might be wishful thinking that prompted Xylo's pronouncement.

"Did she mention Case and Talag?" Widman asked.

Xylo shook his head. "I haven't asked her yet. She's not strong enough right now. If anything has happened to them . . ."

"We'll ask her in the morning," Byid piped up. "She'll feel better then."

Nodding, Xylo passed the bowl of Rucloce to Camilly and Finnan. "I'm sure you're right."

Chapter 38: Xylo

Xylo pressed his lips together tightly. Camilly's report about Lefty and Estray had him worried. "We know the deadbloods are conducting experiments," he said. "Or they were before Gelu left."

"You think it's still going on?" Widman asked. "Wasn't the point of their experiments, their desire for the blood of the Siann Dha, to reverse the gogyvehr and turn Gannoir inside out?"

"Technically it's right side out," Byid chimed in. "I mean, even the scientists agree that Gannoir began as a world with an ice core and a fire exterior."

"The fact that they've kidnapped Case and Talag—two Esh—and tried to kidnap Camilly—a Mayim—is proof enough," Xylo said.

"Maybe it's not about the blood," Finnan suggested. "Maybe it's just a political thing. You know there has been unrest. Some people don't like the idea that the Dynroc is Siann Dha. They'd rather have a deadblood to rule the deadbloods."

Xylo shook his head. "In that case, they wouldn't have tried to take Ceres. Or Camilly. It's the blood. They're doing something."

"But what?" Camilly asked. "They wouldn't keep trying to reverse the gogyvehr, would they?"

"There are a million reasons they could want the blood of the Siann Dha. There's power in the blood. Even if their goal isn't to reverse the gogyvehr, they could be trying to use the power. Maybe they're experimenting to see if they can make their own blood be like ours," Xylo answered.

"That makes the most sense," Byid said with a grin. "The deadbloods want to become Siann Dha."

"Or they want to eliminate the Siann Dha. They could be trying to discover a way to make our blood ineffective," Widman suggested.

"That sounds more likely," Finnan admitted.

"That's horrible!" Byid exclaimed.

"It is horrible," Xylo agreed, "but it makes sense. It would align with what we know about the factions that are opposed to my leadership."

Their speculations were interrupted by a scuffling in the corridor. All four looked toward the doorway.

"Gaoth?" Xylo called. He opened the door.

Gaoth entered. Even though Xylo was accustomed to the presence of the invisible being, he still had a sense of wonder. Gaoth swirled around Xylo, guiding him into the hallway. Xylo followed him through the tunnels and out onto the Orbokth, wondering what was going on. It was rare for Gaoth to summon him in this manner. He tried not to hope that he would see Case and Talag coming over the Orbokth toward him.

In the distance he could see someone coming. He squinted his eyes to see who it was. One person, too short to be Case and too stocky to be Talag, was hurrying over the rocks. As the man came closer, Xylo could see that it was not someone he knew. The man approached him.

"Yes?" Xylo asked.

"I've brought word from Luca," the man panted. "You're Xylo Xalantaka, aren't you?"

Xylo nodded.

"Would you invite me in?" the man asked. "My journey was long and I'm tired."

Xylo noticed that the man had the extensive body-tala of the Esh. His blue tunic was of a costly fabric and was embroidered at the cuffs and hem. Esh-maor, he thought. Educated. Wealthy. Not the type to become a humble messenger.

"Who are you?" Xylo asked.

"My name is Engesyth Nerhial," the man said.

"Nerhial . . ." Xylo mused. "You are one of the sons of Cy Nerhial?" Xylo had gone to school with Cyfeg Nerhial. Cy had been a good man.

Engesyth nodded. "He was my father."

"I went through school with him," Xylo replied. "Follow me." His heart felt numb. The man was bringing word from Luca. Xylo did not assume the word was good. Good news travels slowly. Bad news is expedited with a messenger. Was Ieska all right? What about Dano and Yasamina? Were those on Cudth Deorth safe? The food he had eaten earlier rolled uneasily in his stomach.

Widman, Camilly, and Finnan rose when Xylo brought the man to the sitting room. Byid was already standing, rifling through some books on a shelf.

"This is Engesyth Nerhial," Xylo introduced him.

"Thank you for having me," he said politely. His face assumed a grave expression. "I bring news from Luca."

"Please sit," Finnan gestured toward the table where they had been eating.

Engesyth sat.

"What brings you to us? What is your news?" Xylo asked.

"I work at the university," Engesyth began.

Xylo felt fear rise like vomit inside him. If Engesyth worked at the university, his news must be about Ieska. He found himself mentally reaching out toward Tel-Maor, the invisible ruler of Gannoir. *Please,* he thought, *please let Ieska be all right.*

"Ieska sent me with word," he continued.

She's okay, then, Xylo thought, relieved.

"Her message didn't make sense to me," Engesyth said, running a hand through his faded black hair nervously. "But she said you would know what I was talking about." He looked from one face to another. "She also said it was important to send a messenger who didn't understand the message."

"What is it?" Finnan pressed.

"Here is the message." Engesyth pitched his voice in a high singsong and continued as though reciting a passage in a foreign language. "The fourth-born child of the un-man has given the enemy's child to him. Suspect the crippled one was involved. There is power in the blood. There is darkness in the air and the sea. I am coming to you, but so is the enemy. Beware."

Xylo made the man repeat the message. Then he had Byid escort him out through the tunnels. It would be best if the man didn't hear any discussion that might follow.

Xylo tossed the words around in his head. The part about the fourth-born child was easy. There were nine children of Methiant Migas. Ninach was the fourth. Xylo knew Ninach was a worry to Ieska. Ninach's heart was bitter and angry. If he had to guess which of the Triads would turn against her family, he would have placed his bets on Ninach. But who was his enemy? Gelu? Nadim? One of them was coming. And Ninach had given him a child. Was Ninach expecting Gelu's child? He shook his head. He hadn't been away from Cudth Deorth that long. He would have noticed if Ninach had been pregnant. What child? What did it mean?

The others were, apparently, thinking his thoughts with him.

"Mailu's baby," Finnan whispered. "Gelu's child. Ninach has spirited the child away to Gelu!"

"You believe the enemy she mentions is Gelu?" Xylo asked.

"Who else?" Widman said.

"It could mean something less . . . tangible," Xylo said. "A more spiritual meaning. The darkness is an enemy, for example."

"I think it means Mailu's child," Finnan said. "Mailu must have had the baby. And Ninach took it and went to Gelu. Now Gelu is on his way here. And so is Ieska."

"Why wouldn't she just come herself instead of sending a messenger?" Widman wondered.

"The elders don't know she is involved with me—with us," Xylo said. "She probably couldn't leave right away. In order to keep up appearances at the university, she sent a messenger instead."

"But she says she's on her way," Camilly argued.

"That could mean she's coming in a few days, not right now," Finnan said. "She must have thought this message was too urgent to wait."

"Gelu's coming," Xylo said heavily. "He's coming. And his people have Case and Talag."

"We have to rescue them!" Camilly cried.

"And the baby," Widman said.

"What was the part about the cripple?" Byid asked as he came back into the room.

"The cripple helped her," Xylo remembered. "There are two on Cudth Deorth who could fit that description. Gudall and Tass. They were both crippled when the skyboulder hit."

"Gudall wouldn't participate in a kidnapping," Finnan declared.

"I agree," Widman said. "He's a good man. He never participated in Ninach's schemes, no matter how trivial they were."

"She's always been trouble, then?" Xylo asked.

"She's always had a bitter streak," Finnan said. "When she was four, her mother abandoned her because of her tri-casteing."

"Others were also abandoned," Camilly pointed out.

"Like me," Byid said. "My dad left me and Pax when we were little. I don't think it was because of Pax's casteing. It was just . . . when my mom died, he kinda lost his mind. Pax is still upset with him. That's why he uses his Triad last name. Pax Nayru. I still use my dad's name—Pendefeth."

"It's not an excuse for bitterness," Finnan reassured Byid. "I'm just stating a fact. Ninach was always deeply angry."

"So angry she would betray her brothers and sisters?" Xylo asked.

"I didn't think so," Finnan said sadly. "But it seems that's what happened."

"And Tass joined her in it," Widman agreed.

"Tass also is bitter and angry," Xylo noted.

"The good news is that Tass must be getting better," Camilly said.

Xylo's face relaxed into a smile. Camilly was always looking on the bright side. "That's true," he said. "And I'm glad to hear that much. But if Gelu has the baby and is on his way here, we must act quickly."

"What about the messenger?" Finnan queried. "Are we to send him back to Luca? Or make him part of our plan to find Case, Talag, and the baby?"

"And possibly Ninach," Widman added. "Don't forget, if she spirited Mailu's baby away, then she wouldn't have gone back to Cudth Deorth. If Gelu has Ninach and the baby both, then he's got some very powerful blood for his experiments."

"And if it's Gelu, wouldn't he go back to his plan to reverse the gogyvehr?" Camilly asked.

"And . . . we're back where we started," Byid noted.

"Let's get to work," Xylo said. "We need a plan."

Chapter 39: Tass

Tass lay curled in a ball on her bed in the cave on Cudth Deorth. Ninach and the baby were gone. She had done her part. She knew she should feel satisfied. She had avenged her sister's death. She had gotten rid of her vile half-breed offspring. But instead of satisfaction, she felt only emptiness. Mailu was still gone. There was no one who loved her. And Ninach, the first person with whom she had felt any sort of connection on Cudth Deorth, was gone too. Of course, the others purported to love her—Bridima, Rhyder, Gudall, even Torcalon, who said he was her grandfather. She shook her head. They didn't care about her at all.

The voices murmured their agreement in her ears. Her father was a rapist. She was unwanted and unloved. Mailu was dead and it was the fault of the elders who had sent her to Garradh Gannoir. It was Gelu's fault for capturing and injuring her. It was Xylo's fault for not bringing Mailu back from her trip to the chaos safely. It was the fault of everyone in Cudth Deorth for not keeping Mailu alive, for prioritizing the baby and saving the ugly child instead of her mother. And now Mailu was gone. Everyone had done her wrong.

The voices' laughter echoed in Tass's gills. The laughter stung and increased her bitterness. She was utterly alone.

Chapter 40: Ieska

Ieska smiled at the young woman who brought her the day's news. It was business as usual at the university. Ieska had been conducting experiments on ribbon snails, trying to isolate the mechanism by which they were able to regenerate their tentacles. It was a benign experiment designed to eventually improve life for the citizens of Luca. All in a day's work.

In the back of her mind, however, she was planning her trek to Garradh Gannoir. She had sent Engesyth to the other side of the Orbokth with a message for Xylo and the others. Her heart had been nearly wrenched from her chest when she'd heard what Ninach had done. Kidnapping Mailu's baby was horrible. Giving the child to Gelu was treasonous. She had betrayed them all. This girl whom Ieska had known since she was a four-year-old child had taken sides, and the side she'd taken hadn't been Ieska's. It hurt. It hurt worse than Ieska could explain. She longed to go to Cudth Deorth to be with Bridima, with whom she'd co-parented the Triads for over a decade. She knew Bridima must be drowning in the same sorrow that had flooded her own heart. But if she left in the middle of the work cycle, someone might investigate her reasons for doing so. The political climate was unstable. A rudimentary check into Ieska's life would reveal her recent marriage to "Xylo Sapor." That itself would invite further investigation. It would not be impossible for someone to discover that she was currently the wife of Esh-Maor Nadim's prime enemy. She must not be noticed. Not until she was ready to leave the university for good. And she didn't want to do that. Not all the Esh-maor were on Nadim and Gelu's side. There were some who were loyal to Luca and the Siann Dha, who didn't want to reverse the gogyvehr or experiment on criminals of the lower castes. There were people she could recruit to her side.

Engesyth had legitimate business in Garradh Gannoir. The species of fuuegn he had been researching was suspected to exist in other varieties there. He had been planning a trip for some time, and his paperwork was in order. He was ready to go. She had given him her cryptic message with the hope that Xylo and the others would be able to decipher it. Ninach and Tass had betrayed them. The baby was gone.

What would Gelu do when he saw his disfigured daughter? Ieska knew Gelu had been hoping for a son. Even after the disappointment of discovering that his offspring was girl, he would have wanted a beautiful girl. Mailu had been beautiful. Gelu himself was not bad looking. The baby, with her mottled skin and deformed skull, would not be a delight to her father. They could blame her condition on the fact that her mother was dead during most of her pregnancy, or on Mailu's trip in the skyboulder, or even on Mailu's confinement to an airless coffin before the birth. Any of those could have been contributing factors.

But the truth remained. Gelu would have no love for such a child. He might destroy her. He might—and this was an even more harrowing thought—experiment on her. She had the blood of Mailu—the blood of a Gulot Siann Dha. And if her speculations were correct, the baby may also have Case's blood—the result of experimentation by the scientists of Garradh Gannoir before anyone even knew where Case, Ceres, and Mailu had gone.

She would go to Garradh Gannoir once the work cycle was over. She knew she couldn't take the normal tunnel. It was still heavily guarded. She would take the route over the top of the Orbokth. She hadn't spoken to Xylo since he'd gone, but word had come back to her ears that he had been seen in Garradh Gannoir. Going over the top, then, was possible. She was Esh. If her husband could cross the heights, then so could she. Maybe she'd take someone with her. Hauk, maybe, or Ofnus and Timmia. Among her co-workers she knew them to by disgruntled with the elders and possibly sympathetic to the cause she would present to them. She still had a full day to wait. A day and a night. Then she would go. It would be for good this time. She would not return to the university. She had to act now, and she had to take as many with her as she could—but only those she could trust with her life.

Chapter 41: Unaleah

Unaleah was discouraged. She had been in the women's quarters with Sadi for hours. The Tehom women were not intelligent. Sadi's outrage at the Tehom men's treatment of females was unjustified. The women were mentally deficient. She wondered if they were born that way or if the lack of education and respect had rendered them helpless and foolish. She rather thought it must be the former.

Sadi was still angry. She seemed to be on a campaign to educate the women, to make them understand the world around them. Unaleah looked at her sister across the chamber. Sadi was not having much luck. The women were laughing at her. They were trying to help Sadi fix her hair so her flat face would appear more protruding, more like the Tehom ideal of beauty.

Unaleah longed for home. She longed to see her mother and her siblings. She longed to feel something other than wetness against her skin. She could breathe and live under the water, but she was tired of it. She wanted to go home. As the hours passed, she held out hope that the Tehom would release them, that they would decide she and Sadi were both worthless and helpless and could pose no danger to the Tehom.

When the door to the chamber slid open, she was surprised to see Gelihr, the Tehom man who had found her and Sadi in the hydrolock. He led Pax and Laetu into the room. Unaleah's heart filled with hope. She hurried toward her little brothers.

"They want us to go back to Luca," Laetu reported. "They want to talk to Ieska."

Unaleah took a deep breath. Deep breaths through her gills were not as relaxing as deep breaths with her air lungs, but she was relieved, nonetheless. She was going home. Why did the boys look so worried?

Pax's next words gave her the answer. "They want us to go alone. They're going to keep you and Sadi here as hostages to make sure we come back with word from Ieska."

"We can't bring Ieska here because she's Esh and can't breathe underwater," Laetu explained unnecessarily. "We're going to take messages back and forth."

"Why do they want Ieska?" Sadi asked. She had swum up behind Unaleah silently.

"Because she made Methiant Migas out of Mantais Nayro," Pax explained. "They've been working on a similar project, and they want her advice."

"Even though she's a woman?" Sadi asked wryly.

"I think they're getting the idea that our women are capable and intelligent," Pax said.

"These women would be intelligent and capable if they'd let them," Sadi spat.

"Maybe not," Unaleah said hesitantly. "They're not very smart, Sadi."

"That's because no one ever gave them the chance," Sadi retorted. "If we can just rally them against their men, make them understand that they have the ability to be mentally strong too, then we . . ."

"Sadi!" Pax interrupted. "Didn't you hear what I said? They've been experimenting on someone. A woman. They're trying to make her into a Fossa—the fire-water caste. They're going to destroy her just like the scientists destroyed our dad."

Sadi's eyes narrowed to slits. "They're misogynists."

"What does that mean?" Laetu asked.

"They treat women badly. They hate them," Sadi explained.

"It's not about women," Pax said. "It's about Maor. Spirit. They're destroying someone's spirit."

"We shouldn't be helping them," Unaleah pointed out. "How is becoming a messenger to tell them Ieska's scientific procedures going to do any good?"

"It'll get us out of here," Laetu pointed out.

"It'll get you and Pax out of here," Sadi grumbled.

"That's not the reason," Pax said. "Ieska can make them understand. She can make them see that experimenting on a person is wrong. She can help them. Ieska did the wrong thing at first, but then she realized what she was doing was wrong. She stopped. Ieska's not evil. Maybe the Tehom scientists aren't evil either. They just don't understand. We can help them."

"This isn't going to help us get out of here," Sadi said.

"But it might help Gannoir," Pax said. "And it might help this woman they've been experimenting on."

"And it might help us too," Unaleah added. "Once they see that it's wrong to experiment on living people, they might see that it's also wrong for them to keep us prisoner."

Sadi snorted and then choked. She'd used her nose and air-lungs for her snort. She spat the water out of her lungs and then said, "Doubtful."

"Well, we don't really have a choice," Laetu pointed out. "We have to do what they say. Otherwise, we'll be prisoners too. This way at least we can tell someone where we are."

"He's right," Unaleah said.

"Go, then," Sadi said.

"That's what we came to tell you," Pax said. "Gelihr is taking us out. We're going to Luca to find Ieska."

"Are you sure she's in Luca?" Sadi asked.

"Where else would she be? She works at the university," Laetu said.

"Cudth Deorth?" Unaleah asked.

"Technically, Cudth Deorth is in Luca," Laetu pointed out. "We'll check the university first. Then Cudth Deorth. We'll find her," Pax promised.

Gelihr beckoned to them from the doorway. With parting hugs for their sisters, Pax and Laetu followed their guide out the door.

Unaleah watched them go. It was something, she tried to encourage herself. It wasn't enough, but it was something.

Chapter 42: Pax

Pax pushed his head out of the water and took an experimental breath. Air filled his lungs. It felt weird after so many weeks in the water. Laetu surfaced beside him.

"Is that Nozoffi?" he asked, looking at the enormous clatry in the distance.

"It must be. Remember Ieska told us she worked on an orange clatry with four big buildings?"

"And the buildings are all Lachar, the university?"

"They must be. There's not much on Nozoffi except Lachar," Pax said.

The gentle rocking of the sea caused the orange clatry to bob up and down. The four skyscrapers heaved along with it. The suspension bridges that connected the towers swayed.

"Where do you think we'll find Ieska?" Laetu wondered.

Pax shook his head. "Could be anywhere. We can ask. We just can't let anyone see us getting out of the water."

"That's going to be hard," Laetu noticed. "There are people walking about. How are we going to get out of the water without them noticing?"

Pax frowned. "I'm not sure. But you know we can't let them see people with Esh-tala getting out of the sea. They'd be on us in an instant, ready to experiment on us."

"Maybe they'd take us to Ieska?" Laetu suggested cheerfully.

"Being taken prisoner is not an ideal plan," Pax sighed.

"But . . ."

"No," Pax said firmly. "We can figure this out by ourselves. We'll wait until it's dark to get out of the water. Hopefully the people will be inside by then."

"Do they all live here?" Laetu wondered. "I can't remember what Ieska said."

"Many of them do," Pax told him. "Ieska lives here. I bet more than half of the floors on the buildings are apartments, not part of the university."

"So when night comes, they'll be going home?"

Pax sighed. "That's a good point. And they won't go right when it gets dark. They'll have to wait for the sea to fill up with water so they can use their boats to leave. We'll have to try to go ashore just before dawn."

"After the boats have left, but before the next round of people come in the morning," Laetu extrapolated.

"Yeah. And then we can look for Ieska."

Chapter 43: Camilly

"It was here?" Finnan asked her daughter.

Camilly nodded. "See that window up there?" She pulled her arm out of the sea and pointed at an opening high on the Orbokth. "That's the window I went out of."

"And you didn't see or hear anything that made you think their other prisoners were nearby?"

"Mom, I don't know. I heard them say there were others. I don't know why they brought me to that part of the Orbokth. I didn't see Case or Talag. I didn't hear them. But it's the Orbokth. Any of the corridors could have gone a long way into the hillside. There could have been more rooms. Lots of rooms." Camilly climbed out of the water. "We should explore."

Standing beside her daughter, Finnan wrung the seawater out of her red hair.

Camilly's gaze idly followed the dripping water down to the rocks beneath their feet. The liquid didn't look right somehow. Maybe a trick of the light, she thought. She shifted her weight and looked again from a slightly different angle. "Mom," she whispered.

Finnan looked where Camilly was pointing.

"Do you see it?" Camilly asked. "The black blobs . . . they were caught in your hair!"

Finnan flinched and shook her head violently.

"Stop! Let me help you!"

Camilly gently picked three dga out of her mother's hair. The black spots clung to their tiny hosts.

"Did you get them?" Finnan asked.

Camilly frowned and inspected Finnan's head. "I got the dga out. The black blobs must have been scraped off them when you wrung out your hair. There may be more stuck in there, though."

Together, Finnan and Camilly unbraided her hair. Camilly carefully flicked the smudges of darkness into the sea. Finally, she pronounced her mother's hair clean. "I think I got them all."

Finnan sighed. "Thank you." She checked her daughter's hair, but Camilly did not seem to have any of the bleak, miniscule visitors. "It's getting worse," she commented.

"I know," Camilly said. "We have to do something."

"We're trying," Finnan reminded her daughter. "Dwoyra is holding things together below so that no more darkness can get in. And we're all working together to stop Gelu and whatever experiments he has planned."

"Then let's do this. Let's go in there. Let's find Case and Talag."

"It's dangerous," Finnan commented with a worried gaze at her daughter. "And with Pax and Laetu still missing . . ."

Camilly could see the pain in her mother's eyes. "We have to do this. Even if we never find Laetu and the others. Our lives are less important that the fate of Gannoir."

"I know. I know," Finnan said. "May Tel-Maor protect us."

Camilly and Finnan climbed the uneven rocks of the Orbokth until they were standing before the smooth whitewashed walls of the dwelling. Camilly stealthily peered into the window. She saw no one, heard nothing. Carefully, she climbed through the opening into the room. Finnan followed her.

"It's a nice enough place," Finnan whispered. "Clean . . . large . . ."

"And evil," Camilly grinned wickedly, crossing her eyes at her mother.

They tiptoed across the room and entered a corridor. The smooth walls and floor were a contrast to the nature of the Orbokth. Camilly, who was used to Cudth Deorth where the dwellings were half Orbokth and half reed hut, was impressed. She ran a hand over the wall. "How'd they get it so smooth?" she asked.

"Shh!" Finnan reminded her. "Maybe the rock is different here than it is in Luca."

The tunnel went on and on, branching into other hallways and other empty rooms. It grew darker and darker.

"Do you remember anything about this place?" Finnan whispered. "How you got in, or where they were working?"

Camilly shook her head. "It's all hazy. There are so many tunnels. I don't know how anyone could find their way around in here."

They climbed a short stairway that curved sharply to the left.

"I think I see a light ahead," Camilly noted optimistically.

"Careful," Finnan cautioned. "That may mean someone is here."

Camilly pressed her back against the cool, dry wall. They moved slowly toward the light. The silence encouraged them, soothing their fears. Another sharp turn in the passageway brought them to a room full of light. Columns of seawater rose like pillars extending to the ceiling throughout the room. They glowed with brilliant blue ymolenegth.

"Son of a vauzigk!" Camilly exclaimed. "How much blood does it take to make those light up?"

Finnan turned to chastise her daughter for swearing, but she was too late. They were not alone.

Chapter 44: Xylo

"I don't understand," Xylo said. Widman, Engesyth, and Byid stood behind him, a formidable army of Siann Dha.

"She's been moved. Relocated," the young man told him. "She's no longer at this facility."

"This is the only hospital in Obumbro," Xylo noted sharply.

"You can draw your own conclusions," the man said with a shake of his dark hair. "All I am authorized to tell you is that she is not here." He said the last four words slowly and with patronizing emphasis.

"What about her husband and son," Widman said. "Do you know where they've gone?"

The dark-haired man looked at Widman and then at Xylo. "Her husband and son were not patients here. Only Rahela Barat was being served. Her husband and son are free to go where they please."

"Did they go with her to the other facility?" Xylo asked. "You must tell me. I'm the acting Dynroc of Garradh Gannoir and I'm here on official business."

"I know who you are." The young man's dark eyes were hard and cold. "And let me just say that things are about to change around here. Change for the better."

"What is your name," Xylo asked.

"Nehglon Maraena Suergas," the man said crisply. "My older sister was one of the people you killed when you brought the skyboulder back." He glared at Xylo.

Xylo recognized the name. "You're Gelu's brother-in-law," he said. "Your sister was his wife. I'm sorry for your loss."

"Your compassion would be more meaningful if you had managed to preserve my sister's life."

Xylo looked curiously at the young man. He was much younger than Gelu and his wife, Ceci. He looked healthy and strong. He wondered why Gelu had not chosen this young man, a relative, to be one of the inhabitants of the skyboulder. Gelu knew that if his plans succeeded, only those aboard the rocky spaceship would have had a chance to live. He had elected his brother-in-law to death. It was only because of Gelu's failure that this young man was alive. And it was only because of Gelu that the young man's sister was dead. Yet Nehglon Maraena Suergas was still on Gelu's side—Gelu, who had left him for dead. Xylo marveled at the propaganda powerful enough to banish reason and logic and leave this man thinking it was Xylo who was evil and Gelu who was good.

"Again, I'm sorry for your loss," Xylo said. Then he turned to Widman, Engesyth, and Byid. "Let's go. We'll have to look for Rahela elsewhere."

Outside, the four conferred.

"Where would they have taken her?" Byid asked.

"Where indeed," Xylo said grimly. "The only other place in Obumbro or the surrounding areas where the sick are treated is at the caves of the Dynroc. And we all know she's not there."

"What if she's not at a hospital," Widman suggested. "What if she's been taken to a research facility? She's Siann Dha, after all. They could be holding her, hoping to use her blood for their experiments."

Xylo nodded. "I should have thought of that myself. And if they presented it as 'moving her to another facility,' Laso and Peodar would have blindly walked into the trap. Instead of having one Siann Dha at their mercy, they would have three."

"Do you know where the research facilities are," Engesyth asked.

"They do have a university, small though it is," Xylo reflected. "But my guess is that their real research is done in another place. A secret place."

"How are we going to find it?" Byid asked.

"Many of the people who would have known died in the crash of the skyboulder," Xylo noted. "But there's one person . . . for the right price, she may tell us what we need to know."

Xylo led the others down the main road in Obumbro. With the short vegetation on the left, the hills in the distance beyond the fields of green, and the whitewashed buildings of the city on the right, they made their way through the city. Crowds milled about, shopping, talking, working, and eating. Xylo pushed through a hanging curtain of sea reed and entered a lavish shop on the first floor of one of the whitewashed buildings. A flat brown sign carved with letters proclaimed it to be a wood shop.

Engesyth gasped as they entered. Byid's eyes shone. Widman wordlessly fingered the carved objects that lined the shelves.

"It's really wood . . . from trees!" Engesyth marveled.

"Even though they're extinct in Luca, trees are abundant in Garradh Gannoir," Xylo explained. "I was surprised when I first saw wooden objects for sale too, not just by their existence, but by their beauty." He touched an expertly carved statue of a yovod, one of the big cats of the heights. The woodgrain had been oiled and polished until it was smooth and shining.

"It's beautiful," Widman breathed. "Of course, I had heard they had trees here, but I never imagined wood was anything like this."

"May I help you?" a large woman asked. Her arms were laden with intricate wooden bracelets, and she had a chain of wooden links around her neck.

"We're looking for . . . " Engesyth began, but Xylo motioned for him to be quiet.

"We'd like to purchase a gift," Xylo told her. "It's Minnidair, isn't it?" he asked.

The large woman nodded. Her ears were also adorned with wooden baubles. "Who is the gift for?" she asked.

"A woman who has been through much hardship," Xylo said smoothly. "We want something lavish. Something beautiful. Something . . . expensive."

Minnidair's eyes gleamed greedily. "Of course I can help you," she purred. "Are you thinking about personal adornments?" She gestured toward her bracelets. "Home décor? Maybe a jewelry box?"

"Could we see the jewelry boxes," Xylo asked. "Only the best. The best you have."

The woman beckoned to them. "Come into the back," she said. "Have a drink while I'm assembling the best of the best."

Xylo and the others followed her into a room lined with wooden cabinets, all beautifully carved with images of the flora and fauna of Gannoir. They sat on wooden chairs at a wooden table. The woman poured glasses of methyglyn for them to drink and then left the room.

"Does she know who you are?" Engesyth asked.

"She must," Xylo said. "She was on the skyboulder. She lost her husband in the crash. She knows who I am. She's pretending she doesn't, which makes me think she is about to turn us over to those who are not in favor of a Siann Dha Dynroc. Be ready to fight if we need to. But," he said, leaning close to his comrades, "the other thing I know about Minnidair is that she's greedy. She loves money and luxury. The prospect of a lucrative sale may be enough to make her ignore her loyalties to Gelu. We're going to have to be careful and aware. Be ready to flee if it comes to that."

Widman nodded. "I'm ready. I don't understand how she could still be loyal to Gelu after losing her husband and nearly losing her own life due to Gelu's plan to destroy the world."

"It's the darkness," Xylo said. "It's seeped into our world and has blinded people's eyes to truth."

Footsteps from outside the room told them that Minnidair was on her way back. Xylo braced himself. Either she would enter laden with precious wooden wares, or she would come in with an army of deadbloods, ready to take them captive. He leaned forward.

The door opened. Minnidair came in pushing a metal cart. On it were four jewelry boxes, all lavishly carved. She beamed at them.

Xylo relaxed. It was to be money, not politics, that ruled the day.

Minnidair lifted the first box and set it on the table before them. "This box is carved of an ancient hardwood," she explained. "It has two drawers on the bottom half and a lid that lifts on the top." She pointed out the features of the box, its beautiful carvings, and was halfway through the life story of its maker when Xylo interrupted.

"I'd like to see that one," he said, pointing to a spherical box carved with images of scolopendrae, vervol, and other plants and animals of the heights. He emphasized his extensive body tala as he spoke, as if to indicate that the round box was particularly suitable for an Esh.

Minnidair lifted it carefully. "This is over a hundred years old," she told him. Her eyes were blazing, and Xylo assumed that his guess had been correct—this was the most expensive of the boxes she'd chosen to present to them. She demonstrated fourteen secret doors in the box, suitable for storing precious items. When she pushed the head of one of the vervol, the flying worms, music played.

"It's beautiful!" Byid gasped.

"The music or the carving?" Widman asked him fondly.

"Both," the boy blinked.

"What is the price?" Xylo asked.

Minnidair's smile grew wider. She named her price. "Who is such a precious gift for?" she asked. "I hope the recipient has a proper place to keep it where it will be safe from the damp."

"Oh, she does, she does," Xylo reassured her. "It's a gift for a friend of mine. She's from Luca. Rahela Barat. Do you know her?"

Minnidair smiled. "Of course I do. The woman who was injured in the return of the skyboulder."

"You and many others owe your life to her," Xylo pointed out. His fingertips tingled. It was now or never. Either his plan would work or it wouldn't. "The problem is," he continued, "that she's been moved. She was at the hospital in Obumbro. They've relocated her. I need to know where she is so I can take her this beautiful gift." He stared at Minnidair, mentally pleading with her to tell him what he needed to know.

Minnidair's eyes narrowed. "You'll only purchase the box if I tell you where she is?"

Xylo nodded silently.

Minnidair played with the links on her wooden necklace. Xylo could see the indecision in her face. Her eyes flickered to the spherical jewelry box, then to Xylo's face.

"You can't tell them how you found out," she said, biting her lip nervously.

Xylo smiled. "You have my word."

Chapter 45: Tass

"Tass! Tass!" someone was calling.

Tass groaned. She had been trying to sleep. Since she had helped Ninach kidnap her deformed little niece, the voices in her gills, in her ears, in her mind, had gotten louder and more belligerent. She couldn't rest. All night long, all day long, the voices told her she was unloved and unlovable. One moment they would tell her that she had done wrong to betray her sister by turning her child over to the enemy, and then next moment they would be telling her that the true evil came from Bridima and those who lived in isolation in Cudth Deorth—that they would never love her and that she'd done right to help spirit the baby away from these evil ones. Back and forth, back and forth the voices went, arguing with each other in her mind and making her feel unsteady, exhausted, confused, and angry. The anger was the most pervasive thing in her mind. It seemed to encompass her entire body. Her fingers glowed with it. Her mottled skin, still full of the darkness that had almost taken her life, tingled with her rage. Even her hair seemed to stand up more stiffly on her head.

"Can you come out here, dear?" the voice asked.

Bridima. It was Bridima forcing her to wakefulness and demanding her presence.

Tass rolled over and sat up, putting her feet on the rocky floor of the room that was now hers alone.

"Tass! Ninach has come back! Come out here!" Bridima called.

Ninach? Ninach had come back? Tass thought Ninach was going to stay away. After all, she had just kidnapped Mailu's child. Ninach had to know that the others would be angry with her. She wouldn't just come back, would she?

Tass painstakingly pushed herself to her feet. She could walk, but the weakness in her body still crippled her with agonizing pain and stiffness. She straightened her tunic and wiped her face with a cloth. Then she went out into the clear morning air.

They were already assembled—Bridima, Gudall, Rhyder, Dynny. And Ninach. Ninach was a mess. Her mousy hair was stringier than usual. Her face was tearstained and pathetic. Tass approached slowly, of necessity because of her infirmity, but she would have been slow anyhow. She didn't understand what was going on. What kind of game was Ninach playing?

She's going to betray you, the voices smirked in Tass's head. *She's going to blame you for the kidnapping. You watch.*

None of them love you, another voice told her. *Watch out for yourself and don't worry about the others. They'll only take care of themselves. They'll never take care of you.*

Tass drew near.

"Ninach has returned," Bridima said. Her eyes were full of tears, something that Tass had seen too often since the baby had disappeared. It was annoying.

"I just . . . I just . . . Ninach blubbered. "It was Gelu . . . he came in the night. He had a knife. I had no choice. He made me carry the baby. He made me go with him." She wiped at her streaming eyes with her fist.

"It's okay," Bridima soothed. "It wasn't your fault. Tell us everything you can. Help us find the baby. She's one of us, after all. She's Triad. I'm sure of it."

"Baby . . ." Dynny mumbled. "Gelu might hurt the baby." His wrinkled face was sad and worried.

"She's lying," Tass said. It was important to tell the truth, the voices told her. And tell it quickly, before Ninach could reveal Tass's role in the kidnapping. If Ninach would lie about her own part in the crime, mightn't she not lie and say that it was Tass had been part of Gelu's kidnapping plot? After all, Tass's recent injury, though legitimate, had provided the opportunity for the baby to be spirited away.

Ninach's against you! the voices exclaimed. *Protect yourself. She calls herself sister but she's going to backstab you.*

Your only sister was Mailu . . . Mailu . . . Mailu . . . The voice echoed in her head and with each repetition of Mailu's name, Tass grew angrier.

"Ninach tricked me!" she shouted. "She told me she was going to give the baby medicine." It sounded lame even as she said it. She hoped fervently that the others would believe her. "She told me Dynny wouldn't let her give the baby what she needed to get better. I had to help. The baby is my sister's child. I had to help! Ninach and I planned my injury on the shore that day. But I didn't know she was going to kidnap the baby. I swear I didn't."

They all looked at Tass in surprise.

"Ninach planned the kidnapping all along," Tass said. "I knew it from the moment the baby was missing. She tricked me! She's evil! She's a traitor to Cudth Deorth!"

The shock on Ninach's homely face was balm to Tass's bitter soul. "I didn't!" she shouted. "It was Gelu! He forced me! I don't know why Tass is lying, but she is!"

Tass shook her head. "You really think they're going to believe that?"

The voices guffawed at the spectacle. Tass's head rang with their jeers.

"You're evil, Ninach." Tass glared at her half-sister.

Rhyder came up behind Ninach. He grabbed her upper arms and restrained her, preventing her from fleeing.

"How could you do this?" Gudall asked.

Ninach looked like she'd been slapped. Tass remembered that Ninach was in love with her half-brother.

"I only want what's good for Cudth Deorth," she whispered. "And the baby wasn't. Gelu was coming for her. The baby is his daughter. He was going to find her. He was coming for her, for all of us! If anyone betrayed Cudth Deorth, it was the baby and everyone who wanted to hide her here. By keeping her here, you"—she looked around—"have betrayed us all. Not I."

"You gave the baby to Gelu?" Bridima asked quietly.

Ninach nodded. She was crying real tears now, not the fake ones of her earlier performance. "I did. I was just trying to protect us all."

"And you came to us with lies," Bridima clarified.

"I did what I thought I had to do," Ninach said. "It was for your own good. For all of us."

"Lies are never good," Bridima said severely. "Your father will be disappointed when he learns what you've done."

Ninach's face blazed. "My 'father' was a rapist and a deadblood. Not only that, he's dead."

"I wasn't talking about Mantais Nayro," Bridima interrupted. She was careful to use the dead man's original name, Tass noticed, instead of the name he'd been given after his moral destruction. "I was talking about Widman. He raised you. He loves you. He's your father in every way that matters."

"We should lock her up," Tass suggested.

Everyone looked at her. Tass wondered if she'd gone too far.

"Jail?" Dynny looked at her quizzically.

"Something like that," Tass said. The voices in her head chortled with glee. "After all, what will she do next? Will she turn me over to Gelu or someone ever worse? She doesn't like me. I'm a stranger here. And what about Dynny? You all know Gelu wants Dynny." Actually, Tass didn't know any such thing. It was a suggestion the voices made in her ear as she spoke. But as she thought about it, it made sense. Dynny was the Dynroc, or he had been. He knew things, simple as he was. He had knowledge and power that had been denied to Gelu. The voices told her Dynny's story in bits and pieces, just enough for her to continue her argument. Tass could see the others being swayed to her side.

"I think she's right," Bridima said.

Rhyder tightened his hold on Ninach.

"We'll tether her," Bridima said. "And keep her under guard." She turned to Tass. "And thank you," she said, "for confessing and telling us the truth. We all appreciate it." She nodded at Tass, dismissing her. Rhyder and Gudall took Ninach away and Tass hobbled back to her bed. As she went away, she could hear Dynny mumbling unintelligibly, and she wondered if maybe there was one person she had failed to convince.

Chapter 46: Ieska

Ieska set out for the heights as soon as the crescent glow of the Ghalon slipped away for the night. It hadn't even begun to rain, but she was waiting at the shore for the boat that would take her from the clatry to the Orbokth on the pretense of doing scientific research on the midnight release of spores from a rare species of fuuegn. Her companions would meet her there on the heights.

She sighed as the raindrops began to batter her eyelids. Her skin glowed with the rainbow iridis of the Esh, in contrast to her long gray hair. It was in these moments of quiet, moments of waiting, that she felt her age. She was an old woman. She knew that—once in a while. She was attempting a perilous journey that no one had ever survived, except her husband. Would the laws of probability relent enough to allow two elderly people to miraculously survive the heat and dangers of the heights? She thought of the fiery Ghalon, of the giant, vicious yovod, and of the mythical dangers of the giant scolopendrae and the vervol. Ieska pressed her lips together and stood up straighter. She would overcome. She would make it. She would survive against the odds.

A nagging thought reminded her that she was much more likely to die on the journey from slipping while trying to cross the mountains than from a fierce battle with a horrific monster. She was old . . . old . . .

"Ieska!" a voice called.

Ieska turned quickly. "Hauk! I thought we were meeting on the other side!"

"We were. That was before Ofnus and Timmia backed out. Timmia got scared. She wouldn't come, and Ofnus wouldn't come without her."

"And they're the ones with the boat," Ieska remembered, thinking back to her conversation with her young scientist friends, the only ones she could convince to leave with her.

"Ofnus said he'd still take me across, but I told him I'd go with you. It's better for both of them if they don't know any of the details of the journey, you know, since they're not going."

Ieska nodded. "So it's just the two of us?"

"Less meat for the yovod this way," Hauk retorted with a grin. "You're old and I'm skinny. We'd be a poor meal."

Ieska had to smile at this.

"I'm excited, actually," Hauk continued. "I've only seen a yovod from a distance. I couldn't even make out which part of his coat was spotted, and which part was striped. It was just a blur."

"What about the giant scolopendrae and the vervol?" Ieska asked, her eyes twinkling. "Aren't you just as eager to encounter them?"

"Of course," Hauk said. "If they exist, we can befriend them. Maybe they'll allow us to ride on their backs. They can fly us over the Orbokth to Garradh Gannoir."

Ieska laughed aloud at the thought of the fearsome beasts of mythology serving as a taxi service for ambitious Esh travelers. "It's a thought," she admitted. "I'd never thought about that possibility."

"Glad I could be of service," Hauk said with a flourish.

The rain was falling in earnest now, drenching the pair and rendering the acid sea navigable. They boarded the first of the ferries for the Orbokth. When asked, Ieska explained to the pilot that she and Hauk were scientists at the university, on a quest for rare fuuegn. The man seemed uninterested. He took their money and moved on to the next passenger. When the boat was loaded, they crossed the sea. Most of the passengers headed for the bright blue lights of the small settlement at the edge of the sea. There were restaurants there as well as shops. It was primitive—everything on the Orbokth was—but even the Esh-maor like to visit for a taste of the old days.

Ieska and Hauk headed directly into the hills. Ieska had brought no luggage, though she knew she might not be able to return to Luca for her things—ever. Hauk also traveled lightly, with only a slender crossbody bag slung between his shoulders. Ieska had the same. It was uncomfortable. The downside of having Esh-tala was that you couldn't wear a bag slung under your arm. She and Hauk both had the straps of their bags anchored between their legs. An opening in her tunic let her slide the compartmented section of the bag from her back to her front. She had never liked the feeling, and usually she carried a handbag instead. On this journey however, she knew she would need both hands to steady herself for the climb. Not only that, she would need the full use of her arms to glide down into Garradh Gannoir once they reached the top.

"Do you think Ofnus and Timmia are regretting their decision by now?" Ieska asked. "Things are going to get bad in Luca with Nadim and Gelu working together."

Hauk grimaced. "They're probably not sorry yet, but they will be. I agree that something's going to happen. I'm not sure when or what it will be, but it's not going to be good. They'll wish they had come with us."

They hiked quickly, stooping to pick fuuegn along the way. That way if anyone happened to encounter them in the heights, their story about research would ring true. Hauk tasted the different varieties as they walked.

"Is it good?" Ieska asked, wrinkling her nose. The rain had soaked the fungus, and the sweet stench was more than she could bear.

"It's not bad," Hauk said.

The Orbokth was slippery with the wet vegetation. Ieska slowed to make sure she didn't slip. She knew if she fell, she could extend her arms and coast on her tala, but she didn't want any setbacks. She wanted to get up an over in a night, a single night. She concentrated on placing her feet in places where she would have a sturdy foothold.

"What's that?" Hauk asked suddenly.

Ieska looked up. In the distance, far above them, she could see a golden glow. "I'm not sure," she said. "Reflection of the convenalations on the wet rocks?"

Hauk shook his head. "The convenalations glow red, not gold. This is something else."

The distant glowing spot seemed to seethe with life. It could be a fire, Ieska reflected, although on account of the heavy rain it seemed unlikely.

"Could there be a settlement up here?" Hauk wondered.

"Never heard of one," Ieska replied. She had stopped watching the pulsating glow in favor of focusing on her footing.

"Doesn't mean there's not one here," Hauk answered. "I don't think it's an animal. It's too big. Looks more like a small village."

"They'd have to be Esh," Ieska noted. The water that was hitting her skin sizzled pleasantly on her luminescent Esh-skin. She knew that no Gulot or Mayim would have been able to bear the boiling rain.

"For sure," Hauk agreed. "I like it up here though. The hot rain feels good. I feel like a real Esh now."

Ieska laughed despite her worry. "Weren't you feeling like a real Esh before? You've spent your life being trained as an Esh-maor. You've been to school. You're a professor and a scientist. You need a little burning water to make you feel alive?"

"You know what I mean. Down on the clatry, there's no difference. We could be Gulot for all it matters. Up here, it's an exclusively Esh world."

Ieska looked up toward the sky. The burning rain seared her skin and drizzled over her outer eyelids. Each raindrop held a perfect image of the box fish convenalation reproduced in miniature. At the edge of the individual droplets, she could see a golden glow. She turned her face toward the flickering light. "Is it getting closer?" she asked.

"We're walking toward it, if that's what you mean," Hauk joked.

"I'm being serious," Ieska said. She swept the water off her tala in case she needed to glide. "I don't think it's just that we're walking toward it. It's walking toward us. This is no village."

Hauk squinted through the rain. "I think you're right," he said slowly.

With its image blurred by the rain, the golden blob rose from the ground into the sky. It grew larger and larger.

"I think we're in trouble," Ieska noted.

"Vervol or scolopendra," Hauk said. "Do the old stories mention a golden aura?"

"Doesn't matter which it is," Ieska said quickly. "We've got to get away from it." She pressed her body close to the rock, feeling around for a crevice she could enter. She found one more quickly than mere luck would have admitted and pressed herself through the narrow opening. Hauk followed her. They climbed down a gravelly path into the depths of the Orbokth.

"I think we're safe in here for the moment," Ieska said, panting.

"Or not," Hauk said. "Look!"

Chapter 47 Unaleah

Unaleah and Sadi hovered in a corner of the women's quarters. Sadi was disgruntled and grouchy. When she got this way at home, Unaleah would leave her alone to seek other, friendlier company. Here, though, she preferred her sister's company to that of the Tehom women.

"They're stupid, stupid, stupid," Sadi muttered.

Unaleah had to agree. The women had been muttering inanities for as long as she and Sadi had been with them. They talked about food (eating it, not preparing it), and other pleasures, but never about anything important. She had listened to their prattle for a while—Sadi had thought they might hear something that would help them figure out how to escape—but eventually she had been driven to block their prattle out of her mind.

"Can you hear them?" Sadi asked angrily.

Unaleah shook her head. "I wasn't listening."

"They're vicious gossips as well as being stupid," Sadi complained. "They're talking about some poor woman who's too masculine for them. They're making fun of her."

"Which one are they talking about?" Unaleah wanted to know. She felt protective toward whoever the outcast was.

"I don't think she's in here," Sadi said. "They said something about her being a tool of the men. Maybe she's a sort of underwater prostitute."

Unaleah made a face. Her mother had taught her, rightly, she thought, that there were some things that were unmentionable. And now Sadi had mentioned one of them. "I'm sure that's not true," she said soothingly.

"Why are you sure that's not true?" Sadi demanded, flicking her floating black hair angrily. "What else would they mean by the woman being a tool?"

Unaleah winced. Sadi's explanation was surely the most likely one, but she wasn't ready to give in yet. "It could be anything. Maybe she's extra small and can work in small spaces, so they're using her for some construction project. Or maybe her hair is extra long and . . ."

"Don't be daft," Sadi groaned. "There is nothing good happening here. Nothing."

Unaleah let Sadi mumble on. She tried to listen to some of the women's talk, to see if what Sadi said could be true. The words of the women pranced about her gills in the water.

"Never talks about anything important," a plump young Tehom woman was saying. "Just talks about the temperature of the water and the writings of the ancients and such foolishness."

"Did you know she cut her hair?" another young woman asked. "Just shaved it all off about this long all over her head." She held up two of her clawed fingers to indicate a two-finger width of hair growth. "She can't even braid it."

"I don't know what she can be thinking." the plump woman sneered.

"She'll never marry and bear children. No male will want her when she's so ugly and strange."

"I heard she doesn't even want to marry. What's wrong with her?"

"She wasn't a proper woman from the start," an older woman said. Her blue hair was intricately braided and coiled about her head. "That's why the men took her when she was a child. It's not her fault. They've been using her, experimenting on her. Doing their little science projects. They've ruined her. She might have been a proper woman if they'd just left her alone."

"I won't believe that," a girl with bright yellow hair declared. "She would not have been right no matter what they did or didn't do. She's just odd. She's just not right."

Unaleah watched Sadi's face to see what her younger sister thought of this dialogue. A woman who thought about things like the temperature of water and the writings of the ancients sounded like someone intelligent.

Sadi's face clearly betrayed her interest. "No wonder they don't like her," she exhaled. "She's smart. These nitwits have no understanding at all. I wonder where they're keeping her locked up."

"Not here," Unaleah pointed out. "They don't seem to know where she is."

"They must be hiding her somewhere. I wonder if we could find her."

"We can't even get out of this chamber," Unaleah pointed out. "How are we going to find her? We don't even know what she looks like."

"We know she has short hair," Sadi noted triumphantly. "That would make her stand out from the rest of the Tehom."

Unaleah frowned. "But it doesn't matter. We still can't get out of here to go looking for her."

"They have to let us out sometime," Sadi said in exasperation. "Once Pax and Laetu come back with word from Ieska, Bridima, and Xylo, they'll have to let us go. We'll find her. We'll rescue her. She sounds like someone worth knowing. She doesn't deserve to be the 'tool' of the Tehom men."

"You're probably right about that," Unaleah said slowly. "I'll help. I don't know what I can do, but I'll do what I can."

Chapter 48: Pax

Pax climbed out of the sea onto the edge of the smooth orange clatry. There was no vegetation on the latticed stone, something that felt odd. The clatries naturally teemed with life, floating reefs marking the barrier between wet and dry. He wished he had more time to explore the underside of Nozoffi, to find out whether any creatures inhabited the dense maze of stone.

There was no time for that now.

"Where do you think Ieska's apartment is?" Laetu asked, looking up at the skyscrapers that balanced on the floating island.

"Someone will know," Pax said.

"But everyone's asleep or they've gone across the water. There's no one to ask."

"In the morning, they will come. And by then we'll be dry and won't have to explain how people with Esh-tala can swim."

"So what are we going to do now?" Laetu asked. "I'm hungry."

"We can't fix that now. It's the middle of the night. We'd best try to sleep," Pax said. He started to walk down the boulevard between the buildings. It was clean and dry. The streets were composed of dried sea plants, woven together. A thin coating of algae knit the fibers together. "We can sleep on the street. It's soft enough."

Laetu grumbled but agreed. He had no choice. They found a small corridor at the base of the first building and tucked themselves in for a night's sleep.

At firstlight they woke. Pax ached all over, and from Laetu's moaning, Pax figured he felt the same way. The little niche they'd slept in was still dark, but the hum of the machines in the city as they began the day's work alerted them to the morning.

"I'm hungry," Laetu said.

"Me too," Pax admitted. "Once we find Ieska, she'll give us some food."

Their efforts to find Ieska ended in defeat, however.

"Where'd she go?" Pax wondered after queries at the university had failed. No one had seen her since the day before. A co-worker had given them directions to Ieska's apartment, but their knocks at her door went unanswered.

"Home?" Laetu guessed. "Home to Cudth Deorth?"

Pax sighed. They could have saved a lot of time if they'd gone directly to Cudth Deorth instead of going to Nozoffi to look for Ieska.

"We're swimming again, right?" Laetu sighed.

"We should wait for night. We can't let anyone see us get in the water. Our Esh-tala . . ." Pax began.

But Laetu only snorted at his protestations. With a running head start, he leapt from the clatry into the sea. Pax heard a shout behind him. It was too late to pose as an Esh. He had to get away. Sprinting as fast as his legs could carry him, he followed Laetu into the sea.

Chapter 49 Camilly

"What are you doing here?" the red-haired man shouted. His tall frame blocked the doorway.

Lefty. Camilly swallowed her fear. Left and Estraya had kidnapped her. She'd walked right back into their hands, and she'd brought her mother with her.

"What have you done with Case and Talag?" Finnan demanded.

A smile caused Lefty's mouth to curve upward but there was no friendliness in it. "You're looking for your friends, eh?"

"Are they here?" Camilly asked. She glanced around the room looking for a weapon.

Lefty's smile grew broader. "I'll take you to them," he offered.

I'll bet you will, Camilly thought. *If Lefty and Estraya were holding Case and Talag prisoner, they'd be only too glad to have us as well.* She glanced at her mother, but Finnan hadn't taken her eyes off the pale, beady-eyed man barring the path to freedom.

"Talag is the Dynroc," Finnan complained. "Holding him against his will is illegal. He's the rightful ruler of Garradh Gannoir."

"He's Siann Dha," Lefty pointed out. "Garradh Gannoir has never been ruled by one of the Old Ones. It should not be so now."

"Keeping them captive doesn't change the fact that he is the Dynroc. There's nothing you can do about it. The Dynroc, 59th of that name bequeathed the title and the power to him months ago. You can't just declare someone else to be the Dynroc. It doesn't work like that."

"We don't need a Dynroc at all," Lefty said. "That's been the problem with Garradh Gannoir all along. We've let ourselves be ruled by magicians. We've trusted in all the foolishness of the ancients. There is no such thing as magic. There is no god in the Ghalon. There is here and there is now. That's all."

Finnan took a step toward Lefty. "If it's all foolishness, if there's nothing special about being Siann Dha or about being the Dynroc, then let us go. Let Case and Talag go."

"I never said there wasn't anything special about being Siann Dha," Left said lightly. "You yourselves know that your blood has a different chemical composition than the blood of the citizens of Garradh Gannoir. Your blood makes light. Your blood has power. It's our intent to find out what gives your blood that ability and to harness that ability for the good of Garradh Gannoir."

"You want our blood," Camilly spat.

"Of course," Lefty admitted.

"You'd kill us in the name of progress? Progress for Garradh Gannoir?" Finnan asked.

If she was hoping to appeal to Lefty's integrity and honor, she failed. Lefty had his own system of morality.

"Your blood is important," Lefty said. "We don't want you dead. Dead blood has no power. We want you alive. All of you. Withholding your blood is selfish. Would you have us flounder in the dark, subject to diseases and ills that could be prevented by the application of the blood of the Siann Dha? That's incredibly prejudiced. You could be doing something for the good of Gannoir. Instead, you want to rule us, keeping your powers to yourselves."

This gave Camilly pause. Was Lefty right? Was there good that could be done that they were ignoring? Did the Siann Dha consider the deadbloods less important than themselves? She had never been part of Luca at large. She had been isolated on Cudth Deorth. She had been taught right from wrong. Was it possible that the others in Luca had not learned to do good to others? She closed her eyes. It could not be. The elders she knew—Bridima, Widman, Ieska, and her parents, had been raised in Luca. They were the ones who had taught her right from wrong. They must have learned it somewhere.

A wave of horror lapped at the edges of her mind. Ieska had experimented on Mantais Nayro. She had been part of the quest to change him, to make him a Triad. She had participated in the evils that had turned him into Methiant Migas and destroyed his soul. Maybe, she thought, Ieska had learned to do good because she had done incredible evil and found it to be vile. Maybe in Luca they were teaching the superiority of the Siann Dha over the deadbloods. Maybe they were teaching that the deadbloods were expendable just like the deadbloods were teaching that the Siann Dha were to be used for their blood. Was it possible?

"It's never right to take blood from people by force," Finnan was saying. "It's not right to hold Case and Talag against their will. If you want Gannoir to be a more peaceful world where everyone is sharing and working toward the common good, you won't accomplish it by kidnapping, imprisonment, and bloodletting."

Camilly wanted to hug her mother. Of course, Finnan was correct and Lefty was wrong—horribly wrong.

Lefty rubbed his forehead with his hand. "I . . . I never thought of it that way," he said. He sounded contrite. "I want what's best for

Gannoir, of course. And I believe it's right for the Siann Dha to share their blood, to make things better for the people of Garradh Gannoir. But I never thought about it being wrong to force good to happen. Good is good. But now, you've made me stop and think. You've opened my eyes."

Camilly and Finnan looked at each other. Lefty sounded humble and apologetic. He sounded like he really understood what Finnan had said. Was it possible? Had they changed his mind?

"You'll let them go, then?" Finnan asked.

Camilly stared at her mother. Was she buying this? She shook her head. Finnan was up to something. It was her job to play along.

"Of course. Of course," Left said, nodding vigorously. "They're weak from the bloodletting, so you'll need to accompany them, help them home. But I'll let you take the on one condition."

"What is it?" Camilly wondered.

"You must come back regularly to discuss an alliance between Luca and Garradh Gannoir," Lefty said smoothly. "We can talk about how the power of the blood of the Siann Dha can be used to benefit all."

Camilly bit her lip. It sounded good. It sounded right. It sounded rational.

"Take us to them," Finnan requested.

Lefty stepped back into the corridor and gestured for them to follow. "Come this way."

Camilly and Finnan walked into the passageway. Lefty still made Camilly uneasy. His body was tense, like a yovod ready to spring on its prey. She wondered if her own fears made her hold her body with the same strict uprightness, wondered if Lefty bore the same suspicion toward her that she bore toward him.

They walked down the hallway and Lefty followed, pointing out different rooms and explaining their purpose. The dwelling was a sort of hospital and research laboratory, he told them. They sought much knowledge here. It was an education beyond that offered at the university in Obumbro, he said.

Camilly grew interested despite herself. What might the deadbloods have discovered? Would it shed light on what the Siann Dha knew about Gannoir? Collaboration would be a good thing, she reflected. Ieska would like it. Ieska always wanted to know more, wanted to understand the world around her. Her heart lightened as she walked.

Lefty gestured toward a room on their right, and Camilly and Finnan walked in.

It was a mistake.

Lefty pushed a button in the corridor and bars slid down, trapping them in the room.

"I appreciate your contribution to science," he said genially. And with a little bow, he left them there.

Chapter 50: Xylo

"We should wait," Widman said. "We need more people on our side. If we try now, we'll only fail."

"I agree," Engesyth said.

Xylo shook his head. "No matter how many of the Siann Dha we can convince to accompany us, it won't be enough. You know they want to arrest me. At best, we will only have a handful of allies. The only thing we have on our side is surprise. They don't know we're coming."

"Minnidair will tell them," Byid pointed out.

"That's why we have to act quickly," Xylo said. "We know where they've taken Rahela. Laso and their son will be there as well if I know anything about them. They've probably got Case and Talag at the same place."

"Rahela's ill," Widman noted. "It's likely she won't be able to get away on her own. She'll need at least two of us to carry her."

"With Laso and Peodar, plus the three of us, we can do it," Xylo said.

"We can't wage a direct attack," Engesyth said. "We need to sneak in and sneak out. Do you think it can be done?"

"We have to try!" Byid said. "We can't just let the deadbloods keep them."

Widman nodded reluctantly. "I'm in. I still think it's foolhardy, but I understand your arguments. And you're the acting Dynroc. Your authority stands."

The four Siann Dha climbed into the heights above Obumbro. Xylo's plan was to get as close to the research facility as possible before nightfall so that once the rain began to fall and darkness hid them, they could sneak in. By late afternoon, they could see the entrance Minnidair had revealed to them. Xylo tucked the intricate wooden jewelry box into a niche in the rock of the Orbokth to protect it. It was a beautiful thing. He would come back for it if he could. He would give it to Rahela. She deserved it after risking and almost losing her life for Gannoir. Once things were better, once peace had been established, he would make sure that all the Triads and their families were safe—permanently safe—and able to admit their tri-casteing publicly.

As the light of the Ghalon grew to a slim crescent of red over their heads, Xylo, Widman, Engesyth, and Byid lay low, peering over a boulder toward the opening to the research facility a long distance below them.

"You and Engesyth must restrain the guards," Xylo said. "Byid and I will go in and find Rahela, Laso, and Peodar. We'll get them out. Once we pass through the doorway again, keep holding the guards until we are out of sight. Then let them go and run. Do we have a plan?"

"What if there are more than two guards?" Engesyth asked. "I'm confident that we're stronger than any deadblood guards, but we may not be stronger than four or six men combined."

"We'll incapacitate them one at a time," Widman said grimly. He showed Engesyth the place on the neck where he could apply pressure to make a person pass out. Xylo was surprised. He had not known Widman long, but he would not have guessed that Widman had any knowledge of such things. Engesyth, who was a scientist, might have been expected to know anatomy well, but he seemed to be avidly interested in Widman's techniques.

The four crept closer to the opening in the Orbokth. The last sliver of light slid from the sky as the bright side of the Ghalon hid itself for the night. A faint blue glow emanated from the doorway as the guards inside lit the ymolenegth lamps for the night.

"Now?" Byid whispered.

Xylo was about to nod when he heard something in the distance. He turned toward the noise. A large boat was approaching. It was well lit and noisy, as though a crowd were on board. He held up a hand to stay his companions.

They watched as the boat rolled up to a flat area of shoreline. A man jumped out and tied a rope to a metal post against the wall of the Orbokth. By the dim glow of the sea, Xylo could see that at least fifteen people were aboard the boat. His heart sank. Whatever this expedition was, it was ruining their plans. They would have to wait. And the longer they waited, the greater the chance that Minnidair would have time to alert the other deadbloods to their coming. His heart clenched with fear and anger. The deadbloods were keeping Rahela captive. They probably had Case and Talag as well. He had lost three of his children already. Was he going to lose a fourth? Case, the son of his old age, his comfort after the death of little Dochym.

He took a deep breath and let it out slowly. Maybe the boat was full of tourists ready to go into Obumbro to shop and feast. Maybe it was deadbloods coming back from a holiday in Luca. There were possibilities. He had to relax. He had to be patient. Once the passengers disembarked and scattered, they could resume their plan. He blinked his outer eyelids to wash away the blurriness caused by the incessant rain.

The people getting off the boat waited on shore. They acted like a group, not like strangers back from holiday. Their expectant eyes watched the boat. Whoever disembarked next was important. Xylo felt it in the air.

A woman clutching a bundle to her chest got off next. She huddled over her parcel protectively. Her cowed, submissive demeanor gave Xylo the impression that she was acting on orders. Xylo heard a wail. The woman shifted the bundle in her arms, patting it. It was a baby.

A man got out of the boat after the woman. He was tall and wore a voluminous cloak. Xylo knew him.

Gelu.

Gelu had arrived. And if it was Gelu, then the child, the baby, was Mailu's.

They were too late.

Chapter 51: Tass

Tass lay in her cot with her face to the wall. The voices in her mind jeered at her. One minute they told her that Ninach was to blame for the heartbreaking loss of Mailu's baby, her niece. A second later they were telling her that the baby was evil and that she had been right to help Ninach with the kidnapping. Tass let the voices roll over her like waves on the edge of the clatry, flowing through the holes in the latticework without having any effect. Her mind was exhausted. She didn't have the strength to sort out the rational from the irrational, her own thoughts from those imposed on her by the voices.

A commotion outside alerted her that something unusual was happening. Tass rolled over and crawled off the cot.

"Let me help you," Dynny offered.

Tass allowed Dynny to assist her.

"We should go outside," Dynny said. "Something's happening. Can you hear it?" He smiled winsomely at Tass, and she struggled against the instinct to want to like and protect the little old man.

Dynny guided Tass out of the hut and helped her climb down to the tiny meadow that bordered the water. The others were already there—Bridima, Gudall, and Rhyder—Ninach was still locked up. Gudall and Rhyder were pointing and gesturing toward the passageway that led to the outside world. Bridima had her hand over her mouth and tears in her eyes. What was going on?

Dynny eased Tass down to sit on a boulder. She rubbed her fingers, trying to extinguish the light that had slowly come back. She did not want to be tri-casted. She was Mayim—the best among the Mayim. Nothing more. She sat on her hands and looked in the direction the others were looking.

Three forms slipped into the lush world of Cudth Deorth. The first she knew. It was her supposed grandfather, Torcalon. The other two were boys around her own age. She thought she knew who they were. The missing Triad boys, Pax and Laetu. Who else would be allowed to come to Cudth Deorth?

The boys ran across the meadow. Torcalon followed at a more subdued pace. Bridima ran toward the boys, embracing them almost before they met. Her tears were flowing freely now. Gudall and Rhyder joined the celebration.

"You're back! You're safe! By the grace of Tel-Maor, you're alive!" Bridima cried over and over again.

"Where were you?" Gudall asked. "How come you didn't come home sooner?"

"I'm sure they would have come if they could, right boys?" Rhyder asked, his arm around his son.

Laetu looked up at his father, his face a mix of excitement and relief. "We were prisoners!" he said with shining eyes.

"The deadbloods?" Bridima whispered, holding Pax at arm's length and looking into his eyes.

Pax shook his head. "We've got a lot to tell you. Is Ieska here?" he asked.

Bridima shook her head. "We've got a lot to tell you, too."

Over dinner, the boys told their story, how they had found themselves in the undersea realm of the Tehom, one of the seven castes of Gannoir. How Sadi and Unaleah remained trapped there.

"Seven!" Gudall exclaimed. "I thought there were only three."

"So did we," Pax said as he shoved a chunk of halas bread in his mouth. "Until we met the Tehom." He shook his head. "They're really different. They can only live in water. Not like the Mayim. Mayim is not really a water caste. It's water-land. Mayim can breathe both air and water. Tehom can only live in the sea."

"And they're really ugly," Laetu confided. He raised his hands to his face and cupped them around his nose. "Their faces stick out like this. And their noses are weird. Ears too."

"They have finger tala like the Mayim, but at the ends of their fingers they have claws, not fingernails," Pax added.

"And scales. Their legs are covered in scales like a fish," Laetu said.

"Do their fingers glow?" Tass asked, her face hardening. She hid her hands.

Laetu shook his head. "Not that I noticed. The weirdest part is that their women are really dumb. I mean really dumb. The men have to do everything."

Ninach sat sullenly, eating and not making eye contact with anyone. Bridima had already explained why she was chained up, how she had stolen Mailu's baby and given her to Gelu. She had not bothered with the joyful greeting the others had given the boys. "Where's Kari?" she asked suddenly.

Pax shook his head. "She wasn't with us."

"She swam down with us before the skyboulder crashed," Gudall reminded Ninach. "The boys disappeared long before that."

"So where is she?" Ninach pressed.

The light left Bridima's eyes.

"We'll find her," Rhyder said. "We thought the boys were lost, but here they are. We'll find Kari as well. She'll turn up."

"You said that they Tehom are still holding Sadi and Unaleah prisoner? What do they want for a ransom?" Gudall asked.

Bridima winced. "You're sure they're safe?"

"The Tehom never harmed us," Pax assured her. "They're holding Sadi and Unaleah because they want to talk to Ieska. They want to know about her experiments. How she made Methiant Migas who eventually made us. They've been working to create a Fossa for many years now and they think her knowledge will help them."

"What's a Fossa?" Tass asked, interested despite herself.

"Another of the seven castes," Laetu told her. "Fire-water. Someone who can breathe the hotness on the top of the Orbokth near the Ghalon and who can breathe underwater . . ."

". . . but who can't breathe normal air," Pax finished. "Sadi said the women mentioned that they've been experimenting on a woman, trying to increase her toleration of heat."

"Esh, Mayim, Gulot," Bridima mused. "It's all we've ever known. Three castes, not seven."

"Add Tehom to the list," Pax said. "That makes four."

"And Fossa makes five," Laetu added.

"What are the other two?" Gudall asked.

Dynny looked up suddenly. "Arros said seven." He looked around expectantly.

"Arros said seven castes?" Gudall repeated.

Dynny nodded. "He said seven. Seven makes Gannoir."

"Seven castes?" Gudall pressed.

Dynny looked confused. "I can't remember seven what. Seven something. It's in the hidden literature. He showed me one time. Hidden room."

"Does Xylo know about the hidden room?" Bridima asked.

Dynny shook his head. "I never showed him."

"Do you know what the other castes are?" Gudall looked at Dynny hopefully.

Tass blinked. Her brain whirred with activity. It was painful and satisfying at the same time. "If Tehom is pure water, Gulot is pure land, Mayim is water-land, Esh is fire-air and Fossa is fire-water, then one of the others must be pure fire."

"Pure fire . . ." Rhyder contemplated. "People who dwell on the highest heights of the Orbokth."

"They'd be able to communicate with the Fossa," Bridima realized.

"And the Esh," Torcalon noted.

"That's only six castes," Gudall said.

"The other one was pure spirit," Laetu said with a shrug. "I don't know what that means. It didn't make sense to me."

"This is a lot to digest," Rhyder said. "It changes everything. It will change the entire social and political structure of Luca."

"Are the deadbloods a caste?" Pax wanted to know.

"They're not Siann Dha," Bridima told him. "So, no, they're not casted. That's what being a deadblood means."

Bridima and Torcalon explained the problems in Luca, how Gelu and Nadim wanted to arrest Xylo for the deaths caused when the skyboulder crashed, how Xylo had fled over the top of the Orbokth, and how Ieska had followed in his footsteps.

"But the Tehom want to talk to Ieska," Pax wailed. "They sent us to set up communications between Ieska and themselves."

Bridima shook her head. "You'll have to go to Garradh Gannoir to find her. She's left Luca, maybe permanently." She looked worried.

"I need to go to Garradh Gannoir," said Dynny suddenly. "I need to show Xylo the hidden room, the hidden books. It's important."

"You could just tell me where they are," Laetu offered. "I can show Xylo."

Dynny wrinkled his face in concentration. Several times he began to speak, to try to explain, but each time he shook his head. "I have to show. The telling part in my mind isn't working so good."

"I'm worried about Ieska," Bridima said. "Going over the heights alone . . . or even with a few other scientists. She's elderly, even though she won't admit it. I'd like to go to Garradh Gannoir as well."

"You come with me." Dynny nodded at Bridima. "We'll go see Xylo and Ieska."

"I'd like to go," Gudall said. "I'm strong enough now. I can help search for Kari."

"Me too," Rhyder said. "I'm not letting these boys go out on their own again. I want to be there when Finnan sees that our son is alive."

"We'll all go!" Dynny chortled happily.

Ninach glared at him in stony silence.

"Tass isn't well enough to travel," Bridima pointed out.

Tass disagreed, but she didn't argue. She didn't want to go to Garradh Gannoir. She didn't want to be anywhere.

"I'll stay here with Tass and Ninach," Torcalon volunteered. "I can keep an eye on things. Tend to Tass. Make sure Ninach stays out of trouble."

Bridima made a face. "Do you think it's wise with the political climate being so volatile?"

"They don't know about Cudth Deorth," Torcalon said. "And even if they find it, all they'll find is a reclusive old man, a crippled girl, and a . . ." He looked at Ninach.

"Traitor?" Gudall spat.

Ninach drew in a sharp breath. "I did what I did for the good of Cudth Deorth."

"Angst-ridden young lady," Torcalon finished. "It's not unusual in youth of her age. They won't suspect anything."

"And we'll leave her tied up," Gudall said with grim satisfaction.

"It stands to reason," Bridima agreed.

"We'll leave in the morning," Rhyder said.

"By land or by sea?" Laetu asked.

"The rest of you can go by sea," Bridima said. "I'm the only one who can't swim. I'm Esh."

"We'll all go by land," Rhyder declared. "They're not looking for us. We'll pose as just another vacationing family."

Tass grimaced. Just another happy family on vacation. Sure. Bunch of freaks. Children of a rapist. Children of an uncasted, ruined man. She was glad she was going to be staying on Cudth Deorth. She wanted no part of what was to come.

Chapter 52: Ieska

Ieska grabbed Hauk's arm. "This way," she cried, pulling him into a niche in the cave. She looked beyond him toward the main chamber, toward the beast whose lair they had inadvertently discovered. A trickle of interest penetrated her terror. What was it?

The creature was enormous. She couldn't see all of it through the opening in the wall in which they'd secreted themselves. What she could see was terrifying. Hundreds of short, hairy legs lined an armored, elongated body. It glowed with a golden light that enabled her to see the details clearly, if not the whole. Membranous wings flapped as it moved toward them. Its face was a concatenation of prickly, moving jaws and beady eyes, arranged with an unthinkable randomness.

"What is it?" Hauk whispered.

Ieska's fright grew less as her motherly instinct took over. She wanted to protect the young man who had trusted her enough to leave everything and come with her on her mission. "Scolopendra, I think. There are stories about them in the ancient literature. No one was sure if they were mythical or merely extinct."

"I'd say neither," Hauk noted.

Ieska nodded. "That's for sure."

"Is it dangerous?" Hauk wanted to know.

"No one knows. And I don't want to find out the hard way."

"Do you think the light we saw outside the cave was another of these creatures?"

"It makes sense," Ieska said. "It may have even been trying to chase us into its den." She pressed her body as far back into the crevice as she could, trying to get away from the snapping jaws that now plied the narrow opening.

"What are we going to do?" Hauk asked.

"Stay alive," Ieska said firmly. "Wait for it to get tired. It can't get to us in here. The opening in the rock is too small. Eventually it will realize that and go away. Then we make a run for it."

The snapping jaws quieted for a second. Hauk experimentally reached toward the glowing beast.

"Don't!" Ieska said.

Hauk stroked the mandible. The creature jerked and pulled its face out of the opening.

"I think you scared it," Ieska said, hope rising in her heart.

"I wasn't trying to," Hauk whispered.

"Maybe it will go away."

But a few seconds later, the scissor-like jaws returned, snapping even more aggressively than before.

Chapter 53: Xylo

Xylo clutched a cup of hot tea. It warmed his hands, and he felt guilty for enjoying the sensation. He wondered how far back in his life he would have to go to change things, to not arrive at this moment. If he had only gone looking for Case and Talag sooner. If he'd only enlisted the help of the elders of Luca sooner. If he had told Afa about Methiant Migas's confession. If he had helped Afa, Tass, and Mailu before things went badly with them. If he'd chosen a different location to hide with little Dochym. If he'd never married his first wife, Aythylla, at all. If he'd understood from the beginning that Kleibald was dangerous . . . And now everyone he loved was in danger.

"We need a plan," Byid said. "We have to get our people back. They can't just hold them prisoner."

Widman nodded. "We need to rally our allies. Find out what our assets are. We can't stand against Gelu and the deadbloods without help."

"We have to think carefully," Engesyth said, running a hand through his faded black hair. "Who is on our side?"

"Me," Byid piped up.

"All of us from Cudth Deorth are on the same side," Widman said quietly. "Though there are fewer of us than there once were."

"Once we find Kari, Pax, and Laetu, we'll be the same number we always were," Byid said cheerfully.

"We can't count on Ninach," Widman reminded him. "Remember the message. Ninach took the baby to Gelu. She's sided with our enemy."

"But there's Tass," Byid said. "We might have lost Ninach, but now we have Tass."

"Tass can't fight," Xylo reminded him. "She's sick."

"She's getting better," Byid said.

Ceres smiled wanly. "You have us, Father."

Xylo smiled back at her. "I know," he said. "But you can't fight. You've done enough. And in your condition . . ."

"Is the baby okay?" Byid asked.

Ceres put a hand over her still slim belly. "I think so. I can feel his tiny flutters as he moves around."

"My grandchild," Xylo said, his eyes growing misty. What kind of a world would this little one inherit? Would they be able to stop the darkness from spreading beyond the dga? Would the skyboulder break apart and cause the implosion of Gannoir? Would Gelu and the others seek to eradicate his family in revenge for the deaths that happened when the skyboulder crashed? Would Nadim, his own son-in-law, force him into exile once again? And if he did, would Xylo be around to see the birth of this, his third grandchild? Xylo's heart burned with pain.

A gush of wind blew through the room. Xylo could feel its frantic, excited energy. Gaoth. He didn't speak. He didn't have to.

All four rose and turned toward the door even before they heard the footsteps in the hallway. A moment later the visitors entered.

Xylo's eyes filled with glad tears. They had been praying for help, and help had arrived. Not much of it, but it was something.

"Pax! Laetu!" Byid exclaimed, running toward them. "You're back! You're safe!"

"Kari?" Widman asked hopefully, looking around for his daughter. "Is Kari with you?"

Bridima shook her head. "We haven't found Kari. The boys came home, though. There's hope."

Gudall, Rhyder, and Dynny came into the room last.

"Did the others stay back on Cudth Deorth?" Xylo asked.

"We left Torcalon there to take care of Tass and keep an eye on Ninach," Bridima told him. "Tass is doing better, but she is still very weak. And Ninach . . ."

"She stole Mailu's baby," Gudall said. "She gave him to Gelu."

"I know," Xylo said. "Engesyth here brought a message from Ieska. It was cryptic, but we figured out what she meant. We saw them. Gelu and the baby. They're here."

"Where are Unaleah and Sadi?" Widman asked. "Did they stay behind too?"

Pax explained about the Tehom, how they were holding Unaleah and Sadi until they were able to talk to Ieska about her experiments.

"They're trying to make a Fossa," Laetu told them. "A water-fire casted person. They want Ieska to help them."

"Ieska will never participate in mutilation again," Xylo retorted fiercely. "She would rather die."

"It may come to that," Widman said wryly.

Xylo winced.

"Ieska is on her way," Bridima said. "She was going to bring whomever she could convince to come along with her over the top of the Orbokth."

Xylo paled.

Widman noticed. "You made it. So will she," he said.

Laetu looked around the room. "Where are Mom and Camilly?" he asked.

Xylo groaned. "They should have been back by now."

Widman explained the search. "I think we can assume things went wrong. Our rescue mission has expanded. Now it's not just Rahela, Peodar, Laso, Case, and Talag."

"And the baby," Byid added.

"We've got to assume they have Finnan and Camilly as well," Widman continued.

"Why? What do they want with them?" Bridima fretted.

"The baby is the key to all of this," Gudall said quietly. "The baby is the link between Garradh Gannoir and Luca. She's the link between the deadbloods and the Siann Dha. Gelu was holding Case and Mailu prisoner. He's said to be the father of Mailu's baby."

"And we have reason to believe he was experimenting with the blood of the Siann Dha," Xylo said.

"Do they have people of all the castes now?" Bridima wondered. "Rahela, Laso, and Peodar are Gulot. Case and Talag are Esh. Finnan and Camilly are Mayim." She looked around the room grimly.

"Seven," Dynny piped up, adding to the conversation for the first time since they had arrived. "Seven. Not three. Arros said it too."

Everyone looked at him.

"He's right," Rhyder said. "Seven castes, not three. They don't have them all. They don't even know the other castes exist." The heaviness in the room grew suddenly lighter.

"What other castes?" Xylo asked sharply. "What are you talking about?"

"The Tehom, for one," Pax reminded him. "They're pure water. They can't breathe air at all."

"And the Tehom are trying to make a Fossa," Laetu said. "That's a water-fire caste."

"Come," Dynny said, standing suddenly. He shuffled into the corridor. "Come."

The others followed him.

Dynny led them through the labyrinthine tunnels in the caves of the Dynroc. Even Xylo hadn't explored so far from the main sections of the caves that they had been using. Dynny slid behind a slab of rock leaning to the side of one particularly narrow tunnel. A narrow zigzag of passageways led them to a little library.

Dynny smiled proudly. "Secret room. Ancient documents."

"Why didn't you show this to me before?" Xylo asked, amazed. He fingered one of the dusty books that lined the shelves.

"Forgot," Dynny told him. "Arros said seven. Seven castes."

"And it's in these books?" Xylo asked.

Dynny shrugged. "I can't read them. I don't know."

Xylo took a deep breath. His desire to preserve Gannoir grew even stronger. He wanted to know, to understand the mysteries of his world. He wanted to find out the truth about Tel-Maor, the creator, and about the inhabitants of Gannoir, both past and present. The discovery of the Tehom was mind blowing. If they could find the others, the other three missing castes, who knew what was possible?

Picking up a book, Xylo opened and read silently. The paper was fragile and old. It would be a lifetime's labor to copy these old books, to preserve their contents. He was old. He hadn't a lifetime left. But his grandson had. Talag was the Dynroc, the keeper of the precious books now. And there were others.

Xylo carefully slid the book back into its slot on the shelf. "Let's go back upstairs," he said. "We have to eat. We have to get ready for our mission."

"To save the others from Lefty and Estraya?" Widman asked.

Xylo nodded. "And from Gelu."

Chapter 54: Ieska

"What'd ya find?" a voice hollered.

Ieska opened her eyes groggily. Her body ached. She wondered how she'd even come to be asleep. Hauk, beside her, snored uncomfortably. Ieska stretched her legs and wiggled her toes, trying not to wake her companion. The snapping jaws were gone. They had been replaced by a probing tail, a much more effective tool for penetrating the narrow chasm in which she hid.

"What's in there, eh?" the voice said.

Ieska heard footsteps approaching. Someone, it seemed, had no fear of the scolopendra.

"Hello?" she called weakly.

Hauk opened his eyes. "What? What's going on?"

"I heard a voice," Ieska told him. "Hello?" she shouted toward the opening.

"Who's in there?" the voice asked again.

The scaly tale withdrew from the opening and a person appeared, backlit by the golden glow of the scolopendra. All Ieska could see were two glowing eyes and the fact that the shape didn't look like the shape of anybody she'd ever seen.

"Hello!" Ieska cried. "Help us, please!"

The golden eyes turned toward her, blinding her. "You're not one of us!" the voice exclaimed.

"Who are you?" Hauk asked.

"I'm Boskoe," the voice said. "Who are you?"

Ieska pushed herself to her feet. "My name is Ieska Thayl. I'm a scientist from Luca. My associate and I were in the heights doing research on a rare species of fuuegn," she told him, falling back on her old cover story. "A scolopendra outside forced us to take refuge in here. He's been keeping us trapped in this crevice."

"Aw!" the boyish voice said. "Flippy won't hurt you! He wouldn't hurt a vervol! He just wants to play."

"Flippy?" Ieska repeated incredulously.

"Because he likes to do somersaults," Boskoe told her. "He twirls in the air when he flies. He's the cutest thing."

There was an agreeable rumble from Flippy.

"He's friendly?" Hauk asked.

"Come see," Boskoe beckoned.

Ieska and Hauk cautiously followed Boskoe out of the crevice. It took Ieska's eyes some time to adjust to the bright light in the larger area of the cave. The scolopendra emitted a brilliant golden light. Boskoe too, Ieska noted, was glowing. She examined him, wondering what caste he was. He had Esh-tala, the membranes connecting his body and his arms on both sides. He also had the extensive finger tala of the Mayim. For a second, she thought he must be tri-casted like the children of Methiant Migas. But the children of Methiant Migas did not have glowing eyes. And they did not have the additional tala that Boskoe sported on his back.

Flippy bent his alien head down to look at them. Ieska held her breath. The creature's eyes and mouths were not where she thought they ought to be. It was like someone had created the beast out of spare parts with reckless disregard for symmetry and cohesion. The beast clicked a set of mandibles at her.

Boskoe reached out a hand and patted the giant beast. "See?" he said.

"Who are you?" Ieska asked. "Are you Esh?"

The boy shook his head. He looked scarcely older than Pax and Laetu, certainly not an adult by any means. "I've heard of the Esh. But I've never met one." Then his eyes widened as the realization struck him. "You're Esh?"

Ieska nodded. "We are."

"No one is going to believe me when I tell them I've seen Esh!" the boy whispered ecstatically.

"Who are your people?" Hauk asked. "What caste are you?"

"Pihr," the boy said. "We're the Pihr. There are stories about the Esh, those who can go down into the lower lands, down near the sea. But some people don't believe the stories are true. Who could breathe such cold, heavy air? And why have we never seen any of them?"

"Pihr," Ieska repeated. "You can only live on the heights?"

Boskoe nodded. "We're one of the three original castes of Gannoir. Pihr, Fossa, and Esh. We're the only ones left."

Ieska gave him a pointed glance.

Hauk laughed. "Not really."

Boskoe blushed. "I guess that's not right. Not since you're here. Esh! Real Esh! Wait until I tell everyone!"

"Can we come with you?" Ieska asked. "I would like to meet your people."

"This is awesome!" Boskoe exclaimed. "I'll be the one to bring the Esh to my people!"

"You don't know the half of it," Hauk grinned.

Chapter 55: Tass

Tass rolled over in her cot. Torcalon had insisted on staying in the same dwelling where she and Ninach were. To take care of her, he had said. And to keep an eye on Ninach. He had looked at Ninach, his granddaughter, with love in his eyes, despite her betrayal.

Torcalon was still sleeping. Tass could hear him snoring from the next room. She pressed her blotchy hands against her eyes. If she pressed hard enough, she could see spots of light, even though her eyes were closed. She wondered if everyone could do that, or if it was a Triad thing.

You're not special, you know, the voices hissed inside her mind.

"Shut up," Tass growled aloud.

You betrayed your sister.

"Shut up," Tass said again.

She will never forgive you. Not in a million years. Not in all eternity. Traitor. Hypocrite. Backstabber . . .

"I don't want Ninach's forgiveness. She's the one who kidnapped the baby. She should be chained up," Tass growled.

Silvery laughter rang through Tass's gills, through her limbs. Her fingers glowed with eerie light. *Not Ninach . . .*

Tass shook her head. "I don't know what you're talking about then."

Mailu . . . the voices trilled, sounding sweet and mournful this time. *Mailu . . .*

Tass's heart wrenched painfully at the thought of her sister. "Mailu was dead long before I found her," she reprimanded the voices. "There was nothing I could have done."

Other than protecting her child . . . your niece . . . You're a traitor . . . a hypocrite . . .

Tass scratched her head viciously through her shorn hair, as though she could physically rid herself of her tormentors. "I did what I had to do. That baby has nothing to do with me."

She's your blood. Your kin. Your very own niece . . . The voices were truculent, accusing, woeful.

"Ninach was the kidnapper. Not I."

You helped her. Traitor . . . Hyp . . .

"There's nothing I can do about it!"

A subtle change came over the aura in the room, almost like a wash of color in her mind's eye.

"What?" Tass asked. "What can I do?"

She felt the triumph in the air. The voices knew what they wanted her to do. They knew she would comply. They knew they had won.

Listen carefully . . .

Chapter 56: Pax

They were back—back in the place of their captivity. Xylo and Widman had thought it best that they return to the Tehom. The plan was to stall for time, to try to make the Tehom understand that Ieska would come when she was able, but that because of events on the surface, it wouldn't be soon.

"That went well," Laetu commented fretfully.

"Be quiet," Pax said. He leaned his chin on his hands, elbows on his knees.

"You shouldn't have said anything about the baby," Laetu continued. "They know all our secrets."

Pax grimaced at his half-brother. "Don't you think I know that? I was trying to make them think that the deadbloods could help them. You know, because they experimented on Mailu, and the baby came. If they know it's not just Ieska who knows how to do that stuff, they might leave her alone. They might let us go."

"Well, all we got for it was locked up," Laetu said.

"I am aware of that," Pax spat. "Do you think I wanted to get locked up? Now who's going to rescue us? They still have Sadi and Unaleah, and now they have us as well."

"We have to rescue ourselves," Laetu said.

Pax shook his head. Usually, Laetu was the one who was scared and reluctant to take risks. Now he wanted to be some sort of hero? "We're stuck. They've locked us in."

"We have to think," Laetu said. "We're Triad and they're not. There must be something we can do that they can't do."

"Breathe air?" Pax snorted. "It's not going to help us down here."

"Something else then," Laetu countered. "Something we can do that they can't."

Pax shrugged. Laetu was right. He had to admit that. Whatever was going to be done was going to have to be done without anyone else's help.

Later—how much later Pax wasn't sure—two of the Tehom scientists, Rannasc and Ayruno, came into the holding cell.

"We need your help," Ayruno told the boys. His eyes were kind, but Pax knew that he was ordering, not asking.

"What do you want?" Pax asked suspiciously.

"By your own admission, you are multi-casted," Ayruno said. "We have need of your services."

"Do we have any choice?" Laetu asked.

Rannasc gave a sort of snort. Bubbles rose from his gills. Pax cringed in disgust at the old man's brittle, yellowed claws and stringy hair. All the Tehom were sublimely ugly, but Rannasc was the worst among them.

"Come on," Ayruno ordered. He clipped a sea-string chain to the wrist cuffs that Benjo had ordered placed on Pax and Laetu after they reported that Ieska was not available. Then he gave a sharp tug.

Pax and Laetu moved through the sea toward the opening of the holding cell.

"Unaleah! Sadi!" Pax exclaimed as soon as they were outside.

Unaleah's expression said it all. She had not known the boys were back. She had expected to be freed when Pax and Laetu returned with Ieska. Now, she could see the boys were back and were as much prisoners as she and Sadi. Sadi's face was contorted into a wrathful grimace.

"Come," Ayruno said. He tugged at the cords attached to all four of his captives. They had no choice but to accompany the dark-haired, fish-faced man. He led them through the undersea world of the Tehom, in and out of the rock and ice columns to a place where the water was blue and they could see the underside of the Orbokth above them.

"We've been excavating the Orbokth," Ayruno told them. "Going farther and farther up. According to Rannasc's calculations, this is the place where the Orbokth extends the highest—the closest to the Ghalon. The water is too hot now. Too hot for Tehom diggers."

Pax thought he knew where the conversation was going. If the water was too hot for the Tehom, it might still be okay for a Triad who had an Esh tolerance for heat as well as the Mayim ability to breathe underwater.

Ayruno pointed to a circular opening in the Orbokth above them. "Up there," he said. "Your job is to excavate the Orbokth. Go as high as you can, but not all the way through, you understand. Conditions must be perfect, and all the preparations must be made in advance before we can punch through to the air above." Seeing Pax and Laetu exchanging a hopeful glance, he gave the sea-string chains a sharp tug. "Don't think you can ruin this experiment and get away with it," he said sharply. "You will remain in your chains. We know exactly how far away the surface is. You won't be able to escape, even if you do dig all the way through. And the tunnel is narrow," he said with a brutish expression. "Tugging you back down will likely do serious damage to your limbs, if not the rest of you. Understand?"

Pax and Laetu nodded. Unaleah shivered. Sadi glowered.

Rannasc and Ayruno pushed the four Triads one by one into the hole in the underside of the Orbokth. He was right—the tunnel was narrow. At the opening, it was barely large enough to squeeze through. Pax, who was the last one to enter, kept a hand above his head so he could feel Laetu's foot above him.

As the tunnel ascended, it widened. After what seemed like forever, they came to a place where all four Triads could float side by side.

Unaleah hugged her brothers. "What happened?"

The boys explained that because they had not brought Ieska back with them, the Tehom had locked them in a holding cell.

"I thought they were allies," Pax said sadly. "One more caste to work together with the Siann Dha. But they're not. They're awful."

"Maybe they're not all like that," Unaleah said soothingly. "Even in Luca, there are some who side with Gelu and against Xylo. Even there the Siann Dha are not unified. Maybe it's like that here too."

Sadi frowned in disgust. "We met the women. They're idiots, all of them. Do you really think there's any good to be found here?"

"It's possible," Unaleah said staunchly.

"What are we going to do?" Laetu asked. He looked down at the sea-string chains binding him to his captors like the string on a kite.

"Cut the sea-string?" Unaleah suggested.

Sadi shook her head. "It's sea-string. You can't just cut sea-string rope. Not without a hideously sharp knife."

Pax looked up. The chamber narrowed as it rose. "Do we dig?" he asked.

"What else are we going to do?" Laetu asked.

"It's probably our best chance of escape," Sadi noted. "Dig through, then crawl out onto the Orbokth."

"They said they'll hurt us if we try that," Unaleah protested.

"How're they going to know?" Pax retorted.

Sadi frowned. "Unfortunately, it'll be obvious. And not just because we'll run out of rope."

"Why?" Pax asked blankly.

"The water pressure. The Orbokth isn't naturally full of water. The place we're swimming right now is above sea level. The liquid has only been able to rise this high because it's a sealed chamber. If we pop a hole in the top, the water will rush downward as the air rushes in. They'll know the minute one of us breaks through," Sadi said with a frown.

"And then they'll tug on the chains, pull us down, and mangle us in the process," Unaleah realized.

"We're going to get mangled no matter what we do," Pax realized.

"So what are we going to do?" Laetu repeated.

Sadi pointed to a pile of blocky hammers sitting on a shelf on one side of the chamber. "Dig. We'll think of something. There must be a way. We can think while we dig."

"And if we get close enough to the outside . . ." Pax said.

"We have to escape. But digging through is going to take some time. By the time we're close, we'll have a plan. I'm sure of it," Sadi said.

Chapter 57: Tass

When the night was half done, Tass crept off her cot. Her limbs were still weak, and she knew she had to work quickly before her strength left her. Her mind was strong, however. The voices, the spirits of the darkness that indwelt her, were the glue that gave her strength. They upheld her, supported her, and helped her know what she had to do.

She tiptoed to Ninach's bunk. A sea-string and metal chain, doubly strong because of the combination of materials, attached Ninach to the metal bed frame. "Ninach!" she hissed. "Ninach! Wake up!"

Ninach opened one eye. Her shoulder-length brown hair, which she usually wore in a tight ponytail, was loose and wild around her face. A trickle of drool ran from her chin to the pile of blankets under her head.

Tass shook her. "Ninach!"

Ninach opened one eye and glared at her half-sister. "Haven't you gotten me in enough trouble?" she muttered.

"I'm going to get you out of this," Tass told her.

Ninach opened her other eye and looked at Tass. "Really?"

"They shouldn't have locked you up," Tass said. "You were only doing what you thought was the right thing."

"You betrayed me," Ninach accused Tass. "Why should I trust you now?"

"Do you want me to get you out of here or not?" Tass countered.

Ninach frowned. "Out. But it doesn't mean I'm going to believe anything you say."

"I've got the key," Tass told her. She held up the little metal key to the padlock on Ninach's chains. "And a knife for the sea-string."

Ninach sat up and reached for the key, her green eyes flashing. "Give me that!"

"Shh!" Tass cautioned. "We can't let Torcalon hear us."

"What's he going to do?" Ninach snorted. "He's old and frail."

"Old and strong is more like it," Tass said.

Ninach sighed. "You're right about that. He is stronger than he looks."

"So be quiet."

Ninach took the key and opened the padlock. She stood up. "It's still around my wrist," she said. "It'll take more than a key to get that off."

"We'll worry about that later," Tass said. "For now, we just have to get away." She cut the sea-string easily.

Ninach wound the chain around one hand and climbed out of bed. "Let's go, then."

Tass and Ninach tiptoed through the small hut, past a sleeping Torcalon. His snoring took on a syncopated rhythm as they went by. They paused, knowing that on some level, the old man had registered their presence in the outer room.

Tass held a finger to her lips to remind her older half-sister to be quiet.

Ninach rolled her eyes.

Tass pushed at the fibrous curtain that served as a door. Rain was falling softly outside, trickling down from the heights of the Orbokth onto the verdant greenery that lined the interior of Cudth Deorth. The red glow of the convenalations, along with the heightened emotions of their task, leant an ethereal atmosphere to the night. Ninach went through the curtain. Tass swayed. Her strength was waning. Her knees buckled. Not now!

The voices laughed in her gills. As Tass fell to the ground, her anger gave her new strength. She hit the floor and then rolled over, pushing herself to her feet.

"What's going on?" Torcalon asked. He was sitting up, looking Tass square in the face. Tass grabbed her knapsack and swung it at the old man as hard as she could. He collapsed on his cot, and Tass pushed her way into the night.

"Where are we going?" Ninach asked. There was nothing about her manner that indicated she knew what had just happened inside the hut.

"Outside," Tass said. "Into the sea. We'll be safe there."

Ninach nodded. Together, they climbed to the other side of Cudth Deorth and slipped through the nearly invisible passageway in the Orbokth that led to Luca.

"Come on," Tass said. She dove into the sea.

The rain was falling more heavily here. Ninach pushed her hair out of her face, plastering it to her head so she could see. Then she leapt into the sea.

Chapter 58: Xylo

A crowd gathered in the forest behind the mine. Xylo, watching from a distance, looked on with approval. It was more people than he had expected. At least half of the deadbloods, then, were on his side—his and Talag's.

He was grateful that he had remembered the deadblood women who had expressed their support months earlier. He had sent Engesyth to them with his message. They had done the rest, gathering the crowd to support him against Gelu.

He perused the crowd, looking for Mara, her daughter, Rio, and Rio's friend Juli, their first allies. There were others there, people he had not expected to join his cause—Solet, the innkeeper; her perpetual customer and sometime suitor, Bardan; Fionn, the young man who had delivered Case to what he had believed was certain death, and who had, apparently, repented of his actions; and others too—people whom he had had assumed would follow Gelu blindly but who were not. He was grateful.

Engesyth lifted his arms to get the attention of the people.

Then Xylo came forth. "My people," he said. "Loyal followers of the Dynroc. We had only recently restored the real power behind the office of the Dynroc. Arros, 58th Dynroc and one of you, kept faith with you all his days, but he was violently killed by his protégé, Gelu, who became your political leader, but never the Dynroc."

The strategy was important. The people had loved Arros, had gone to him for wisdom and advice even though he had not held power over Garradh Gannoir. His death at the hands of Gelu was a well-known fact, and one that Xylo could use in more strongly binding the people to his cause.

"Arros, just before his death, bequeathed the office of the Dynroc to Dynny, his longtime servant. Dynny, in turn handed that power over to my grandson, Talag, now the 60th Dynroc and the first Dynroc to be of the Siann Dha in modern times."

There were murmurs at this. Even though these people had rallied to his side, Xylo could tell they were still uncomfortable at the idea that an outsider, a Siann Dha, could be their ruler, their Dynroc. He was hoping that the way he had phrased his statement had made them question whether there had been Siann Dha Dynrocs in ancient times. He thought it likely, but he had no proof.

"My grandson has been abducted by Gelu and his henchmen," Xylo told the people. A gasp rippled through the crowd. "Many of you may know Lefty Binsaid and his wife, Estraya Androkas," Xylo said. "We have an eyewitness who has named them as the kidnappers."

Another round of murmurs shuddered through the assembly. The tone was filled with disapproval.

"Now, Lefty and Estraya have amassed many of the Siann Dha in their laboratories, preparatory to using the blood of the Siann Dha for their vile experiments. They have taken Rahela, Laso, and Peodar Barat."

At this, the crowd broke into angry shouts. Everyone knew that Rahela had risked her life and sacrificed her wellbeing for the sake of Garradh Gannoir—for the whole world—and they loved her for it.

"They have taken my son, Case, and my grandson, your Dynroc, Talag. We have reason to believe that they have also abducted two others of our company, Finnan Ruadhi Louloudi and her daughter, Camilly Louloudi Efteri. We ourselves have seen that Gelu himself has returned to Garradh Gannoir with a company of Siann Dha, ready to reclaim his power over you all."

More angry murmurs. Bringing up that powerful Siann Dha were on both sides was a good strategy, Xylo reflected. If any wanted to reject Siann Dha leadership, siding against him wouldn't accomplish it.

"We need your help. We need to put a stop to Gelu, Lefty, and Estraya. We must prevail. We must restore the balance of power in Garradh Gannoir. The power of the office of the Dynroc rests in Talag Dineaweth Xalantaka, and order will not be properly restored to Garradh Gannoir, and indeed, to Gannoir itself, unless Gelu's evil plans are thwarted. Are you with me?" Xylo's voice rose in a gradual crescendo throughout this speech, and his efforts were rewarded with the resounding cheers of the people.

He began to detail his plan.

Chapter 59: Ieska

Fearsome Flippy reared up and gnashed his multiple jaws. Ieska looked at him warily.

"All aboard, right?" Hauk said cheerfully.

"Yep," Boskoe said with a grin.

Flippy spun in a circle.

"He's just excited," Boskoe explained. He took hold of one of the plates in the exoskeleton of the massive arthropod and heaved his leg over the side of the creature. "Come on!" he said.

Hauk copied Boskoe, landing behind the boy. He extended a hand to Ieska.

Ieska shook her head. "I appreciate the compliment," she told them, "but I'm an old woman. I can't just fling myself through the air and land gracefully mounted on a scolopendra." She smiled wryly.

"You can do it," Hauk encouraged her. "After all, you made the trek into the heights of the Orbokth. You can do anything."

"And what else are you going to do?" Boskoe added.

Ieska looked around. "I have an idea." She climbed carefully and slowly up one of the uneven walls of the cave. When she was sufficiently higher than the writhing scolopendra, she stretched out her arms and flung herself through the air. Using her Esh-tala, she was able to glide gently, if awkwardly, onto the back of the beast. Hauk and Boskoe helped her situate herself on its back, no easy task since Flippy was apparently exceedingly excited by the prospect of carrying not one, but three people.

"We're off!" Boskoe cried. He reached out and grabbed a rope encircling Flippy's neck—if any part of the creature could be called a neck—and kicked his legs against the hard plates on its side. "Let's go!"

Chapter 60: Pax

"I'm hot," Laetu complained.

"It's no wonder," Sadi retorted. "It's boiling in here."

"Feels nice," Unaleah said. "It's so hot it feels almost like being in the heights."

"Except it's wet," Pax said. He set the mallet on a shelf and rubbed his skin. Unaleah was right—the heat did feel nice. He liked the water, but he had spent most of his life living on the Orbokth in the air.

"Keep digging," Sadi ordered.

"I am," Pax grumbled. "I just needed a rest. A little one." He wondered why Sadi was in such a hurry. They didn't have a plan yet. And without a plan, they could only dig so far before they had to stop.

"Why don't we all take a rest," Unaleah said. "We've been digging for hours, seems like."

"Can we swim lower?" Laetu asked. "It's so hot here. I don't like it."

"Suit yourself," Sadi said. She tossed the mallet she'd been using on a shelf of rock near the ceiling of the chamber.

Pax badly wanted to sit down, to feel the normal sensations of resting, reclining, to have the heaviness of his limbs upheld by something solid and sturdy. It just wasn't the same underwater. He swam through the acrid water toward the shelf where Sadi had discarded her mallet. The platform was large. If he contorted his body just right, he could imagine it was supporting him, even if he was floating just above it. He could pretend.

The protrusion of rock was larger than he had thought. There was enough room for all four of them to lie down side by side. A hole in the wall caught his eye. It was round and sized so that if he wanted the sensation of solid ground underneath him, it could not be avoided in there. He grabbed the rocky edge of the hole and climbed inside. The hole was more than a hole—it was a tunnel.

Pax explored, swimming more and more deeply into the tunnel. He wondered who had created it. Perhaps it was an organic feature of the Orbokth at this height. The tunnel was rough and rocky, just like any natural tunnel would be.

He could hear the voices of the others in the distance ringing faintly in his gills. They were calling him back to work. Didn't they know what resting was? He'd only been away from digging for a few minutes. He needed more time. Ignoring the voices, he pushed himself through the tunnel with his arms and legs. He was not swimming now. The tunnel was too narrow. He was crawling, slithering, climbing . . . anything but swimming. It felt good.

Then he saw it.

A mallet lay on the floor of the tunnel. Someone had been here, had been excavating this tunnel purposefully. He wondered who had done it and why. It seems contrary to the goals that Rannasc and Ayruno had expressed. Dig up, they had said, not sideways. He picked up the mallet. There was nothing to indicate who the digger had been. The tunnel narrowed even more as he pressed on. He swung the mallet, breaking off a bit of rock and widening the tunnel so he could keep going. A second swing of the mallet opened the wall in front of him. Instead of finding himself in a new section of tunnel, he was in a wide chamber. It extended for what seemed like miles and miles beneath him. What was going on? Had the previous diggers been trying to escape just like he and his siblings were?

His heart pounded. Whatever it was he had stumbled upon just might be their best chance of escape. He turned and went back to find the others.

A short while later, all four Triads were swimming in the second column of water. For that was what it was—a tunnel identical to the one that they'd been told to excavate. It extended just as high as their tunnel and no further, and it had the same features as the other column—a narrow base, widening as it rose, and then narrowing as it neared the ceiling. Sadi swam down and reported that there was a sealed door at the bottom.

"Did they try the same experiment earlier?" Pax wondered. "Trying to make a tunnel nearly to the top of the Orbokth?"

"Looks like it," Laetu said. "I wonder why they stopped and made the other tunnel."

"Maybe the rock was too hard here or something. Or they discovered the other area went higher . . . closer to the Ghalon?" Unaleah suggested.

"It's just as hot over here," Sadi said. She had brought her mallet with her. She swung it experimentally at the ceiling of the new tower of water.

"Does it matter?" Pax asked.

"Well, it lets us know something important," Sadi said with a frown.

"What?" Pax asked.

Sadi tugged at her sea-string bonds. "No one is tugging us back down through the Orbokth," she said. "When they asked us to dig, they said the cords would extend until just before we broke through at the top. It's much farther away than I thought if we can come all this way through that tunnel and no one down below cares."

Discouragement washed over Pax. "We'll be digging forever," he said.

"I have an idea," Sadi said. Her fingertips glowed with fervor. "This new chamber is the answer. It's what we've been hoping for."

"What do you mean?" Unaleah asked.

"It's sealed at the bottom. If we break through the top in here, the water won't rush down. No one will be any the wiser," Sadi replied.

"But we're still tied up," Laetu pointed out. "How are we going to get away if we can't cut the sea-string?"

"Not only that," Unaleah said quietly, "we've just connected this chamber to the other one. This chamber was sealed before we made a passageway through the last layer of rock separating the two, but now that it's connected to the other one, the water will rush out the bottom of the other one. It was a good idea though," she said.

Pax frowned. "We could seal it back up," he said slowly. "We could pile the rocks up and block the tunnel."

"Tightly enough that water won't get through?" Sadi made a face.

"Maybe not," Pax said. "But tightly enough that the water will drain slowly. We can get out before they realize what's going on."

"What about the sea-string?" Unaleah asked. She rubbed the band around her wrist.

"We can try to break it with the mallet," Laetu said.

"We tried that as soon as we had the mallets in our hands," Sadi reminded him. "It didn't work, remember?"

"Something has to work," Pax said.

"What about bashing the wrist bands," Unaleah said. She tugged at the woven fabric.

"We'll bash our wrists in the process," Sadi snorted.

"But we'll be free," Unaleah said.

"And badly injured," Sadi reminded her.

"But free," Pax said, throwing in his vote with his oldest sister.

Laetu put a hand on Pax's shoulder. He pointed into the cloudy seawater below them with his other hand. "Someone's coming," he hissed through his gills.

Chapter 61: Tass

"Are you sure this is right?" Ninach asked through her gills. She was not yet adept at gill-speech, and her words were nearly inaudible.

It made it easy for Tass to ignore her. Tass pressed on through the water. Her head ached. The voices, her constant companions in darkness, were not speaking words now. Their presence weighed on her, influenced everything she did. She could not get away from them. Oh, how she longed to be free of her tormentors. She hadn't realized how heavy the burden of their constant presence was until she was back in the water, back in her rightful realm. She was home, if anything in her world could be called that, but she wasn't, really, because she wasn't herself. Not with the voices hanging onto her soul.

Did she want the voices to go away? She wasn't sure. It was only because of their help that she had been able to bring Mailu home. And it was only with their direction that she would be able to rescue Mailu's unnamed baby. She needed them.

She pushed herself through the sea, enjoying the sting of the acrid water on her skin. Her limbs, so weakened on land, were much more capable in the water. They were close to Garradh Gannoir now.

Tass had intended to go to Luca. That was where Gelu was stationed now, working closely with Nadim. She had learned as much during the time she'd spent on Cudth Deorth. But the voices told her to go to Garradh Gannoir. That was where she would find Gelu. And when she found Gelu, she would find the baby. Fish-face. That was what she'd been calling the ugly little thing. She didn't know why no one had given the baby a name, but no one had. What were they waiting for?

Tass felt the water change around her as she dove deeper. The liquid swirling around her changed from yellow to tangerine. Deeper. Tangerine gave way to a salmon-color and then magenta.

"Tass . . ." she heard the thin thread of Ninach's voice warbling through the water. Ninach was scared.

A wave of satisfaction washed over Tass. She had considered Ninach an equal, a rival. Ninach had the courage to kidnap the baby and take it to Gelu. But now, Ninach was scared. And she, Tass, was not. She was only twelve—many years younger than nineteen-year-old Ninach, but she was in control. She would be able to do what the voices told her to. It would be easy. Ninach was not the person she'd thought she was.

"Tass . . . Tass . . ."

Tass spun to look at Ninach. "What?"

"This can't be right. It's too cold. The seawater is strange. It stings my skin."

"We have to go up through the waters of the mine," Tass explained with exaggerated patience. "It will put us near the city center. That's where we'll find Gelu. But to get there, we have to dive deep. We have to go under the deepest parts of the Orbokth in Garradh Gannoir."

Not because it was necessary, but only because she knew it would make Ninach nervous, Tass stretched downward toward the purple fire in the distance, the fire of the Bec.

Suddenly her mind and heart reared up. It was like an electrical shock coursing through her soul. Something had happened.

The voices were speaking words now, placating words, words intended not to force Tass to bend to their will, but to coax her, to win her.

Another, stronger voice sounded around her, its words too big to fit inside her mind. She could feel them, though. If she had to describe them, she would have said they were a long straight line, rigid and inflexible, in comparison to the tangle of words from the voices.

She knew what it was.

It was the Bec.

And it was speaking to her.

She had forgotten the Bec.

Now the voices of the darkness and the voice of the Bec clashed within her.

"Tass! Tass!" Ninach called faintly in the distance above her.

Her voice became part of the spiraling battle for Tass's mind. The spiral grew, leaving the center of the vortex hollow save for Tass's own self. She was alone in the center—alone for the first time since she had invited the darkness to infiltrate her physical body in order to bring Mailu home. She could think her own thoughts, go her own way. Even breathing seemed to be filled with clarity. She drew the caustic seawater into her gills, enjoying the sting.

"Tass!" Ninach cried.

Tass looked toward her companion. She remembered her mission. She was on her way to rescue her ugly little niece, that deformed little fish-face, from Gelu. And she was going to accomplish this by betraying Ninach, by handing her over to the man who had caused her sister's death.

Don't do it, came the straightforward voice of the Bec. ***Ninach is your sister too.***

You're fickle, the voices accused her. *Ninach is nothing. She would betray you in an instant. Mailu was the one who loved you. You don't owe Ninach anything.*

You don't belong to the darkness, the Bec insisted. **Don't do this.**

Mailu. Not Ninach, the darkness pressed. *You owe it to Mailu.*

"Tass!" Ninach's terrified voice called. "Tass!"

Ninach was a sniveling coward, Tass reflected. Even a fish-faced baby would be better than bratty Ninach. She closed her mind to the voice of the Bec. The darkness was right. She didn't owe Ninach a thing. It was only Mailu who had earned her allegiance. Only Mailu . . .

The spiral of thought around Tass narrowed and consumed the empty space in which she'd been able to make her decision. She was one with the darkness again.

Chapter 62: Xylo

Xylo looked toward the forest where the various teams were assembling. Widman was leading one group, with Byid by his side. The other units were led by Engesyth, Bridima, Gudall, and Rhyder. Five groups. Three would approach the research facility. The other two would stand guard in town.

Gaoth swirled around Xylo's head. Xylo took a deep breath and let it out slowly, glad of the presence of the rational wind. It reminded him that there were powers, forces, on his side. Forces that Gelu did not have. The wind seemed to splinter into little pieces, prodding and poking Xylo, irritating him.

"What are you doing, Gaoth?" he asked.

A strand of wind infiltrated his fire-gills. "Ieska . . ."

Xylo's heart stood still. "What about Ieska?"

Gaoth suddenly fled. Then he came back.

Xylo frowned as he realized what Gaoth was trying to say. "She's gone?"

"Ieska . . . can't find . . ." Gaoth managed to say. Putting ideas into words was difficult for him.

Pain shot through Xylo's frame. "You were with her? But now you can't find her?"

An affirmative hiss rattled through Xylo's gills.

Ieska had to be okay. She had to. She was infinitely precious to him. She was his wife. She was his hope for his old age. She must be okay. If Gaoth couldn't find her, it didn't mean she was dead. If she were dead, Gaoth would have found her body. That wasn't the case. She just . . . wasn't there.

Xylo reflected for only a second before making his decision. "Go to her," he ordered. "Find her. Look everywhere. Find my wife!"

Gaoth was off with a gust of his airish body. The backdraft hit Xylo with such force that he knew Gaoth was almost as concerned about Ieska as he was.

The groups began to head for their posts. Widman brought his people to Xylo. "Are you ready?" he asked.

Xylo nodded. "Let's do this."

Chapter 63: Pax

Someone was coming. Pax could see the figure through the murky water.

"They figured out what we were doing," Unaleah worried softly.

"Looks like it," Sadi added mercilessly.

"Shh!" Pax said. "Go back into the tunnel."

The four Triads swam into the hole that connected the new column of water with the old. Then they waited. And waited.

"Is it still coming?" Laetu hissed.

"Probably," Pax noted.

"Pile up the rocks," Sadi whispered. "Make it look like nothing happened."

Quickly, they began stacking the rocks they had spent so much effort to break apart. When the rocks were piled to the ceiling of the tunnel, they started filling the gaps with smaller rocks, trying to make it seem like they had never broken through at all.

"Hurry!" Sadi cried.

Pax looked at their rock wall. "We're too late," he said without taking his eyes from what he saw.

Eyes.

Someone was peeking through one of the gaps in their hastily constructed wall.

The eye disappeared and a hand began scrabbling at the rocks, enlarging the hole.

With Pax and Unaleah working at the wall, and Sadi and Laetu handing them rocks from the floor of the tunnel farther away, they scrambled to fortify the wall.

"Oof!" Pax grunted as the wall exploded into his gut.

"Sadi!" Unaleah cried. "Are you all right?"

Sadi crawled out from under a pile of rock. "I'm fine. It's not like we're on land. Rocks in the water land softly," she noted.

In what seemed like slow motion, they all became aware that they were no longer alone. Someone had kicked down the wall from the other side. And now she was standing in front of them.

She was the ugliest woman Pax had ever seen. She was even uglier than the women of the Tehom, and they were not an attractive bunch.

Her eyes bulged. Scars crisscrossed her face as though she'd been cut a thousand times, bones broken, blood vessels redirected, nerves cut. Half of her face sagged, making the bottom of one eyelid expose its reddish underside. Her hair was cropped to a finger's width above her scalp, and it grew in uneven patches separated by more scars. She wore the typical garments on the Tehom, but Pax could tell that her body also was deformed and ugly. She had one leg covered in scales, the other, with lumpish scars. One hand had the extensive finger tala and fierce claws of the Tehom, but the other was curled in a lumpish mass that could scarcely be called a hand.

She reached toward them, and Pax noticed that she could not raise her arm far from her body. With horror, he saw that it was attached to the skin of her side in a grotesque mockery of Esh-tala. Her tunic was not the usual clothing of the Tehom, but was more like Esh clothing, with its accommodations for body-tala.

Unaleah was staring at her open-mouthed. She reached a hand toward the woman, her own Esh-tala contrasting with the woman's like light and darkness, like day and night, like good and evil.

The woman reached toward Unaleah.

"No!" Pax cried. He pushed Unaleah back.

Sadi came forward. "Who are you?" she asked.

The woman's intelligent eyes glittered. "Who are *you*?" she asked, her words coming out thick and garbled.

"I'm Laetu Louloudi Efteri," Laetu volunteered.

"You're not Tehom," the woman correctly assessed.

"Are you?" Pax asked. He tried to look at her eyes and not at her deformed body.

The woman pressed her lips together. "I was," she said bitterly.

"I know who you are!" Unaleah exclaimed. "You're the woman. The one they've been experimenting on. The one they're trying to make into a Fossa!"

"Nice to meet you," the woman said, and despite her speech impediment, Pax could hear the bitterness in her voice.

"What's your name?" Sadi asked.

"What's yours?" the woman retorted.

Sadi grinned suddenly. "You're smarter than the other Tehom women. By far."

"That's for sure," the woman said with a sudden grin that was almost more hideous than her resting face had been.

"I'm Sadi," Sadi said. "And these are my brothers, Pax and Laetu, and my sister, Unaleah."

"You're not Tehom," the woman noted again.

"No," Sadi said, assuming the role of spokesperson for the Triads.

Pax thought Sadi was smart not to give away their true caste.

"You're in the water," the woman pressed, "but your faces tell me you aren't Tehom. They're too flat. You're Mayim. Except you all have body tala."

Pax lifted an arm, stretching out his tala.

The woman saw him and winced. "They're trying to give me body tala," she told them. "They sewed my arm to my side, hoping that as I used my arm, the skin would stretch and become tala. That was two years ago." She lifted her damaged arm. "That's as far as I can move it."

"What's your name?" Pax asked.

"Falmakad," the woman said. "That's what they call me, anyway. My parents named me Dulci. That means sweetness. Falmakad means evaporation. That's what they're trying to do to me. Make me fit for the dry air." She grimaced. Or maybe she grinned. Pax wasn't sure.

"We're going to get you out of here," Sadi announced. "The Tehom suck zigk moak."

"Sadi!" Unaleah exclaimed. "You can't talk like that."

Pax giggled. Unaleah was always sensitive to swearing. And "suck zigk moak" was almost as bad as it got—in Cudth Deorth, at least.

"They do suck zigk moak, though," Laetu agreed with a relish.

"I'm with them," Pax told Unaleah. "Sorry."

Falmakad snorted. "Same."

Unaleah sighed. "I agree with the sentiment. But you could have said it differently."

"I'm not going to argue that right now," Sadi told her older sister with irritation. "What we have to do is get out of here. All five of us, right Falmakad?"

"Would you rather be called Dulci?" Unaleah asked kindly.

The ugly woman shook her head. "I'm used to Falmakad. It's all I've been called since I was a toddler when they took me away from my parents. I wouldn't even know what to do if someone called me Dulci. I'm not her anymore." She frowned.

"You want out, right?" Pax asked.

Falmakad pressed her scarred lips together. "I would love to leave the Tehom. But I'm not sure where I can go."

"We're going out on top of the Orbokth," Laetu volunteered. "Up in the fiery parts of the Orbokth."

"Can you breathe out of the water?" Sadi asked.

"That's what they've been working toward," Falmakad told them. "But they haven't tested it yet. They've just been making the water hotter and hotter. The higher you go in this funnel, the hotter the water is, and the more fire-air content it has. But I don't know. I don't know."

"Well, we'll find out," Sadi said. "And if you can't breathe out there, we'll leave you in the funnel. But we'll come back for you. I promise."

"So what's the plan?" Falmakad asked.

They told her. And then they began to work.

Chapter 64: Tass

Tass sat on the shore shaking the water out of her gills. Ninach was doing the same. It was close to firstlight. The rain had stopped, and the mist glowed golden.

"Come on," Tass said. "We have to go into town."

She got up and strode across the grass toward the white buildings of Obumbro. Ninach looked at the city in wonder. Tass knew the older girl had never seen a city before—at least not since she was four years old and had come to Cudth Deorth. Tass was irritated by Ninach's fascination. She couldn't let herself like her half-sister or want anything good for her, not even a wondrous new experience.

"Come on!" Tass said again, more insistently this time.

"Where are we going?" Ninach asked.

"We have to find Gelu. It shouldn't be that hard," Tass noted.

The voices murmured their agreement in Tass's ears, switching easily from gill-speech to the airish sort.

A quick inquiry of a deadblood woman told Tass what she wanted to know. Gelu and his people had arrived the night before.

"He's on the other side," the woman told her. "Everyone is glad he's back. Now we can have a proper government. Not like the old superstitious thing about the Dynroc and his imaginary powers."

"Hmm," Tass said in a way that could have indicated agreement. She had reason to believe that the powers of the Dynroc were real. She knew enough not to doubt. But she needed information from the woman, and disagreeing with her wasn't the way to get it.

"Where can I find him?" Tass asked.

The woman gave her instructions.

Tass was annoyed. She had purposely surfaced from the waters of the mine so she would be nearest the city center. Now this woman was telling her that she should have taken the easier route through the sea. Gelu, it seemed was on the opposite side of Garradh Gannoir, across a high stretch of the Orbokth.

"You're Siann Dha," the woman noticed with a gleam in her eye.

"So?" Tass asked.

"Gelu will want to see you. You'll have no trouble at all," she said.

"I have no doubt of that," Tass retorted.

Tass and Ninach dove back into the water of the mine, Tass having decided that the underwater route to the sea would be quicker and more comfortable than the trek over the mountains. Despite her apparent Triad status, Tass had trouble in the extreme heat of the heights. *I'm not Triad,* she told herself. *I'm not like them. I have no body tala. I can't endure the heat. I'm Mayim. I'm Mayim.*

They found the teaching laboratory easily by following the directions the deadblood had given them.

A woman greeted them at the door. "You're Siann Dha," she noted.

"We wish to speak with Gelu Pagos," Tass told the woman.

"Come in," the woman said in her extraordinarily deep voice. "I'll take you to him."

Nooooo howled the voices in Tass's mind.

"No," Tass replied immediately. "Bring Gelu out here."

The woman started. "He's not going to like that. He won't come."

"I don't care what he likes," Tass shot back at her. "He'll want to talk to us."

"Who are you?" the woman asked.

"Tell him the spirits sent me," Tass repeated after the voices.

Moments later, a tall man with a long, gray-blue ponytail strode out of the facility. "Who are you?" he demanded. Then his eyes narrowed. "I've seen you before," he said, staring intently at Tass.

"You have something I want," Tass said, looking at him steadily.

"What difference does that make?" Gelu asked smoothly.

"The voices of the darkness led me to you," Tass told him. "You will give me what I want."

Gelu looked back at her. Tass could see that he was rattled by her mention of the spirits and the darkness. Gelu, she saw, knew the voices as well as she did. If the darkness wanted the exchange to happen—Ninach for the fish-faced baby—it would happen. They would see to it.

"What do you want?" Gelu asked.

"I think you already know," Tass told him.

Gelu's expression did not change. "What will you give me for her?" he asked.

Tass jerked a thumb over her shoulder. "This is Ninach. You've met her before, I understand. She's tri-casted. You give me the baby, my niece, and you can keep Ninach for yourself."

"Tri-casted?" Gelu's eyes gleamed.

"What?" Ninach yelped. "What are you saying, Tass? What?" She turned to run, but the woman caught her by her upper arms and held her.

"Is it a deal?" Tass asked.

"The baby is my child," Gelu said. "I am its loving father. I would never trade her away."

"The baby is my sister's child," Tass retorted. "And," she repeated what the voices were telling her, "she is no kin to you."

"That's not true," Gelu answered.

Tass could see in his eyes that he was unsure. "You know it too," she said. "You can hear the darkness. I know you can. Look at your hands." She pointed to Gelu's hands, which were blotched with darkness in the same way Tass's were. "You know I'm right."

"The baby is mine," Gelu retorted.

Tass shook her head.

"The baby is deformed. Useless," Tass argued. "With Ninach, you could have more children. You could have healthy children who have the genetics to become Triad like Ninach. Mayim, Esh, and Gulot."

Ninach struggled to free herself from the strong woman, but it was no use. She started to cry.

Gelu rubbed his fingers together as though he were trying to rub out the darkness . . . or stimulate it so that it spoke to him.

"Is the baby still alive?" Tass asked.

"Yes," Gelu told her. "Wait here. I'll get the baby for you." He disappeared into the depths of the facility built into the rock of the Orbokth.

A moment later, strong hands grabbed Tass from behind, binding her as completely as the woman had bound Ninach. Gelu appeared in the doorway holding the ugly little baby.

"Let me go!" Tass spat. "She is my niece. Mailu was my sister. The baby is more mine than yours!"

"Then you won't mind staying here with her," Gelu said smoothly. "Lefty, Estraya, bring them inside with the others."

In her prison, Tass paced angrily. She was alone, Ninach having been taken somewhere else. She gripped the bars that prevented her from escaping and shook them, wondering how they had been attached to the rocky floor and ceiling and how she could break them out of their foundations.

The voices had led her into a trap! She hadn't exactly trusted the voices, but she had listened to them because she thought it would bring her what she wanted—Mailu's baby. Instead, they had delivered her to Gelu.

Mocking laughter rang in her ears. *Worthless . . . unlovable . . . stupid . . .*

They were right, Tass reflected. Anyone who blindly followed voices in her head was stupid and worthless. She had fallen into their trap. What the voices wanted, she did not know. Gelu was a deadblood. That the spirits should side with a deadblood was unfathomable to her. Anything in the spirit world should have been more accessible to the Siann Dha than to the deadbloods.

Maybe, she thought, the voices were tricking Gelu too. She was sure he was even stupider than she—and more worthless. The voices were using him. In her own relationship with the voices, she was as much a user as the one being used. The voices were helping her get what she wanted. She didn't blindly adore them just because they were unbodied spirits. Gelu, as a deadblood, was lower than she.

He might think he was using the voices for his own purposes, but she knew the voices were the ones using him. In the end, it was Gelu who would be defeated. She would rise amid his defeat, claim her sister, and get out. It had to happen. It just had to.

Chapter 65: Camilly

Camilly didn't like the red light that had settled in the chamber like a haze. It lit the captives eerily, made it seem like they were dead, like they'd already been sent up to the Ghalon in flames. She shuddered.

She could see their faces clearly—her mother by her side, holding the tiny, ugly baby; Peodar and Laso sitting on either side of Rahela; Case and Talag. For a prison, the space they occupied was large. And it was hot.

"What are we going to do?" she asked her mother.

Finnan snuggled Mailu's baby. "Wait. For now, we wait. Xylo and the others knew where we were coming. They'll come for us. When that moment comes, we'll act."

"They want us alive," Case noted optimistically. "They've been feeding us."

Talag snorted. "And taking our blood."

"Do you know why?" Camilly asked.

"They're trying to find a way to change deadblood into the living blood of the Siann Dha," Case told her.

"We think that was their motive in impregnating Mailu," Talag said, sounding older than his thirteen years. "To create someone who was half deadblood and half Siann Dha. From there, they could figure out how the blood was different."

"And Mailu's baby is different?" Peodar asked, coming over to peer at the infant. He gasped.

"I know," Camilly said. "It's awfully ugly."

"She," Finnan corrected her. "Not 'it'." She stroked the baby's smooth, piebald skin.

"What's wrong with its—her—face?" Peodar asked.

Camilly shrugged. "Maybe that's what happens if a deadblood has a baby with one of the Siann Dha."

"Or it's because Mailu was dead for so long before she was born," Finnan suggested.

The baby started to fuss.

Finnan cooed over her, but the baby refused to be comforted. Her fussing turned into full-fledged wailing.

"What's wrong with her?" Peodar asked, looking worried.

Finnan shook her head. "I'm worried. She's burning up. She must have an infection."

"Could be teething," Laso suggested. "Igracio and Peodar always had fevers from teething."

"The baby's too young," Rahela chided him.

"She's sick," Talag noted.

"We've got to get out of here," Rahela said.

Laso squeezed his wife's hand. "We will. We all will."

"Unless they drain all our blood first," Talag frowned.

"Xylo and the others will come before that happens," Camilly said. She made herself sound certain.

But at heart, she was worried.

Chapter 66: Xylo

Xylo looked up. They had timed the rescue to begin in accord with the movement of the convenalations above them. The wingtip of the winged man was only a sliver from the edge. When the wingtip disappeared, they would begin.

Tension gave his old body energy. He tried not to think about Ieska.

"Almost time," Widman whispered. He had tied a dark cloth over his blond hair, the better to proceed unseen.

Xylo nodded without taking his eyes from the dark side of the Ghalon above his head.

The crowd behind them was as quiet as a mass of people could be. They had brought tools from their homes. They were ready to force their way in.

The glowing red wingtip was touching the edge now. Xylo could feel the energy coursing throughout his army. Widman held up his hands, ready to give the signal.

It's not supposed to be a battle, Xylo reminded himself. We go in, overpower them, rescue our friends, and get out. No one gets hurt.

There are enough of us to do the job without bloodshed on either side. He pressed his lips together, knowing that plans don't always work the way they are intended to work—almost never, in fact.

Widman held up five fingers.

Four.

Three.

Two.

One.

The people surged forward toward the door of the facility, ready to break it down to get in.

It wasn't locked.

Widman, Xylo, and the people poured into the hollow spaces in the Orbokth. They filled the passageways, some going right, some left, and some down a staircase straight in front of them. Xylo knew that the same thing was happening at the other two entrances. They would pour in like water, filling in all the miscellaneous corridors until they couldn't help but find the others and overpower their captors.

Xylo went with one group to the right, while Widman took the passageway to the left. About twenty of their companions flowed into the corridor with him, peering into rooms and heading down tunnels and up staircases. It wasn't long before his group had split into groups of twos and threes, exploring the rooms and hallways.

The corridor Xylo had chosen ended in one final room. Xylo entered it alone. The room was small, little more than a large closet, really. Cabinets lined the walls. He opened one metal door to examine the contents.

Metal jars labeled with the names of chemicals and medicines were neatly arrayed in the cabinet. Xylo recognized some of the substances. There were more that he had never heard of. All the cabinets were the same—jars, large and small. It was well-organized and irrelevant. Nothing pointed to the insidious experiments they suspected the deadbloods were conducting. He turned to go back out into the corridor, only to find that a dozen of his fellow rescuers were packed into the space.

"What's going on?" he asked.

"It's a trap," a large muscular man told him. "Once we came through, the passageways closed."

"Doors come down from the ceiling," another man said. "We must have triggered some kind of emergency defense system."

Xylo's heart sank. He had not expected a medical research facility to have such an elaborate system of defense. "How many of us are in this corridor?" he asked.

"It's sealed off halfway back," a woman with long, dark hair said. "There are fifteen of us here."

"But it's likely the others are experiencing the same thing all over," the muscular man added. "We're trapped."

Xylo shook his head. "If we're trapped, so are our enemies. At some point, they'll have to open doors. And in the meantime, we must press on. If the doors came down, they can go back up. We just need to find out how to make that happen."

"But . . ."

"Just do it," Xylo barked. Then he softened his voice. "Together we will do it."

The men and women with him began banging, pounding, prying, poking, and experimenting. It had to work. It just had to.

Chapter 67: Tass

Tass could hear the faint blat-blat of alarms in the distance. What was going on? Did it have something to do with her and Ninach? Or Mailu's baby?

She pounded at the door of her cell. "Let me out!" she yelled. The faintest glow lit her blackened fingertips. Hiding her fingers, she pounded at the door with her fists.

To her surprise, the door opened. Estraya was on the other side of it. "I came . . ."

Tass shoved the plump, dark-haired woman aside and bolted into the corridor. She had no idea where she was going, other than away from Estraya. She hadn't gone far before strong arms grabbed her. She kicked and bit, but it did no good. Lefty's grasp was too strong.

"I just want my niece!" she shouted. "Then I'll leave. Just give me the baby."

Lefty ignored her. "Estraya!"

"I'm here," Estraya said huffily. Tass wasn't sure whether Estraya was angry or if she'd had the wind knocked out of her when Tass burst past.

"Put her with the others," he ordered his wife.

Estraya approached, shaking her head as she skirted Tass's kicking and spitting. "She's strong. You'll have to do it."

Left slapped Tass's face. "Stop it. Stop fighting." He swore. "This is all I need. We have enough problems right now. Attacked by deadbloods." He spat on the floor in disgust. "I told Gelu that using this facility for a headquarters was a stupid idea. We should have picked somewhere father from civilization."

Tass, reeling from Lefty's slap, barely took in what he was saying. Hazily, his words sunk into her consciousness. Attacked by deadbloods. Lefty was being attacked by deadbloods? What deadbloods? Where were they? Slowly, she realized the meaning of the alarms she'd heard.

"It's too late for that now," Estraya said quickly. "Just stick her in with the others and we'll worry about them when this deadblood thing is over."

Lefty's grip on Tass's arm tightened painfully. Tass leaned toward him and clamped her teeth down on his fingers.

This time it was Estraya who slapped her. "If you want to be toothless in a very short time, keep this up," she hissed.

"Grab her other arm," Lefty ordered.

Estraya grabbed Tass's arm, and together, they led her through the corridors of the labyrinthine research facility. Tass tried to orient herself, keeping a possible escape in mind. Once she had the baby . . .

"Tass!" someone exclaimed as Lefty rudely shoved her into a room and slammed the door.

Chapter 68: Ieska

"This is as far as I can go," Boskoe told them. "But Flippy can take you down to the sea. He can breathe air as well as fire. He'll listen to you."

Ieska looked down through the rain. Boiling water streamed off the rocks at the highest point of the Orbokth above Garradh Gannoir. She couldn't see the acidic sea below her, couldn't see the land, but she knew they had come to the right place. And she had a new set of allies in the Pihr.

"We were glad to meet you and your people," Hauk said. "We look forward to collaboration in the future. After all, we Esh can meet with you in the heights. We'll bring the people of Gannoir back together—all seven castes."

Boskoe grinned. "Taking you two back home with me was amazing. I'll never forget the faces of the leaders when they realized what you were. Esh! Esh! I was the first of my people to meet a real Esh!"

"We'll meet again," Ieska promised, hugging the young man. "I promise."

"Shall we?" Hauk asked, cupping his hands so he could boost Ieska back onto Flippy's armored back.

Ieska lifted her foot to step into Hauk's hands.

The ground beneath her feet shook, and she stumbled.

Boskoe grabbed her arm and steadied her.

"What's going on?" Hauk asked.

Flippy sidestepped to get away from the disturbance in the rock. Cracks radiated from the place where he had been standing.

"It's breaking up! The Orbokth is cracking!" Boskoe cried.

"Hurry!" Hauk ordered. "Get aboard!"

Ieska stepped into Hauk's hands and mounted the giant beast. Hauk and Boskoe threw themselves onto its back behind her. Flippy flapped his wings, and they were airborne. The cracks in the Orbokth spread.

"Is this the end of the world?" Boskoe whispered.

"No," Ieska told him with certainty. "The prophecies have not been fulfilled. You know as much yourself. Your elders know it. All the castes must come together before Gannoir can be redeemed from its inside-out state. When we thought there were only three castes, it seemed like a near possibility. But now, now that we know there are others, that there are seven . . ."

"I thought you didn't believe in the ancient prophecies," Hauk commented.

"I never did before," Ieska told him. "I spent my life believing that the prophecies of old were just myths, the legends of an ignorant people. Science eliminated the need for such things. But now, knowing what I know now . . . A lot of rumors and legends have built up around the prophecies, but the core . . . the original prophecies . . . I believe. I do believe."

The cracks beneath them widened as Flippy hovered in the air.

"And in Tel-Maor? Do you believe in Tel-Maor, the creator, the one who turned the world inside-out?" Hauk asked.

"Tel-Maor exists," Boskoe said. "How could he not?"

Ieska nodded. "If I'm going to believe the prophecies, I have to believe in the one who gave the prophecies to the ancients, don't I?"

"Look!" Boskoe pointed.

Water was pouring from the cracks in the Orbokth. It sizzled on the hot surface of the rock. The cracks became fissures.

A hand seemed to grow out of the rock, getting taller and taller. A hand, then an arm. Then it went back inside the fissure.

A chunk of rock disappeared into the fissure, and then another. And then a person shot out of the hole in the Orbokth, propelled by an invisible force. The hands clung to the rock. Ieska could see the Esh-tala connecting the person's arms to his body.

"Put me down!" she cried. "Put me down!"

Chapter 69: Xylo

The deadbloods did it. They broke through the stone gate of their prison using sheer force. They rushed into the corridor on the other side. The sirens were howling painfully. Xylo realized that this must be Gelu's worst nightmare—his own people rising up against him, even if it was only half of them.

Each time they broke through one of the barriers, it was easier. Each time the people got angrier. As they went, the forces Xylo had assembled met and merged until the corridors were awash in rage, like hot blood flowing through the veins, bringing life and fire to the surrounding tissue, infecting the research facility Gelu's minions had carved out of the rocky Orbokth.

Xylo let them get ahead of him as he carefully checked behind each closed door, looking for Case, Talag, and the others. Most of the rooms were empty and sterile, as though the entire facility had been carved out to house a much larger population than it currently served. Silently, Xylo wondered how many of the Siann Dha Gelu—and before his death, Kleibald—had planned to imprison and use for their experiments. The long, branching tunnels seemed never to end, and Xylo came upon door after door after door, room after room, as he searched desperately for his son and his grandson.

He thought of Ieska, lost somewhere on the heights, and of Gaoth, whose help he desperately needed now. Guilt immersed him. He'd sent Gaoth away because he wanted Ieska. He'd led the raid because he wanted Case and Talag. Did he ever act without putting his own interest first? Did he?

You're not fit to be an Esh, the voices hissed in his gills.

Xylo's face hardened. He knew what the voices were saying was true. But he also knew the voices were his enemies. He fought against the temptation to trust them, to believe that the truths they whispered in his gills were an accurate summary of his life, of his essence. His failures, his selfishness, his greed . . . they did not tell the whole story. He was more than his failures. More than his flaws. More than his sin.

Childish laughter rang in his ears and in his gills.

Xylo shut his heart and mind against his tormentors.

Find Case and Talag, he told himself. *Stop Gelu from his cruel experiments. Stop him from imprisoning the Siann Dha. Free Laso, Rahela, and Peodar. Free Camilly and Finnan. Find the baby and bring her home to Cudth Deorth.*

He repeated his task over and over in his mind, and then, as a last resort, as last way to hold out against the voices, he said them out loud, chanting his mantra.

Footsteps echoed in the corridor. Xylo turned aside from the room he'd just confirmed was another empty suite.

"Widman!" he exclaimed as he saw his friend. Blood was running down Widman's face from a wound on his scalp. The trails of blood looked dark and deep in the dim light. Xylo thought they were just streams flowing from the injury higher on Widman's head, but he had to be sure. He reached a hand toward the blond man.

"They've lost their minds!" Widman cried hysterically.

"They're not rational anymore. They're maiming anyone they come against, even other deadbloods. They've become a mob! You've got to do something."

Xylo closed his eyes and drew in a deep breath. What had happened to his orderly plan? Go in, rescue the Siann Dha. Come back out. Violence was to be kept to a minimum, and only in self-defense. How had things gotten so out of control?

"Hurry!" Widman urged him.

He turned and ran toward the cacophonous sounds of the incensed mob, and Xylo hurried after him.

Chapter 70: Tass

"Tass!" someone exclaimed. "Oh Tass!"

Suddenly, someone was hugging her.

Tass pushed her tormentor away and glared.

"It's me! Camilly, remember?"

Tass nodded. It felt like a dream—or a nightmare. She'd been imprisoned in Gelu's headquarters, only to find the horror that awaited her on the other side of her prison door was a bubbly red-haired teenager. It was dizzyingly surreal.

"What are you doing here?" Tass asked with none of her usual rancor.

"We were looking for Case and Talag," Camilly explained. "They captured us and locked us in here."

"Us who?" Tass asked, peering toward the far wall of their prison.

"Lots of us," Camilly said. "We're all here—me and Mom, Rahela and Laso and Peodar, Case and Talag . . . and the baby."

Tass felt a prickle of excitement. "The baby? Mailu's baby?"

Camilly nodded.

"Where is she? Where's my niece?" Tass asked sharply.

"My mom's holding her," Camilly said.

"Why can't I see anyone but you?" Tass asked.

The voices howled in her ears delightedly.

Camilly laughed her silvery sweet laugh. "This room's got a lot of bends in it. Come with me. I'll take you to her. Most of the others are together in the central part of the room. It was way too hot there, so I came this way. My Mayim skin can't take the heat. I don't know how my mom stands it. Maybe because she's older. Maybe she doesn't feel the heat so much."

Camilly chattered to Tass as they made their way through the bends in the room, back to the center where the other captives were.

"Mom!" she called as soon as they burst upon the scene. "Mom! Tass is here! I found her!"

Everyone turned toward Tass, agape. The baby—Mailu's baby—wailed a prognostication of doom.

She's your destiny, the voices whispered to Tass, a saccharine dribble of thought flowing into Tass's ears. *Do whatever you have to do to make it happen. She is yours . . .*

Tass clenched her fists, hiding her fingers, which were now glowing furiously. She glanced down at her forearms to see if the blackness of her skin, the infection of evil, had abated.

It had not.

Tass took a step toward the group. She would have to play her cards carefully, saying just the right things. "Hi," she said in a small voice. "Can I hold the baby?" She made her voice sound as sweet and young as she could—not a difficult task, as she was, thought she sometimes forgot, only twelve.

Finnan bounced the screaming baby. "Yes," she said, handing the squalling bundle to Tass. Then, "How did you get here? How long have you been a prisoner?"

Tass bit her lip, wondering what the most advantageous answer would be. She couldn't tell them about overpowering Torcalon. She'd have to make something up.

She looked at the others, holding the sobbing, hiccupping baby over her shoulder. Finnan looked suspicious, but Camilly, her mother's younger twin, looked ready to trust Tass no matter what she said. Case's face was filled with pain. Of the others, he alone had known Mailu. Was he seeing her sister's face in her own? Tass had never thought she looked anything like Mailu, but she supposed it was possible. Her memories of her sister in life were hazy, culled as they were from her four-year-old brain—the last time she'd been her sister's darling. Talag was staring at her with open hostility. Peodar and Laso were staring at her in shock. And Rahela . . . Rahela's eyes were filled with motherly compassion.

Lie! the voices insisted.

Tass took a deep, deliberately shuddery breath. "Gelu's henchmen came for us, me and Ninach. They brought me here. They want me for their experiments." She spat on the floor to indicate her disdain for the cold-hearted pragmatism of Gelu and his crew.

"Oh honey!" Rahela exclaimed. She hobbled forward and embraced Tass, stroking her hair.

It was almost Tass's undoing. She felt a genuine sob rising in her chest.

Don't believe her. She doesn't love you. She wants to be the sort of person who loves. She loves the idea of loving you. But it's not you she loves. It's herself. Don't be deceived. Don't get sucked in. Stupid . . . worthless . . . unlovable . . .

"What happened to Ninach?" Finnan asked, her expression still unyielding.

Tass closed her eyes. "They brought her here too. They separated us. I don't know where she is now."

"And Torcalon?" Camilly added. "Oh my grandpa! Is he here too?"

Something like guilt washed over Tass, but she shrugged it away and put on a woeful face. "I . . . I don't know," she stammered disingenuously. "It all happened so fast. They didn't bring him with us. That's all I know."

Camilly's perpetually happy face fell. She turned to Finnan. "Mom! Oh Mom!"

"He'll be okay," Finnan reassured her. "Or he won't. May Tel-Maor guard and guide his soul." She pressed her lips together as Camilly found refuge in her embrace. Case put his arms around the pair.

It was too much. Tass wriggled away from Rahela. "What plans have you made?" she asked, looking at the others. "How are we going to escape?"

Her only answer was silence.

Chapter 71: Xylo

The din rose to ear-splitting heights as Xylo and Widman drew near to the destructive mob.

"See?" Widman whispered as they watched the others, Siann Dha and deadblood alike, beating the doors down with hammers they must have acquired from one of the many rooms along the corridor. Now and again, they struck at each other. "What's going on? What happened?"

"The darkness. The tormenting darkness," Xylo said hoarsely. "It's taken hold of the lot of them."

"I don't know what you mean," Widman said. "What darkness? What torment?"

"The voices of the darkness," Xylo said grimly. "As an Esh, they speak into my fire gills. Camilly can hear them in her water gills. I didn't think the deadbloods would be able to hear them. I didn't think they were vulnerable. They have no powers. Nothing. Even you, a Gulot . . ."

"I'm Gulot, but I'm not nothing," Widman said with an icy glare.

Xylo wanted to reassure his friend, but he knew it wouldn't do any good. Widman couldn't hear the voices—not in so many words—but he was absorbing their energy.

It was up to him now.

There was no more question of rescuing the captives, only of escape—escape from the inhuman rage of the mob, escape from Gelu and the others on his side, escape from the murderous voices who had lent their spirit to the attack.

One of the deadbloods scored a direct hit on the skull of the man standing next to him. The man's skull split like a cantaloupe, blood and brains oozing down his neck and torso long even before he fell to the ground.

The others laughed. They continued smashing everything they could see, blinded by the darkness that had overpowered their souls. The triumphant laughter of the voices mixed with the crack of stone and the blat of the alarms to make a devilish symphony in Xylo's senses.

"What am I going to do?" he whispered.

Then he turned and ran in the opposite direction from the bloodthirsty mob.

Chapter 72: Camilly

"What's going on?" Camilly asked. She was both scared and excited. Something was finally happening. The blats of the alarms filled the air, and she could hear the cracking of stone and the shouts of a battle outside in the corridor.

"Xylo's come for us," Rahela said. She clung to her husband and son, helpless but hopeful.

Tass clung to the baby they had finally let her hold.

Case pounded on the door of the enormous chamber. "Hey!" he cried. "We're here! We're in here!"

Camilly and Finnan joined him, adding their voices to his.

"Think they'll hear us over the sound of the alarms?" Camilly asked.

"I don't know," Finnan yelled. "But we've got to try. Xylo! Xylo!" she shouted.

"They may try to break down the door," Laso said. "We ought to stand back."

Laso and Peodar helped Rahela to move toward the rear of the main chamber. The others followed, still shouting to their rescuers.

The stone door slid open.

Slid.

Camilly's heart wrenched within her. She had expected Xylo and whoever was with him to break down the door. It was Lefty and Estraya—and Gelu's other allies—who knew the mechanism to open the door. Maybe Xylo figured out how it worked, she tried to comfort herself. But her heart was heavy with worry.

A dozen people poured through the open doorway. Camilly could see the terror and rage on their faces. She could see, even in the dim red light, the blotches of blackness on their skin and the bloody wounds that covered them, head to foot. She heard the door to their prison slam shut.

Oh no. Oh no. Oh no.

"Gudall!" Camilly cried. She rushed to embrace the young man who was like a brother to her. "Gudall!"

Gudall pushed her away. "Don't touch me," he said. "The darkness has taken over my mind. I can hear it. I can taste it. I can smell it, Camilly. Stay away!"

Camilly backed away, her eyes round with hurt and fear. "What are we going to do?" she asked. She felt dizzy, as though the darkness was closing in on her, affecting her balance, affecting the very molecules of the thick air around her.

The moans and cries of the deadbloods mixed with the screams of the alarms. Only Gudall seemed aware of his tormentors. The others, the deadbloods, had become darkness itself. They beat at each other with their fists as they advanced on the captives.

"Here!" Finnan cried. "Up here!"

She was clinging to the rocky wall of their prison, climbing toward the fiery red light pouring from a small aperture in the ceiling. Camilly shook her head. She couldn't go that way. It was too hot. She was too . . . too . . . too Mayim. She'd never make it. Just being in the room was bad enough, drying out her skin and causing her pain. She couldn't go higher. She couldn't.

She watched as Peodar and Laso dragged Rahela up the wall toward their only escape. Rahela, weak and sobbing, did the best she could. Case and Talag, climbing alongside the others, were the first to push their bodies through the opening. Talag slipped through easily, but it was only just big enough for muscular Case. It was all well and good for Case and Talag, she thought. They were Esh. They were made for the fire of the heights.

"Camilly!" Finnan screamed. "Hurry!"

Camilly felt teeth sink into her upper arm. She kicked at her attacker and ran toward the wall. She would rather burn up than be chewed to death. When she was near the top, she looked back down. From the heights, the blobs of darkness covering the skin of the deadbloods were clearly visible. They were not people anymore. They were just darkness.

Strong arms reached down and drew Camilly through the hole. She coughed as she found herself high on the Orbokth, in such incredible heat as she'd never felt before.

Don't look up, she counseled herself. *You'll burn your eyes.*

Camilly crawled forward, trying to push herself to her feet.

"Hurry," Case said, yanking at her arm.

Camilly winced as his fingers grasped her burning flesh. Case dragged her to a rocky outcropping that provided a bit of shade. Her mother threw her arms around her. It hurt, but it was worth it. Camilly felt like she should be crying, like she would cry if she could, but she couldn't. All the liquid in her body seemed to have been dried up in the awful heat.

"I don't understand," she gasped, looking back toward the crack in the rock she'd just exited. "Why didn't they follow us? Why did they stay in there?"

"I don't know," Case said. "But I'm glad they didn't."

"Me too," Talag agreed. He and Case were standing out in the open, apparently enjoying the searing heat.

"We're out," Laso said. "That's all that matters."

Peodar nodded and looked at his bruised arms and legs. Camilly thought he must have fallen victim either to the deadbloods or to the vicious nature of their climb.

"That's not all that matters," Rahela said sadly, from the place where she leaned against the shaded rock wall.

Camilly sighed. Rahela was right. The deadbloods themselves were victims of the darkness. They mattered. So did whoever had come to rescue them, as well as any other victims Gelu had confined in his scientific prison.

But Rahela continued. "The baby. What happened to Tass and the baby?"

Chapter 73: Xylo

Xylo found his way outside easily—too easily, he thought. He couldn't hear the din of the fighting anymore. He couldn't hear the alarms. The Ghalon glowed with the dim red light of evening. The rains had just begun.

As quickly as he could, he hurried over the rocky Orbokth in the direction he thought the city was. Stumbling, slipping on the wet rocks and vegetation, he made ample use of his tala to keep his balance, to keep him from falling.

Then he heard voices below him. He crouched low to hide from his enemies, which now, he surmised, could include anyone, even his former allies. His true enemy, the darkness, had taken over.

Quietly, he crept toward the voices.

A whimper.

A moan.

An encouraging word.

A faint spark of hope sprang up in Xylo's heart. These did not sound like the bloodthirsty voices of those overcome by the darkness. They sounded friendly. Helpful. Caring.

Should he risk approaching the dim, red-lit forms in the distance? What did he have to lose?

I'll glide down toward them, he told himself. *I'll take them by surprise, landing right in front of them. If they're hostile, I can leap off the cliffside and coast to the city below.*

The climbers screamed as he lit in front of them. First they screamed with terror, and then with gladness.

"Xylo!" Camilly exclaimed. "Oh Xylo!"

She burst into tears.

"What's happened?" Xylo asked.

"The mob lost their minds," Case answered. "We escaped through a crack in the ceiling. It's too hot for Camilly and Finnan, and too hard a climb for Rahela. Our progress is slow."

"And the wind came in a few minutes ago," Laso added heavily. "It was all Peodar and I could do to hang on to my wife."

"The wind . . ." Xylo said, his heart beating faster. "The wind . . ."

"Do you think . . ." Talag began.

Just then, a current of wind swirled around Xylo like a cyclone, pressing fingers of air into his arms and then shooting into his fire-gills.

"Gaoth!" Xylo shouted. "Gaoth!" He looked up. He knew he couldn't see his airish friend, but instinct fought against reason, and it always won. He always looked.

A dark form was silhouetted against the red glow of the misty sky. Hot rain pelted Xylo's face as he looked up. He closed his inner eyelids, trying to see through the watery haze.

Talag clutched at his arm. "What is it, Papa Xy?" He sounded scared.

"It's enormous," Laso breathed. He hovered over Rahela and Peodar protectively.

Finnan and Camilly clung to each other as they stared at the horrendous form coming toward them. It had a long, snaky body, giant wings, and an impossibly vicious-looking head.

"We didn't escape after all," Talag whispered.

"May Tel-Maor have mercy on our souls," Rahela whispered.

The monster came closer, and they looked into its hideous face, transfixed by the plethora of snapping jaws, rolling eyes, and antennae.

"What is that?" Peodar whispered from beneath his father's embrace.

Camilly whimpered.

"Giant scolopendra," Xylo shouted. He was the only one still standing. "Talag. Case. Go. There's nothing you can do to save us. Use your tala. Glide down from the heights. Warn anyone left in the city. Our doom as come!"

The horrible beast cracked its whip-like tail and a sound like thunder permeated the sky.

Case and Talag needed no more urging. They leapt from the heights and disappeared into the darkness below.

The remnant left on the heights huddled together. Xylo and Laso spread their bodies over the others. At least, Xylo thought, when it eats us, only Laso and I will be bitten in half. The others would probably be swallowed whole, not the fate he would have wished to befall his friends, but preferable to being cruelly and painfully bisected.

He cringed, expecting the pain of his death to come with extreme force at any moment.

Instead, the creature lit on the heights thirty yards from where the cluster cringed from it.

"Xylo!" an exuberant voice cried. "Xylo!"

Xylo lifted his head. He wondered if he was dead.

Ieska was running toward him, arms outstretched.

He stood up like one in a trance. "Ieska? Is it really you?"

She threw herself into his arms. "It is. Gaoth told us to come. He said it was bad. You need help?"

Xylo looked toward the incredible monster, so hideously ugly, yet still the bearer of his beloved. "That thing . . . it brought you to me?"

Ieska nodded. "I'll explain later."

If Xylo had been surprised by the sudden appearance of the scolopendra bearing his beloved, he was even more surprised by what happened next. Five people slid from the back of the giant creature and ran toward him.

Pax. Laetu. Sadi. Unaleah. Hauk.

Confusion rattled Xylo's mind. What were the four Triads doing with Ieska? Why were they all riding a scolopendra? Nothing made sense.

"What do you need?" Hauk asked.

Xylo shook his head. "There's nothing you can do. The battle is over. The darkness has won."

"Nonsense!" Ieska retorted crisply. "We have a giant scolopendra on our side. This thing is by no means over."

"She's right!" Camilly grinned, bouncing toward Xylo and the others.

All the former captives had risen to their feet.

"Just tells us what you need," Hauk said.

Chapter 74: Camilly

Camilly raced down one corridor, wishing she wasn't alone. Flippy had already torn the roof from the research facility. The top story was in ruins. She could see his dark form silhouetted against the fiery sky when she looked up. Would he wait until their task was done?

She and the others—all except Hauk and Rahela—had climbed back down into the chaos, intent on rescuing anyone they could before the giant scolopendra took the place down. Hauk, of course, was riding Flippy and would be orchestrating the destruction. Rahela was too weak to be of much use. Hauk and Flippy had taken her far enough away to be safe until it was over.

Already, Camilly noted, the deadbloods were fleeing. They were still rational enough to know that their doom was near—something that gave her hope that the power the darkness had over them might be temporary.

And it wasn't just deadbloods, she knew. Widman and Gudall were still in the fray somewhere. She'd seen Gudall, covered in darkness and despair. She wondered where they were, wondered if there was any hope at all that their lives—and souls—could be redeemed.

Alarms were still sounding. Camilly could feel the darkness around her like a physical presence in the air. Would it get her before she could do the good she'd come to do?

All these thoughts swept over her mind like shards of glass and worry, spurring her to run even more quickly, as though by speed she could escape her invisible tormentors. She glanced into room after room as she ran, trying to find anyone who might need her help. The giant scolopendra wasn't supposed to destroy the next level of the research facility until all the rescuers gave the signal, but she was still scared.

Hearing a scuffling, she slowed her pace and peered into the next room. It was darker than the corridor, the ceiling still hanging in shards over the large space.

"Hello?" she hollered into the shadows. "Is anyone there?"

A figure walked into the dim light in the center of the room. "Who's that?" it asked.

"Camilly Efteri," she told the person, squinting to see who it was, hoping against hope that it wasn't an evil trick of the darkness.

"Help me!" the voice begged.

"Who are you?"

"Estraya Androkas. Oh, please help!"

Estraya. Her kidnapper. Lefty's wife.

Camilly took a step backward. This woman was complicit in the evil that had befallen Garradh Gannoir. She was a kidnapper. She wanted to destroy the Siann Dha—to harvest their blood, and maybe more, "for the good of Gannoir." She wouldn't save her. She couldn't.

Laughter rang in her ears.

Triumphant laughter.

Dark laughter.

A step away from Estraya was a step toward the darkness.

Camilly felt sick. A wave of indignation washed over her. The right thing to do was to forgive, to forget that Estraya had done reprehensible things, to reach out to save her.

She didn't want to do the right thing.

She wanted revenge.

People were dead because of Estraya and Lefty and the others.

They were Gelu's allies—and he was trying to destroy everything.

This was war, and this woman was the enemy.

In war, it would be just to leave the enemy to die.

She could do it.

She could run away as fast as she could, finish clearing the building, leaving Estraya to her well-deserved death.

Or she could help her.

She could shine light in the darkness.

She could fight her real enemy—and Estraya's.

"Come here," Camilly ordered. "Come out where I can see you."

Estraya took another few steps toward the center of the room where the red light and mist swirled around her. Camilly could see the bits of darkness clinging to her.

"I'll help you," Camilly said, "if you promise not to hurt me."

"The building is collapsing," Estraya wailed. "We'll never get out. It's too late!"

"It's not collapsing," Camilly told her. "It's being destroyed, a layer at a time, methodically. "All you have to do is keep going down until you get to the bottom floor. Then get out."

"I can't!" Estraya gasped. "I can't. I'm safer here. If I go down, the whole Orbokth is going to collapse on my head."

"It won't," Camilly told her. "You have to trust me."

"You could be trying to destroy me," Estraya said.

"I could be," Camilly agreed. "I should be. But I'm not. Go downstairs. Go all the way down as fast as you can. Go now."

Estraya's terrified gaze met hers. "Why would you help me?"

Camilly felt a wave of strength surge through her. "Because I can't let the darkness win. And you shouldn't either." She pointed to Estraya's arms and neck. "I can see the darkness on you. It's not what I want for myself."

Estraya looked at her hands in horror. Camilly wondered if the woman really hadn't known the degree to which evil had possessed her. Hadn't she bothered to examine herself, body and soul?

"Go downstairs," Camilly yelled. "Hurry." She pointed upward, toward the gargantuan form flitting in the sky far from them. "See that? It's a giant scolopendra. It's going to take this place down a floor at a time, starting with this one. Now go!"

Estraya turned and fled.

Chapter 75: Xylo

The rain stopped, and the Ghalon had turned its glowing face toward Garradh Gannoir. The golden mist of morning was mixed with the dust of destruction as Xylo and the others stood high on the Orbokth, watching the exodus from the doomed facility.

It was over.

Those fleeing were only hazy silhouettes, but Xylo recognized Gelu's lanky form at the head of a small group of refugees. He pointed him out to the others.

"Who's that with him?" Camilly asked sharply.

Widman, his body ragged and bloody from the fight, but free from dark, oppressive blotches, drew in a sharp breath. "It's Ninach," he said in a low voice.

"We have to help her!" Finnan exclaimed. "She's fighting. She doesn't want to go with him!"

"She chose to come here," Rhyder noted angrily. "She kidnapped the baby. She took the baby to Gelu. Now the baby is gone, dead probably, and she's joined his side for a second time. We don't owe her anything."

"No!" Finnan protested. "Look at her. She doesn't want to be there. Maybe Gelu showed up at Cudth Deorth and forced her to come here with him."

"That's not what Tass said," Camilly pointed out.

"Tass lies," Xylo reminded her softly.

"Tass didn't get out, did she?" Widman murmured sadly.

Xylo shook his head. "I never saw her among the others." His heart tightened with pain. He should have loved Tass better than this. They were all gone now, all the ones he'd sworn to the deviant Methiant Migas to help. Tass. Mailu. Afa. Gone.

"Maybe it's for the best," Rhyder said. "She was beyond hope, Xylo. The darkness had taken over. If the darkness is our enemy, then so was she."

Camilly shook her head, her red hair dulled by dust and debris. "She was a victim of the darkness just like the deadbloods are. It's not her fault. She should have had to die. And the baby too. Mailu's baby was with Tass, last time I saw it."

"Her," Finnan corrected her daughter.

"She was one of us," Camilly mourned.

"So was Tass," Gudall said, coughing. The darkness that had been oppressing him was gone, but he was still weak and sick. He hadn't been strong to begin with, and the battle hadn't helped.

"So much darkness," Ieska said, putting her arms around Xylo.

Xylo's heart ached. He loved Tass like a daughter—an errant one, but a daughter, nonetheless. To think that she'd lost her life, victim to darkness and destruction, was unbearable. He squinted into the distance, trying to make out her twelve-year-old form limping among the others on their trek to the sea.

She wasn't there. And no one was holding a baby.

They were gone.

"What now?" Camilly asked. She'd plunked herself down on the rocks next to Gudall.

Everyone looked at Xylo expectantly.

"We could plan another rescue," Finnan suggested. "Even if Gelu has Ninach right now, even if she wants to be with him, we can get her back. We can reclaim her from the darkness."

"We're not going to plan another rescue. Not right now," Xylo decided. "We've got worse problems."

"What?" Camilly asked.

"Have you forgotten?" Xylo asked heavily. "Remember Dwoyra? She's holding the skyboulder together under the sea, trying to keep it from cracking up. If it implodes, the hole in the Bec that it's currently plugging will be open. The seawater will start to seep into the chaos. We could be looking at the death of all Gannoir."

Camilly frowned. "I did forget that part. But Dwoyra's strong. She's not like us. She can hold the skyboulder together indefinitely, can't she?"

"Maybe. Maybe not," Finnan said. "Remember, she seemed anxious for us to return with a solution to the problem."

"I've got some ideas," Rhyder offered. "Ways to stabilize the skyboulder. Make it last for years and years."

"How quickly can it be accomplished?" Xylo asked.

"With the help of the citizens of Obumbro . . ." Rhyder began.

"We don't have the help of the citizens of Obumbro, remember? The darkness came upon them. Without the blood of the Siann Dha, they couldn't resist." Xylo thought sadly of his loyal supporters among the deadbloods—Juli, Mara, Rio, Bardan, Solet, and the others. Were they lost forever?

When Flippy and Hauk returned, Xylo and the others climbed onto the back of the giant scolopendra. It took time, but they finally found Gelu and his followers. It was not just the six or seven people they had seen fleeing the wreckage with him. Gelu had rallied hundreds to his side. They were on their way to Luca.

Xylo shook his head. Luca. The only home he'd known for most of his years. Now it would belong to Gelu and the elders who had opposed him from the beginning.

The unrest to come, he knew, would be explosive.

It wasn't over.

This was just the beginning.

Chapter 76: Tass

Tass tucked her tiny niece into a crevice in the Orbokth above their heads. The wretched child seemed to enjoy the water, but diapers were completely ineffective under the sea. It was disgusting. At least the baby could breathe in the water. Tass was glad of that.

The voices had stilled to a dim hum in Tass's gills. She knew they were pleased that she'd taken the baby from Gelu, but she didn't know what they wanted her to do next.

Disgusted with herself for looking for direction from the darkness, Tass steeled up her resolve. She would live in the sea like a proper Mayim. She could find food for herself and little Fish-face. They would survive. And the baby would love her just as Mailu had done. She would be the baby's everything, even if the child was ugly, discolored, and deformed. Tass caught sight of her own yellow and black skin. The baby was just like she was. Ugly. Unlovable. Rejected. Despised.

With these comforting thoughts, Tass tucked herself into the crevice under the water beside the baby and went to sleep.

To be continued . . .

A Prelude to

Illumination

Book 4 of the Illumination of the Siann Dha

Tass already knew she'd made a mistake. Mailu's baby, hungry, sick, and unused to being underwater, wouldn't stop howling. At least she was good at gill-speech—if the wailing could be called speech. Too good. The voices of the darkness had abandoned her, or so it seemed. The only thing filling her mind with noise was the insistent howls of her little fish-faced niece.

It had occurred to Tass to leave the baby tucked in a crevice under the Orbokth. Without food and care, and as sick as she was, she would die. Maybe it was better that way. It would serve Gelu right for what he had done to her sister. But whenever she came close to doing it, Igracio's face would appear in her mind, pleading with her on behalf of the child's life. She could lash out viciously at Gelu. She could betray her sister. But she couldn't turn her back on Igracio. He had loved her like no one else. He had died for her.

Tass pushed the image away. She wouldn't leave her niece to die, but she didn't want to think about Igracio. The water pressed pleasurably against her tala, the webbing between her fingers. She was Mayim. She was water casted. Anyone who said differently, who said she was Triad, was crazy. She wasn't part of them, and she never would be.

Rejecting all the thoughts that scraped at the skin of her soul like sandpaper, she swam on through the caustic sea with the ugly baby tucked up against her.

She thought she heard the voices laughing.

Appendix A: Characters

Adam Anuilon "Xylo" Xalantaka (A-dum Uh-NEW-ill-on (ZIE-low) zuh-LAN-tuh-kuh): elderly Esh who is now the acting Dynroc of Garradh Gannoir

Afa (Bracha) Elisus (AH-fuh ELL-ih-sus): Tass's mother, deceased

Ardanach (ARE-dan-ack): Kleibald's current wife; Xylo's ex-wife; mother of Gryf, Aythylla, and Dochym

Arros (AIR-ahs): The 58th Dynroc, deceased

Athayer Sapor (Uh-THAY-er suh PORE): Chwerta's father

Ayruno (eye-ROO-no): Tehom scientist

Aythylla Tolmara Xalantaka (ay-THILL-uh toll-MAR-uh zuh-LAN-tuh-kuh): Daughter of Xylo and Ardanach, deceased

Bardan (BAR-dan): uncasted man from Garradh Gannoir

Benjo (BEN-joe): leader of the Tehom

Boskoe (BOS-koh): Teenage boy of the Pihr caste; scolopendra keeper

Brenina (breh-NEE-nuh): Tehom woman, wife of Benjo

Bridima Iommy Metuenu (brih-DEE-muh EYE-oh-mee met-oo-AY-no): Mother of Unaleah and adoptive mother of Ninach; one of the matriarchs of the band of Triads

Byid Aphanista Pendefeth (BEAD AH-fan-ee-stuh pen-DAY-feth): Pax's twelve-year-old brother

Camilly Louloudi Efteri (kuh-MILL-ee loo-LOO-dee eff-TARE-ee): Mayim daughter of Finnan and Rhyder

Caro Sapor "Case" Xalantaka (CAR-oh suh-PORE zuh-LAN-tuh-kuh): Xylo's son; Esh

Ceci Maraena Suergas (SEE-see muh-RAY-nuh SHARE-gus): Gelu's wife

Ceres Klee (SAY-rees CLAY): Mayim wife of Case

Chwerta Sapor (SHWEAR-tuh suh-PORE): Xylo's second wife; mother of Caro and Yasamina

Cyfeg Nerhial (SIE-feg ner-I-ull): Father of Frigo & Engesyth Nerhial; went to school with Xylo

Dano Eidales (DAN-oh eye-DAL-ess): Xylo's son-in-law; married to Yasamina

Dochym Tolmara Xalantaka (doe-KEEM toll-MAR-uh zuh-LAN-tuh-kuh): Died at age 4; Son of Xylo and Ardanach

Donamys Dineaweth Xalantaka (DOH-nuh-mis din-AY-uh-weth zuh-LAN-tuh-kuh): Talag's sister

Dwoyra (DOO-y-r-ra (roll the "r")): the rational water (pronunciation is approximate; hard to replicate with lungs instead of gills)

Dynny (DIN-ee): Mentally disabled elderly man who has been named the 59th Dynroc

Engesyth Nerhial (enn-GAY-seth—"th" as in "the"—ner-I-ull): Esh-maor man who works at the university; son of Cyfeg Nerhial and brother of Frigo

Estraya Androkas (ess-TRAY-uh AND-roh-koss): Lefty's wife

Falmakad (FALL-muh-kad): Tehom woman subject to experimentation by the Tehom scientists

Finnan Ruadhi Louloudi (FINN-ann roo-ODD-ee loo-LOO-dee): Mother of Laetu and Camilly and wife of Rhyder; Mayim

Fionn (FEE-on): uncasted man of Garradh Gannoir

"Fish-face" or "the Baby": Mailu's baby girl

Flippy: giant scolopendra

Frigo Nerhial (FREE-go ner-I-ull): member of the elder council of Luca

Gaoth (GAY-oth): the rational wind

Ged (GED): Burly Tehom man

Gelihr (GEH-leer): Tehom man

Gelu Pagos (GAY-lue puh-GOHS): Leader of the people in Garradh Gannoir

Gryf Tolmara Xalantaka (GRIFF zuh-LAN-tuh-kuh): Son of Xylo and Ardanach; governor of the Nepell clatry

Gudall Metuenu-Nayro (GOO-doll met-oo-AY-no NAY-roh): Twenty-four-year-old Triad, adopted son of Bridima

Hauk Touma (HAWK TOO-muh): Young Esh scientist who works with Ieska

Ieska Thayl (YES-kuh THALE): Esh-maor scientist in Luca, one of the matriarchs of the band of Triads

Igracio Barat (i-GRAH-see-oh bah-RAHT): Gave his life for Gannoir some months earlier

Juli (JOO-lee): uncasted citizen of Garradh Gannoir

Kari Coffya Ansidla (CARE-ee coff-EE-uh ann-SEED-luh): Sixteen-year-old Triad, daughter of Widman

Kleibald (CLAY-bald): the Esh-Maor; leader of Luca

Laetu Louloudi Efteri (LIE-too loo-LOO-dee eff-TARE-ee): Thirteen-year-old Triad; son of Finnan and Rhyder

Laso Barat (la-SOH bah-RAHT): Igracio's father

Lefty Binsaid (LEF-tee BIN-suh-eed): Friend and advisor of Gelu

Mailu Elisus Harreg (my-LOU ELL-ih-sus hah-REG): Tass's sister

Mara (MAR-uh): uncasted citizen of Garradh Gannoir; Rio's mother

the Master: Runs the Calix, the school for the Mayim

Methiant Migas (Mantais Nayro) (METH-ee-unt MEE-gus/man-TIE-us NAY-roh): Petty criminal subject to nefarious experiments that resulted his destruction, soul and body; father of the Triads

Milis Dineaweth (MILL-iss din-AY-uh-weth): Gryf's wife and Talag's mother

Minnidair (MIN-ih-dayr): uncasted woman of Garradh Gannoir

Nadim (nuh-DEEM): Aythylla's husband and next in line to be the Esh-Maor of Luca

Nehglon Maraena Suergas (NEH-glon muh-RAY-nuh SHARE-gus): Ceci's brother; uncasted man of Garradh Gannoir

Ninach Ansidla-Nayro (NIE-nock ann-SEED-luh NAY-roh): Nineteen-year-old Triad; adopted daughter of Widman

Ofnus (OFF-nuss): Young Esh scientist; married to Timmia

Pax Aphanista Nayro (PAX AH-fan-ee-stuh NAY-roh): Fourteen-year-old Triad; brother of Byid

Peodar Barat (PAY-oh-dahr bah-RAHT): Igracio's brother

Rahela Barat (ruh-HAY-luh bah-RAHT): Igracio's mother, now a member of the team trying to save their world once again

Rannasc (ran-ASK): ugly Tehom scientist

Rio (REE-oh): uncasted citizen of Garradh Gannoir

Rhyder Efteri (RIDE-er eff-TARE-ee): Father of Laetu and Camilly, husband of Finnan; Mayim

Saoradi "Sadi" Thayl Nayro (shore-AH-di "SAY-dee" THAYL NAY-roh): Ieska's daughter, one of the Triads

Solet (so-LET): Uncasted woman of Garradh Gannoir

Talag Dineaweth Xalantaka (tuh-LAG din-AY-uh-weth zuh-LAN-tuh-kuh): Son of Gryf and Milis, grandson of Xylo, step-grandson of Kleibald, and Dynroc of Garradh Gannoir

Talassa (Katurima) Galan (tuh-LA-suh (kah-TUR-i-muh) guh-LAWN): Twelve-year-old Mayim who doesn't want to be wanted just for her blood.

Tel-Maor (TELL may-OR): the god-like being who supposedly lives in the Ghalon

Timmia (tim-ME-uh): Wife of Ofnus

Torcalon Nayro (TOR-cuh-lawn NAY-roh): Father of Methiant Migas and ferryman for the Triads

Unaleah Metuenu Dion (oo-nuh-LEE-uh met-oo-AY-no DEE-on): Twenty-five-year-old Triad, daughter of Bridima

Widman Xunisso Ansidla (WID-man zoo-NEE-soh ann-SEED-luh): Kari's father

Yasamina Sapor Xalantaka (yeah-suh-MEE-nuh zuh-LAN-tuh-kuh): Daughter of Xylo and his second wife, Chwerta; married to Dano

Appendix B: Places

Calix (CA-licks): School for the Mayim

Cudth Deorth (KOODTH DAY-orth): the secret verdant valley where the Triads live

Gannoir (gan-oh-EAR): Heavenly body upon which the story takes place

Garradh Gannoir (guh-RAD gan-oh-EAR): Open area within the body of Gannoir where Gelu is the leader and no one is casted

the Great Sea: Where Luca is

Lachar (luh-CAR): Training college for the Esh-maor

Luca (LOO-kuh): Open area within the body of Gannoir where the four main characters live

Lucedth (loo-SAIDTH): Capital city of Luca

Nepell (neh-PELL): Clatry over which Gryf Xalantaka is the governor

Nozoffi (no-zo-FEE): Clatry that holds the school for the Esh-maor

Obumbro (ah-BUM-bro): Main city in Garradh Gannoir

the Rhosen (ROW-zen): reddish clatries at the far side of Luca, mostly agricultural

Rhosen Faide (ROW-zen FIDE): the farthest clatry of the Rhosen

Sorbel (SORE-bell): Home of the Tehom

Tienged (TEE-en-ged): Clatry in the Great Sea

Zafir (zuh-FEER): Clatry on which the Calix is located

Lisa Pelissier

Appendix C: Glossary

Bec (BECK): Soulish layer of ice on the exterior of Gannoir

beakfish: small predatory fish

Bilik (BILL-ick): Hole in the bottom of the sea

bonefish: fish with a crusty, marbled exoskeleton

cincinny fish: yellow fish with long, curly fins

clatry (CLAT-ree): Lattice of super hard stone that floats atop the water in Luca; cities are built atop it

convenalation (CON-ven-ih-lay-shun): Constellation made by cracks in the dark side of the Orbokth through which red fire gleams

deadbloods: uncasted people; people who aren't Siann Dha

dga (JAW (but the "j" has a little "d" in it)): Insect-like fish with a hard, metallic exoskeleton

dulcimel (DULL-sih-mell): Berries that are made into wine; too sweet to ear without processing

Dynroc (DIN-rock): Spiritual leader of the people of Garradh Gannoir

Esh (ESH): People of the fire caste

Esh-maor (ESH may-OR): Leadership caste

Esh-Maor (ESH may-OR): The title for the leader of Luca

Esh-qadar (ESH kuh-DAR): Ordinary people of the fire caste; often soil miners

finger-eye coral: like coral, but with blubbery projections that look like fingers, each ending in what looks like an eye

Fossa (FOSS-uh): Caste of fire and water

fuuegn (FOO-ain): Sweet-tasting fungus grown in the midlands of the Orbokth

Ghalon (guh-LAWN): Ball of fire at the core of Gannoir

ghloam (GLOWM): The time when the light has just left the sky and night has begun

gogyvehr (GO-gih-vair): The catastrophe that turned Gannoir inside-out

Gulot (GOO-lot): People of the earth or land caste

gwynant (GOO-ee-nant): Whipped sea-tree oil; Usually spread on bread

halas bread (HALL-uss BRED): Plain biscuit-like bread made from pellig flour

hydrolock: gateway to the world of the Tehom

iridis (EAR-ih-dis): Rainbow shimmer that lights the skin of the Esh

lumalaua (LOO-muh-low-uh ("low" as in "allow")): Sea creature shaped like an eel; feathered, with phosphorescent appendages; magenta at the head, fading to pink, orange, and then yellow at the tail;

Maor (MAY-or): caste of pure spirit

Mayim (my-EEM): People of the lowly water caste

mellila shrimp (meh-LEE-luh): make honey

methyglyn (METH-ih-glin): Alcoholic beverage made from mellila

mhowis goat (MOW-iss GOAT): Thick-bodied goat-like mammal that lives in the heights of the Orbokth

Orbokth (OR-bawkth): The rocky borderlands at the edges of the sea

pauluvervol (POW-loo-VAIR-voll): tiny flying salamander-like creatures

pellig (PELL-ig): Type of sea-tree. The bark is stripped, dried, and ground into flour

Pihr (PEER): caste of pure fire

ribbon snails: Mollusks with tentacles

rucloce (roo-CLOWSH): Blue-foliaged plant that produces large, waxy white berries with a variety of flavors and colors at the center

salt orange: grows in the sea

sarxworms: aquatic worms that are a good source of protein

scolopendra (skah-low-PEN-druh): Like giant flying centipedes with membranous wings

sea bramble: aquatic tumbleweed

sea reeds: useful sea plant similar to bamboo but thinner

sea-string: Webbing made by sea spiders

seagrass: They make mats out of it

Siann Dha (shawn DAH): The "Old Ones"—people with fire in their blood

tala (TAH-luh): Webbing either between the fingers of the Mayim or between the limbs and body of the Esh

Tehom (teh-HOME): caste of pure water

ugaz (OOH-gaz): Life-form with a mammalian body and a vegetable soul; has no head

vauzigk (VOW-zik): Blubbery sea creature similar to pinnipeds

vervol (VAIR-voll): flying creatures similar to salamanders

ymolenegth (im-MALL-in-eth ("th" like "the")): Blue glow in the sea; Blood keeps it glowing

yovod (yoh-VAHD): Big cat that roams the heights of the Orbokth

zigk-moak (ZIG moke): Delicacy made from the charred flesh of the vauzigk

Appendix D: Triad Family Tree

Unaleah Metuenu Dion, age 25
>Mother: Bridima Iommy Metuenu
>Acting father: Arx Dipheyn Dion (deceased; not named in book)

Gudall Metuenu-Nayro, age 24
>Mother: not named in book
>Adopted by: Bridima Iommy Metuenu

Saoradi "Sadi" Thayl Nayro, age 22
>Mother: Ieska Thayl

Ninach Ansidla-Nayro, age 19
>Mother: not named in the book
>Adopted by: Widman Xunisso Ansidla

Kari Coffya Ansidla, age 16
>Mother: Tueema Coffya (not named in the book)
>Adoptive father: Widman Xunisso Ansidla

Igracio Barat, deceased at age 15
>Mother: Rahela Barat
>Acting father: Laso Barat
>Half-Brother: Peodar Barat

Pax Aphanista Nayro, age 14
>Mother: Caedi Aphanista
>Adopted by: Finnan and Rhyder
>Half-Brother: Byid Aphanista Pendefeth

Laetu Louloudi Efteri, age 13
>Mother: Finnan Ruadhi Louloudi
>Adoptive father: Rhyder Efteri
>Half-Sister: Camilly Louloudi Efteri

Talassa "Tass" (Katurima) Galan Elisus, age 12
>Mother: Afa (Bracha) Elisus

Lisa Pelissier

About the Author and Illustrator

About the Author

Lisa Pelissier lives in Oregon where she is a homeschool mother of four and self-published author. She also works as a freelance wordsmith. Lisa has a B.A. from Biola University in Christian Education with dual emphases in music and elementary education. In her spare time Lisa enjoys making art, playing the piano, and singing. She has three kids still at home, six cats, two bearded dragons, and a sparse colony of giant hissing cockroaches.

About the Cover Illustrator

Helen Holmes is an aspiring artist and illustrator. At only eighteen, she has illustrated for 12 books (including this one). She was homeschooled and is a self-taught artist. She enjoys drawing, playing with her pug, Shredder, and making up her own stories as well.

346